Golden Face
A Tale of the Wild West

by

Bertram Mitford

Golden Face
A Tale of the Wild West
by Bertram Mitford

Copyright © 2024

All Rights reserved.

ISBN: 978-93-61421-24-2

Published by

DOUBLE 9 BOOKS
2/13-B, Ansari Road
Daryaganj, New Delhi – 110002
info@double9books.com
www.double9books.com
Tel. 011-40042856

ABOUT THE AUTHOR

Bertram Mitford FRGS (13 June 1855–4 October 1914) was a colonial writer, novelist, essayist, and cultural critic who published forty-four books, the majority of which were set in South Africa. He was a contemporary of H Rider Haggard. He was a Mitford family member and the third son of Edward Ledwich Osbaldeston Mitford (1811-1912). In 1895, he became the 31st Lord of the Manor of Mitford, succeeding his brother Colonel John Philip Osbaldeston Mitford. He died in 1912 at Mitford Hall in Northumberland. Bertram Mitford was born in Bath in 1855, educated at Hurstpierpoint College in Sussex, traveled to southern Africa in 1874, lived in Cheltenham in 1881, married Zima Helen Gentle, daughter of Alfred Ebden, on March 9, 1886 in Brighton, had daughter Yseulte Helen on June 3, 1887 (died July 1969), son Roland Bertram on June 17, 1891 (died April 16, 1932), lived in London in 1891, and died of liver disease in 1914 in Cowfold, Sussex. He belonged to four London clubs: The Junior Athenaeum, Savage, the New Vagabond, and the Wigwam.

CONTENTS

Preface

An impression prevails in this country that for many years past the Red men of the American Continent have represented a subdued and generally deteriorated race. No idea can be more erroneous. Debased, to a certain extent, they may have become, thanks to drink and other "blessings" of civilisation; but that the warrior-spirit, imbuing at any rate the more powerful tribes, is crushed, or that a semi-civilising process has availed to render them other than formidable and dangerous foes, let the stirring annals of Western frontier colonisation for the last half-century in general, and the Sioux rising of barely a year ago in particular, speak for themselves.

This work is a story—not a history. Where matters historical have been handled at all the Author has striven to touch them as lightly as possible, emphatically recognising that when differences arise between a civilised Power and barbarous races dwelling within or beyond its borders, there is invariably much to be said on both sides.

Chapter One
The Winter Cabin

"Snakes! if that ain't the war-whoop, why then old Smokestack Bill never had to keep a bright lookout after his hair."

Both inmates of the log cabin exchanged a meaning glance. Other movement made they none, save that each man extended an arm and reached down his Winchester rifle, which lay all ready to his hand on the heap of skins against which they were leaning. Within, the firelight glowed luridly on the burnished barrels of the weapons, hardly penetrating the gloomy corners of the hut. Without, the wild shrieking of the wind and the swish and sough of pine branches furiously tossing to the eddying gusts.

"Surely not," was the reply, after a moment of attentive listening. "None of the reds would be abroad on such a night as this, let alone a war-party. Why they are no fonder of the cold than we, and to-night we are in for something tall in the way of blizzards."

"Well, it's a sight far down that I heard it," went on the scout, shaking his head. "Whatever the night is up here, it may be as mild as milk-punch down on the plain. There's scalping going forward somewhere—mind me."

"If so, it's far enough away. I must own to having heard nothing at all."

For all answer the scout rose to his feet, placed a rough screen of antelope hide in front of the fire, and, cautiously opening the door, peered forth into the night. A whirl of keen, biting wind, fraught with particles of frozen snow which stung the face like quail-shot, swept round the hut, filling it with smoke from the smouldering pine-logs; then both men stepped outside, closing the door behind them.

No, assuredly no man, red or white, would willingly be abroad that night. The icy blast, to which exposure—benighted on the open plain— meant, to the inexperienced, certain death, was increasing in violence, and even in the sheltered spot where the two men stood it was hardly bearable for many minutes at a time. The night, though tempestuous, was not blackly dark, and now and again as the snow-scud scattered wildly before the wind, the mountain side opposite would stand unveiled; each tall crag towering up, a threatening fantastic shape, its rocky front dark against the driven whiteness of its base. And mingling with the roaring of the great pines and the occasional thunder of masses of snow dislodged from their boughs would be borne to the listeners' ears, in eerie chorus, the weird dismal howling of wolves. It was a scene of indescribable wildness and desolation, that upon which these two looked forth from their winter cabin in the lonely heart of the Black Hills.

But, beyond the gruesome cry of ravening beasts and the shriek of the gale, there came no sound, nothing to tell of the presence or movements of man more savage, more merciless than they.

"Snakes! but I can't be out of it!" muttered the scout, as once more within their warm and cosy shanty they secured the door behind them. "Smokestack Bill ain't the boy to be out of it over a matter of an Indian yelp. And he can tell a Sioux yelp from a Cheyenne yelp, and a Kiowa yelp from a Rapaho yelp, with a store-full of Government corn-sacks over his head, and the whole lot from a blasted wolfs yelp, he can. And at any distance, too."

"I think you *are* out of it, Bill, all the same;" answered his companion. "If only that, on the face of things, no consideration of scalps or plunder, or even she-captives, would tempt the reds to face this little blow to-night."

"Well, well! I don't say you're wrong, Vipan. You've served your Plainscraft to some purpose, you have. But if what I heard wasn't the war-whoop somewhere—I don't care how far—why then I shall begin to believe in what the Sioux say about these here mountains."

"What do they say?"

"Why, they say these mountains are chock full of ghosts—spirits of their chiefs and warriors who have been scalped after death, and are kept snoopin' around here because they can't get into the Happy Hunting-Grounds. However, we're all right here, and 'live or dead, the Sioux buck 'd have to reckon with a couple of Winchester rifles, who tried to make us otherwise."

He who had been addressed as Vipan laughed good-humouredly, as he tossed an armful of fat pine knots among the glowing logs, whence arose a blaze that lit up the hut as though for some festivity. And its glare affords us an admirable opportunity for a closer inspection of these two. The scout was a specimen of the best type of Western man. His rugged, weather-tanned face was far from unhandsome—frankness, self-reliance, staunchness to his friends, intrepidity toward foes, might all be read there. His thick russet beard was becoming shot with grey, but though considerably on the wrong side of fifty, an observer would have credited him with ten years to the good, for his broad, muscular frame was as upright and elastic as if he were twenty-five. His companion, who might have been fifteen years his junior, was about as fine a type of Anglo-Saxon manhood as could be met with in many a day's journey. Of tall, almost herculean, stature, he was without a suspicion of clumsiness; quick, active, straight as a dart. His features, regular as those of a Greek-sculpture, were not, however, of a confidence-inspiring nature, for their expression was cold and reticent, and the lower half of his face was hidden in a magnificent golden beard, sweeping to his belt. The dress of both men was the regulation tunic and leggings of dressed deerskin, of Indian manufacture, and profusely ornamented with beadwork and fringes; that of Vipan being adorned with scalp-locks in addition.

These two were bound together by the closest friendship, but there was this difference between them. Whereas everyone knew Smokestack Bill, whether as friend or foe, from Monterey to the British line, who he was and all about him, not a soul knew exactly who Rupert Vipan was, nor did Rupert Vipan himself, by word or hint, evince the smallest disposition to enlighten them. That he was an Englishman was clear, his nationality he could not conceal. Not that he ever tried to, but on the other hand, he made no sort of attempt at airing it.

This winter cabin was a substantial log affair, run up by the two men with some degree of trouble and with an eye to comfort. Built in a hollow on the mountain face, it hung perched as an eyrie over a ravine some thousands of feet in depth, in such wise that its occupants could command every approach, and descry the advent of strangers, friendly or equivocal, long before the latter could reach them. Behind rose the jagged, almost precipitous mountain in a serrated ridge, and inaccessible from the other side; so that upon the whole the position was about as safe as any position could be in that insecure region, where every man took his rifle to bed with him, and slept with one eye open even then. The cabin was reared almost against the great trunk of a stately pine, whose spreading boughs contributed in no slight degree to its shelter. Not many yards distant stood another log-hut, similar in design and dimensions; this had been the habitation of a French Canadian and his two Sioux squaws, but now stood deserted by its former owners.

Vipan flung himself on a soft thick bearskin, took a glowing stick from the fire, and pressed it against the bowl of a long Indian pipe.

"By Jove, Bill," he said, blowing out a great cloud. "If this isn't the true philosophy of life it's first cousin to it. A tight, snug shanty, the wind roaring like a legion of devils outside, a blazing fire, abundance of rations and tobacco, any amount of good furs, and—no bother in the world. Nothing to worry our soul-cases about until it becomes time to go in and trade our pelts, which, thank Heaven, won't be for two or three months."

"That's so," was the answer. "But—don't you feel it kinder dull like? A chap like you, who's knocked about the world. Seems to me a few months of a log cabin located away in the mountains, Can't make it out at all." And the scout broke off with a puzzled shake of the head.

"Look here, you unbelieving Jew," said the other, with a laugh. "Even now you can't get rid of the notion that I've left my country for my country's good. Take my word for it, you're wrong. There isn't a corner of the habitable globe I couldn't tumble up in every bit as safely as here."

"I know that, old pard. Not that I'd care the tail of a yaller dog if it was t'other way about. We've hunted, and trapped, and 'stood off' the reds, quite years enough to know each other. And now I take it, when we've lit upon a barrelful of this gold stuff, you'll be cantering off to Europe again by the first steamboat."

"No, I think not. Except—" and a curious look came into Vipan's face. "Well, I don't know. I've an old score to pay off. I want to be even with a certain person or two."

"You do? Well now don't you undertake anything foolish. You know better than I do that in your country you've got to wait until your throat's already cut before drawing upon a man, and even then like enough you'll be hung if you recover. Say, now, couldn't you get the party or parties out here, and have a fair and square stand up? You'd make undertaker's goods of 'em right enough, never fear."

"No, no, my friend. That sort of reptile doesn't face you in any such simple fashion. It strikes you through the lawyers—those beneficent products of our Christian civilisation," replied the other, with a bitter laugh. "However, time enough to talk about that when we get to our prospecting again."

"If we ever do get to it again. Custer's expedition in the fall of last year didn't go through here for fun, nor yet to look after the Sioux, though that was given as the colour of it. Why, they were prospectin' all the time, and not for nothin' neither. No, 'Uncle Sam' wants to have all the plums himself, and, likely enough, the hills'll be full of cavalrymen soon as the snow melts. Then I reckon we shall have to git."

"Well, the reds'll be hoist with their own petard. It's the old fable again. They call in 'Uncle Sam' to clear out the miners, and 'Uncle Sam' hustles them out as well. But we may not have to clear, after all, for it's my belief that the moment the grass begins to sprout the whole Sioux nation will go upon the war-path."

"Then we'd have to git all the slicker."

"Not necessarily," replied Vipan, coolly. "I've a notion we could stop here more snugly than ever."

"Not unless we helped 'em," said the scout, decidedly. "And that's not to be done."

"I don't know that. Speaking for myself, I get on very well with the reds. They've got their faults, but then so have other people. Wait, I know what you're going to say—they're cruel and treacherous devils, and so forth. Well, cruelty is in their nature, and, by the way, is not unknown in civilisation. As for treachery, it strikes me, old chum, that we've got to keep about as brisk a look-out for a shot in the back in any of our Western townships as we have for our scalps in an Indian village."

The scout nodded assent; puffing away vigorously at his pipe as he stared into the glowing embers.

"For instance," went on the other, "when that chap 'grazed' me in the street at Denver while I wasn't looking, and would have put his next ball clean through me if you hadn't dropped him in his tracks so neatly—that was a nice example for a white man and a Christian to set, say, to our friends Mountain Cat, or Three Bears, or Hole-in-a-Tree, down yonder, wasn't it? But to come to the point—which is this: Supposing some fellow had rushed us while we were prospecting that place down on the Big Cheyenne in the summer and invited us to clear, I guess we should briskly have let him see a brace of muzzles. Eh?"

"Guess we should."

"Well, then, it amounts to the same thing here. We are bound to strike a good vein or two in the summer—in fact, we have as good as struck it. All right. After all the risk and trouble we've stood to find it, Uncle Sam lopes in and serves us with a notice to quit. It isn't in reason that we should stand that."

"Well, you see, Vipan, we've no sort of title here. This is an Indian reservation, and Uncle Sam's bound by treaty to keep white men out. There are others here besides us, and I reckon in the summer the Hills'll be a bit crowded up with them. So we shall just have to chance it with the rest, and if we're moved, light out somewhere else."

"Well, I don't know that *I* shall. It's no part of good sense to chuck away the wealth lying at our very feet." And the speaker's splendid face wore a strangely reckless and excited look. "The scheme is for the Government to chouse the Indians out of this section of country by hook or by crook—then mining concessions will be granted to the wire-pullers and their friends. And we shall see a series of miscellaneous frauds blossoming into millionaires on the strength of *our* discoveries."

"And are you so keen on this gold, Vipan? Ah I reckon you're hankering after Europe again, but I judge you'll be no happier when you get there."

The scout's tone was quiet, regretful, almost upbraiding. The other's philosophy was to end in this, then?

"It isn't exactly that," was the answer, moodily, and after a pause. "But I don't see the force of being 'done.' I never did see it; perhaps that's why I'm out here now. However, the Sioux won't stand any more 'treaties.' They'll fight for certain. Red Cloud isn't the man to forget the ignominious thrashing he gave Uncle Sam in '66 and '67, and, by God, if it comes to ousting us I'll be shot if I won't cut in on his side."

"I reckon that blunder won't be repeated. If the cavalrymen had been properly armed; armed as they are now, with Spencer's and Henry's instead of with the sickest old muzzle-loading fire-sticks and a round and a half of ammunition per man, Red Cloud would have been soundly whipped at Fort Phil Kearney 'stead of t'other way about."

"Possibly. As things are, however, he carried his point. And there's Sitting Bull, for instance; he's been holding the Powder River country these years. Why don't they interfere with him? No, you may depend upon it, a war with the whole Sioux nation backed by the Indian Department, won't suit the Govermental book. 'Uncle Sam' will cave in—all the other prospectors will be cleared out of the Hills, except—except ourselves."

"Why except ourselves?" said the scout, quietly, though he was not a little astonished and dismayed at his friend and comrade's hardly-suppressed excitement.

"We stand well with the chiefs. Look here, old man: I'd wager my scalp against a pipe of Richmond plug—if I wasn't as bald as a billiard ball, that is—that I make myself so necessary to them that they'll be only too glad to let us 'mine' as long as we choose to stay here. Just think—the stuff is all there and only waiting to be picked up—just think if we were to go in on the quiet, loaded up with solid nuggets and dust instead of a few wretched pelts. Why, man, we are made for life. The reds could put us in the way of becoming millionaires, merely in exchange for our advice—not necessarily our rifles, mind." And the speaker's eyes flashed excitedly over the idea.

Chapter Two
A Nocturnal Visitor

No idea is more repellent to the mind of a genuine Western man than that of siding with Indians against his own colour. Contested almost step by step, the opening up of the vast continent supplies one long record of hideous atrocities committed by the savage, regardless of age, sex, or good faith; and stern, and not invariably discriminate, reprisals on the part of the dwellers on the frontier. It follows, therefore, that the race-hatred existing between the white man and his treacherous and crafty red neighbour will hardly bear exaggeration. Thus it is not surprising that Smokestack Bill should receive his reckless companion's daredevil scheme with concern and dismay. Indeed, had any other man mooted such an idea, the honest scout's concern would have found vent in words of indignant horror.

There was silence in the hut for a few minutes. Both men, lounging back on their comfortable furs, were busy with their respective reflections. Now and again a fiercer gust than usual would shake the whole structure, and as the doleful howling of the wolves sounded very near the door, the horses in the other compartment—which was used as a stable—would snort uneasily and paw the ground.

"You don't know Indians even yet, Vipan," said Smokestack Bill at length, speaking gravely, "else you'd never undertake to help them, even by advice, in butchering and outraging helpless women, let alone the men, though they can better look after themselves. No, you don't know the red devils, take my word for it."

"I had a notion I did," was the hard reply. "As for that 'helpless woman' ticket, I won't vote on it, Bill, old man. There's no such thing as a 'helpless' woman; at least, I never met with such an article, and I used to be reckoned a tolerably good judge of that breed of cattle, too—"

His words were cut short. The dog uttered a savage growl, then sprang towards the door, barking. Each man coolly reached for his rifle, but that was all.

"I knew I wasn't out of it," muttered the scout, more to himself than to his hearer. "Smokestack Bill knew the war-whoop when he heard it. He ain't no 'tenderfoot,' he ain't."

Swish—Whirr! The fierce blast shrieked around the lonely cabin. Its inmates having partially quieted the dog, were listening intently. Nothing could they hear beyond the booming of the tempest, which, unheeded in their conversation, had burst upon them with redoubled force.

"Only a grizzly that he hears," said Vipan, in a low tone. "No red would be out to-night."

Scarcely had he spoken than the loud, long-drawn howl of a wolf sounded forth, so near as to seem at their very door. Then the hoof-strokes of an unshod horse, and a light tap against the strong framework.

"It's all straight. I thought I knew the yelp," said the scout. Then he unhesitatingly slid back the strong iron bolts which secured the door, and admitted a single Indian.

The new comer was a tall, martial-looking young warrior, who, as he slid down the snow-besprinkled and gaudy-coloured blanket which had enshrouded his head, stood before them in the ordinary Indian dress. The collar of his tunic was of bears' claws, and among the scalp-locks which fringed his leggings were several of silky fair hair. But for three thin lines of crimson crossing his face, and a vertical one from forehead to throat, he wore no paint, and from his scalp-lock dangled three long eagle-feathers stained black, their ends being gathered into tufts dyed a bright vermilion. For arms he carried a short bow, highly ornamented, and a quiver of wolfskin, the latter adorned with the grinning jaws of its original owner, and in his belt a revolver and bowie knife. This warlike personage advanced to Smokestack Bill, and shook him by the hand effusively. Then, turning to Vipan, he broke into a broad grin and ejaculated—

"Hello, George!"

He thus unceremoniously addressed made no reply, but a cold, contemptuous look came into his eyes. Then he quietly said:—

"Do the Ogallalla dance the Sun-Dance (Note 1) in winter?"

"Ha!" said the Indian, emphatically, grasping at once the other's meaning.

"When I was lost in the Ogallalla villages, all the *warriors* knew me," went on Vipan, scathingly. "There may have been *boys* who have become warriors since."

"Ha!"

The Indian was not a little astonished. This white man spoke the Dahcotah language fluently. He was also not a little angry, and his eyes flashed.

"You are not of the race of those around us," he said, "not of the race of The Beaver," turning to the scout. "Your great chief is George."

"Don't get mad, Vipan," said Smokestack Bill, hastening to explain. "He only means that you're an Englishman. It'll take generations to get out of these fellers' heads that Englishmen are still ruled by King George."

Vipan laughed drily. He had given this cheeky young buck an appropriate setting down. Whether or no it was taken in good part was a matter of indifference to him.

Meanwhile, the scout, having put on a fresh brew of steaming coffee, threw down a fur in front of the fire, and the warrior, taking the pipe which had been prepared for him, sat in silence, puffing out the fragrant smoke in great volumes.

This done, he drew his knife, and proceeded to fall to on some deer ribs provided by his entertainers. The latter, meanwhile, smoked tranquilly on, putting no question, and evincing no curiosity as to the object of his visit. At length, his appetite appeased, the warrior wiped his knife on the sole of his mocassin, returned it to its sheath, and throwing himself back luxuriously, ejaculated —

"Good!"

To the two white men, the visit of one or more of their red brethren was a frequent occurrence; an incident of no moment whatever. They were accustomed to visits from Indians, but somehow both felt that the arrival of this young warrior had a purpose underlying it.

The pipe having been ceremonially lighted and passed round the circle, the guest was the first to break the silence.

"It is long since War Wolf has looked upon the face of The Beaver" (Smokestack Bill's Indian name), "or listened to the wise words which fall from his lips. As soon as War Wolf heard that The Beaver had built his winter lodge here, he leaped on his pony and wasted not a moment to come and smoke with his white brothers."

Vipan, listening, could have spluttered with sardonic laughter. Though he had never seen him before, he knew the speaker by name—knew him to be, moreover, one of the most unscrupulous and reckless young desperadoes of the tribe, whose hatred of the whites was only equalled by their detestation of him. But he moved not a muscle.

"It is long, indeed," answered the scout. "War Wolf must have journeyed far not to know, or not to have heard of Golden Face," and he turned slightly to his friend as if effecting an introduction.

By this *sobriquet* the latter was known among the different clans of the Dahcotah or Sioux, obviously bestowed upon him by reason of his magnificent golden beard.

"The name of Golden Face is not strange, for it is not seldom on the lips of the chiefs of our nation," continued the savage with a graceful inclination towards Vipan. "The hearts of the Mehneaska (Americans) are not good towards us, but our hearts are always good towards Golden Face and his friend The Beaver. To visit them, War Wolf has journeyed far."

"Do the Ogallalla (a sub-division or clan of the Sioux nation) send out war-parties in winter time?" asked the scout, innocently. But the question, harmless and apparently devoid of point as it was, conveyed to his hearer its full meaning. The eyes of the savage flashed, and his whole countenance seemed to light up with pride.

"Why should I tell lies?" he said. "Yes, I have been upon the war-path, but not here. Yonder," with a superb sweep of his hand in a westerly direction. "Yonder, far away, I have struck the enemies of my race, who come stealing up with false words and many rifles, to possess the land—our land—the land of the Dahcotah. Why should I tell lies? Am I not a warrior? But my tongue is straight; and my heart is good towards Golden Face and his friend The Beaver."

Vipan, an attentive observer of every word, every detail, noted two things: one, the boldness of this young warrior in thus avowing, contrary to the caution of his race, that he had actually just returned from one of those merciless forays which the frontier people at that period had every reason to fear and dread; the other, that having twice, so to say, bracketted their names, the Indian had in each instance mentioned his own first. In his then frame of mind the circumstance struck him as significant.

After a good deal more of this kind of talk, safeguarded by the adroit fencing and beating around the bush with which the savage of whatever race approaches a communication of consequence, it transpired that War Wolf was the bearer of a message from the chiefs of his nation. There had been war between them and the whites; now, however, they wished for peace. Red Cloud and some others were desirous of proceeding to Washington in order to effect some friendly arrangement with the Great Father. There were many white men in their country, but their ways were not straight. The chiefs distrusted them. But Golden Face and The Beaver were their brothers. Had they not lived in amity in their midst all the winter? Their hearts were good towards them, and they would fain smoke the pipe once more with their white brothers before leaving home. To that end, therefore, they invited Golden Face and The Beaver to visit them at their village without delay, in fact, to return in company with War Wolf, the bearer of the message.

To this Bill replied, after some moments of solemn silence only broken by the puff-puff of the pipes, that he and his friend desired nothing better. It would give them infinite pleasure to pay a visit to their red brethren, and to the great chiefs of the Dahcotah nation especially. But it was mid-winter. The weather was uncertain. Before undertaking a journey which would entail so long an absence from home, he and his friend must sleep upon the proposal and consult together. In the morning War Wolf should have his answer. Either they would return with him in person, or provide him with a suitable message to carry back to the chiefs.

In social matters, still less in diplomatic, Indians are never in a hurry. Had the two white men agreed there and then upon what their course should be, they would have suffered in War Wolfs estimation. The answer was precisely what he had expected.

"It is well," he said. "The wisdom of The Beaver will not be overclouded in the morning, nor will the desire of Golden Face to meet his friends be in any way lessened."

While this talk was progressing, Vipan's eye had lighted upon an object which set him thinking. It was a small object—a very small object, so minute indeed that nine persons out of ten would never have noticed it at all. But it was an object of ominous moment, for it was nothing less than a spot of fresh blood; and it had fallen on the warrior's leggings, just below the fringe of his tunic. Putting two and two together, it could mean nothing more nor less than a concealed scalp.

"Bill was right," he thought. "Bill was right, and I was an ass. He did hear the war-whoop right enough. I wonder what unlucky devil lost in the storm this buck could have overhauled and struck down?"

The discovery rendered him wary, not that a childlike ingenuousness was ever among Vipan's faults. But he resolved to keep his weather eye open, and if he must sleep, to do so with that reliable orbit ever brought to bear upon their pleasant-speaking guest.

Soon profound silence reigned within the log cabin, broken only by the subdued, regular breathing of the sleepers, or the occasional stir of the glowing embers. The tempest had lulled, but, as hour followed hour, the voices of the weird waste were borne upon the night in varied and startling cadence; the howling of wolves, the cat-like scream of the panther among the overhanging crags, the responsive hooting of owls beneath the thick blackness of the great pine forests, and once, the fierce snorting growl of a grizzly, so near that the formidable monster seemed even to be snuffing under the very door.

The two owners of the cabin are fast asleep; Vipan with his blanket rolled round his head. The scout, however, is lying on his back, and his blanket has partially slipped off, as though he had found its weight too burdensome. The three are lying with their feet to the fire in fan-shaped formation from it: the scout in the centre, their guest on the outside. The latter, too, is fast asleep.

Is? Surely not. Unless a man can be said to sleep with both eyes open.

A half-charred log fell into the embers, raising a small spluttering flame. This flame glowed on the fierce orbs of the red warrior. For a fraction of a second it glowed on something else, before he hid his hand within his blanket. But the still, steady breathing of the savage was that of a sleeping man.

"Tu-whoo-whoo-whoo!"

Nothing is more dismal than the hoot of an owl in the dead silent night. That owl is very near; almost upon the tree overhead. His voice must have had a disturbing effect upon the dreams of the red man, for in some unaccountable fashion the distance between the latter and the sleeping scout has diminished by about half. Yet the white man has not moved.

"Tu-whoo-whoo-whoo!"

That time it is nearer still. Noiseless, and with a serpentine glide, the head of the savage warrior is reared from the ground, in the semi-gloom resembling the hideous head of some striped and crested snake, and in the dilated eyeball there is a fierce scintillation.

The attitude is one of intense, concentrated listening.

Honest Bill slumbers peacefully on. That hideous head raised over him, scarce half a dozen yards distant, is suggestive of nightmare personified. Yet its owner is his guest, who has eaten at his fireside, and now rests beneath his roof. Why should his slumbers be disturbed?

"Tu-whoo-whoo-whoo!"

Again that doleful cry. But—look now! What deed of dark treachery is this stealthy savage about to perpetrate? He is a yard nearer his sleeping host, and his right hand grips a long keen knife. Ah! will nothing warn the sleeper?

The murderous barbarian rises to his knees, and his blanket noiselessly slips off. And at that moment through the intervening space of gloom comes a low distinct whisper:

"Are the dreams of War Wolf bad, that he moves so far in his sleep?"

Vipan has not moved. His blanket is still rolled round his head, but the fierce Indian, darting his keen glance in the direction of the voice, espies an object protruding from the speaker's blanket that was not there when last he looked. It is about three inches of a revolver barrel, and it is covering him. No fresh scalp or scalps for him to-night.

Let it not be supposed for a moment that the treacherous villain was in any way abashed. It was not in him. He merely replied, pleasantly:

"No—I cannot sleep. I am hungry again, for I have ridden far, and it is now near morning. I would have found the 'chuck' (food) without disturbing Golden Face and The Beaver, who are very weary, and sleep well."

And, knife in hand, he deliberately stepped over to the corner where hung the carcase from which they had feasted the evening before, and cutting off a portion, placed it upon the coals to broil.

Vipan could not but admire the cool readiness of both reply and action. He knew that but for his own wariness, either his friend or himself—possibly both—would by now be entering the Happy Hunting-Grounds, yet from his bloodthirsty and treacherous guest he apprehended no further aggression—that night at any rate. The surprise had failed abjectly; the enemy was on the alert; it was not in Indian nature to make a second attempt under all the circumstances. Moreover, he recognised in the incident a mere passing impulse of ferocity, moving the savage at the sight of these two victims ready,—as he imagined—for the knife, combined with the overmastering temptation to the young warrior to bear back to his village the scalps of two white men—men of considerable renown, too—taken by himself, alone and singlehanded. So he calmly laid down again as if nothing had happened.

The scout, who had awakened at the first sound of voices, and who took in at a glance the whole situation, fully equalled his friend's coolness.

"Snakes!" he remarked, "I had a pesky bad dream. Dreamt I was just goin' to draw on some feller, when I awoke."

"The Beaver has slain many enemies," rejoined War Wolf, nodding his head approvingly. "When a man has taken scalps, he is prompt to take more, even in his dreams."

"And to lose his own, you pison young skunk!" thought Smokestack Bill, in reply to this. "I'll be even with you one day, see if I don't."

But the "pison young skunk," unenlightened as to this event of the future, merely nodded pleasantly as he sat by the fire, knife in hand, assimilating his juicy venison steak with the utmost complacency.

Note 1. Part of the initiatory festival during which, by virtue of undergoing various forms of ghastly self-torture, the growing-up boys are admitted among the ranks of the warriors.

Chapter Three
A Tragedy of the Wild West

It may seem strange that on the face of so forcible a demonstration of the treacherous disposition of their guest, yet a couple of hours after sunrise should see our friends starting in his company for the Sioux villages. But the incident of the night, which might have had so tragic a termination, impressed these men not one whit. It was "all in the day's journey," they said, while admitting that they had been a trifle too confiding. That, however, was a fault easily remedied. But to men who habitually carry their lives in their hands, one peril more or less matters nothing.

As they threaded the mountain defiles nothing could be more good humoured and genial than the young warrior's manner. He chatted and laughed, sang snatches of songs in a high nasal key, bantered Vipan on the poor condition of his nag, and challenged him to a race as soon as they were domiciled in the village. He wanted to know why Golden Face had not followed the example of other white men in the matter of squaws. Red Cloud's village could furnish some famous beauties. Golden Face was rich—he could take his choice. There would be great festivities in his honour, and the prettiest girls would be only too glad to be chosen by a man of his prowess. Thus the genial War Wolf—who amid shouts of laughter extended, or, to be more accurate, "broadened" this vein of fun. Now all this was very jolly, very entertaining; but on one point our two friends were of the same mind. Under no circumstances whatever should the sportive young barbarian be suffered to ride behind. When he stopped, they stopped; and one or two crafty attempts which he made to fall back, they, with equal deftness, resolutely defeated.

It was a lovely morning, crisp and clear. A thin layer of snow lay around, diminishing as the altitude decreased. The frosted pines sparkling in the sun, the great crags towering up to the liquid blue; here the ragged edges of a cliff shooting into the heavens, there a long narrow cañon, whose appalling depth might well make the wayfarer's head swim as his horse slipped and stumbled along the rugged track which skirted its dizzy brink—

all this afforded a scene of varied grandeur, which, with the strong spice of danger thrown in, was calculated to set the blood of the adventurously disposed in a tingle.

They struck into a tortuous defile, whose lofty sandstone walls almost shut out the light of day. High above, soaring in circles, a couple of eagles followed the trio, uttering a harsh yell, but otherwise the voices of Nature were still. Vipan found an opportunity of chaffing the Indian, whom he challenged to bring down one or both of the birds with his bow—a proposal which was met by the suggestion that he could do so with a rifle—would Golden Face let him try with his? Then a wide valley, into which boulders and rocks seemed to have been hurled in lavish confusion. Oak and box elder, dark funereal pines and naked spruce, lay dotted in clumps about a level meadow, through which rushed a half-frozen stream. Suddenly a white shape darted through the leafless brake.

Flash—bang! A snap shot though.

"Get to heel, Shanks! Darn yer hide, you've become so tarnation fat and skeery you ain't worth a little cuss, you ain't," cried the scout, dropping the smoking muzzle of his piece. The dog thus apostrophised was a mangy and utterly useless Indian cur, which the scout had picked up in the woods, and which Vipan was continually urging upon him to shoot. "Sho! you gavorting jack-rabbit! A white wolf 'll make a mouthful of you. And he ain't touched," went on Shanks's master, disgustedly, as the dog slunk to heel. Better not to fire at all than to miss in the presence of an Indian. Then something seemed to strike him.

A raven rose from the ground, uttering a plethoric croak, then another, and the pair flopped heavily up to a limb overhead. A plunge or two through the leafless thicket and they were in a small open space. The wolf—the ravens—each had been disturbed in a hideous repast. There, in the midst of their ravaged camp, the remnants of its fire strewn around them, lay the corpses of two white men, half-charred, frightfully mangled, and—scalped.

Looking upon this doleful spectacle the scout was able to locate the warwhoop he had heard the night before. Vipan, for his own part, cherished a shrewd conviction that he could restore the missing scalps—though too late—merely by the simple process of stretching forth an arm. But the matter was no concern of his. On the other hand, to seize and hold on to the chance of monopolising the search after the precious metal here, preeminently was.

The unfortunate men were evidently miners. The implements of their calling lay around, together with their modest baggage; but their weapons had disappeared. Both had been shot to death with arrows, and that at very close quarters, probably while they were asleep. They were rough looking fellows, one red-haired and red-bearded, the other hatchet-faced, but both with skins tanned to parchment colour.

"Reckon we'll give the poor boys a hoist under the sod," said the scout, shortly. Then as for a moment his steady gaze met that of War Wolf, the latter said:

"Wagh! Bad Indians are about. The white men were too reckless. When they come to find wealth in the country of the Dahcotah they should sleep warily. The Beaver is going to bury his friends. Good. When the shadow is there" (about half an hour) "War Wolf will return."

If there was the faintest satirical gleam in the warrior's eyes as he uttered these words, there would be nothing gained by noticing it. Smokestack Bill, seizing one of the murdered men's picks, began to dig, lustily and in silence, every now and again shaking his head ominously. Vipan, who thought this voluntary sextonship a bore, lent a hand to oblige his friend. These two unknown miners were no more his kin than the savage Sioux who had slain them. He had no kin. All the world was an enemy, to be turned to advantage when possible, and defeated at any rate when not. Had he been alone he would merely have looked, and passed on his way.

By half an hour a hole of adequate dimensions received the two mangled and mutilated corpses. Then, having trodden down the last spadeful of earth, the scout, with a knife, marked a couple of rude crosses upon the trunk of the nearest tree. His companion, consistently callous, said nothing.

As they turned to leave this lonely grave in the wilderness, they were rejoined by the young warrior. He had not been idle. A brace of ruff-grouse, shot by arrows, dangled from his saddle, and the three moved forward in silence, seeking a suitable midday camp.

Chapter Four
The "Squarson" of Lant-Hanger

The Rev. Dudley Vallance was "squarson" of Lant with Lant-Hanger, in the county of Brackenshire, England.

Know, O reader, unversed in the compound mysteries of Mr Lewis Carroll, that the above is a contraction of the words squire-parson.

On the face of this assertion it is perhaps superfluous to state that the Rev. Dudley was a manifest failure in both capacities—superfluous because if this is not invariably the rule under similar circumstances, the exceptions are so rare as to be well-nigh phenomenal.

As squire he was a failure, for he had a pettifogging mind. He was not averse to an occasional bit of sharp practice in his dealings, which would have been creditable to an attorney after the order of Quirk, Gammon, and Snap. Moreover, he was lacking in geniality, and for field sports he cared not a rush.

As parson he was a failure; for so intent was he upon the things of this world that he had neither time nor inclination to inspire his parishioners with any particular hankering after the things of the next. Now this need not seem strange, or even severe, since the fiat has gone forth from the lips of the highest of authorities—"Ye cannot serve God and Mammon."

In aspect the Rev. Dudley was tall and lank. He had a very long nose and a very long beard. Furthermore, he had rather shifty eyes and a normally absent manner. When not absent-minded, the latter was suave and purring. His age was about fifty.

In the matter of progeny he was blessed with a fair quiverful—eight to wit—of whom seven were daughters. His spouse was nothing if not fully alive to a sense of her position. This she imagined to consist mainly in a passion for precedence, gossip, cliquerie, and deft mischief-making at secondhand. If she fell short in one thing it was in that aggressive and domineering fussiness habitually inseparable from the type, but this was only because she lacked the requisite energy. Howbeit, she never forgot that she was "Squarsina" of Lant with Lant-Hanger—if we may be allowed to coin a word. This was not wholly unnecessary, for others were wont to lose sight of the fact.

Lant Hall—commonly abbreviated to Lant—the abode of the Vallances, was rather an ugly house; squat, staringly modern, and hideously embattled in sham castellated style. But it was charmingly situated—dropped, as it were, upon the side of a hill, whose vivid green slope, falling to a large sheet of ornamental water, was alive with the branching antlers of many deer. Overshadowing the house lay a steep wooded acclivity—or hanger—at one end of which lay the village, whence the name of the latter. "A sweetly pretty, peaceful spot," gushed the visitor, or the tourist driving through it; "a nook to end one's days in!"

Scenically, the prospect was enchanting. On the one hand, line upon line of wooded hills fed the eye as far as that organ cared to roam, on the other, softly undulating pastures, with snug farmhouses and peeping cottages here and there. Skirting the village on one side, the limpid waters of the Lant sparkled and swirled beneath the old grey bridge—which bore the Vallance arms—and then plunged on, to lose themselves in a mile of dark fir wood, where the big trout lay and fattened. A lovely champaign, in sooth; small wonder that the aesthetic stranger should be smitten with a desire to end his days in so sweet a spot.

But this sweet spot had its disadvantages. It was frightfully out of the way, being five miles from the nearest railway station, and that on a branch line. The necessaries of life were only to be obtained with difficulty, and farm and dairy produce was expensive, and in supply, precarious. There was one butcher, and no baker, and a post-office chiefly noteworthy for the blundering wherewith Her Majesty's mails were received and dispensed. Moreover, the Brackenshire folk were not of a particularly pleasant rustic type. They were very "independent," which is to say they did what seemed right in their own eyes, irrespective of such little matters as honesty or square dealing. They were, as a rule, incapable of speaking the truth, except accidentally, and they had very long tongues. Suffice it briefly to say, they excelled in the low and sordid cunning which usually characterises the simple-hearted rustic of whatever county.

The Rev. Dudley Vallance had a shibboleth which he never wearied of pronouncing. This was it:—County Society.

Now, at Lant-Hanger this article, within anything like the accepted meaning of the term, did not exist.

It was a crying want, and like all such so capable, it must be supplied. Our "squarson" set to work to supply it by a simple device. He went into bricks and mortar.

His jerry-built "bijou residences," and tinkered-up rustic cottages soon let, and let comfortably—for him. Not so for the tenants, however, for the honest Brackenshire craftsmen "did" their employer most thoroughly, and the luckless householders found themselves let in for all sorts of horrors they had never bargained for. Thus the Rev. Dudley "did" as he was "done." But he got his "County Society."

This, at the period with which we have to deal, in the year of grace 1875, consisted of a sprinkling of maiden ladies and clergymen's relicts, who leased the delectable dwellings aforesaid; a retired jerry-builder, who knew better than to do anything of the kind; the village doctor; a few neighbouring vicars of infinitesimal intellect; a couple of squireens evolved from three generations of farmers, and, lastly, Mr Santorex of Elmcote; all of whom, with the notable exception of the last-named, constituted an array of satellites revolving round the centre planet, the Rev. Dudley himself.

The Lant property, though comparatively small, was a snug possession. Aesthetically a fair domain, it was all of it good land, and the five to six thousand acres composing it all let well. Wholly unencumbered by mortgages or annuity charges, it was estimated to bring in about 7,000 pounds a year, so that in reckoning the present incumbent a fortunate man, the neighbourhood was not far wrong. There were, however, half-forgotten hints, which the said neighbourhood would now and again let drop—hints not exactly to the credit of the present squire. For it was well known that the Rev. Dudley had inherited Lant from his uncle, not his father, and that this uncle's son was still living.

Chapter Five
The Santorexes of Elmcote

"Now, Chickie, hurry up with the oats, and we'll go and try for a brace of trout before the sun blazes out."

"Mercy on us, do let the child finish her breakfast! It's bad enough being obliged to have it twice laid, without being hurried to death, one would think."

But the "child" stands in no need of the maternal—and querulous—championship.

"I'm ready, father," she cries, pushing her chair back.

"Right. Get on a hat then," is the reply, in a prompt and decisive, but not ungenial tone, and the head which had been thrust through the partially opened door disappears.

"That's your father all over," continued the maternal and querulous voice. "How does he know I don't want you at home this morning? But no, that doesn't matter a pin. I may be left to toil and slave, cooped up in the house, while everybody else is frisking about the fields all day long, fishing and what not—"

"But, mother, you don't really want me, do you?"

"—And then your father must needs come down so early, and, of course, wants his breakfast at once, and then it has to be brought on twice; and he must flurry and fidget everyone else into the bargain. Want you? No, child, I don't want you. Go away and catch some fish. If I did want you, that wouldn't count while your father did—oh, no."

Yseulte Santorex made no reply. She did the best thing possible—however, she kissed and coaxed the discontented matron, and took a prompt opportunity of escaping.

One might search far and wide before meeting with a more beautiful girl. Rather above the medium height, and of finely formed frame, it needed not the smallness of her perfectly shaped hands and the artistic regularity of her features to stamp her as thoroughbred. It was sufficient to note the upright poise of her head, and the straight glance of her grand blue eyes, but surer hall-mark still, she was blessed with a beautifully modulated voice. When we add that she possessed a generous allowance of dark brown hair, rippling into gold, we claim to have justified our opening statement concerning her. Her age at this time was twenty; as for her disposition, well, reader, you must find that out for yourself in the due development of this narrative.

Losing no more time than was necessary to fling on a wide straw hat, the girl joined her father in the hall, where he was waiting a little impatiently — rod, basket, landing-net, all ready.

"You shall land the first fish, Chickie," he said, as they started. "It isn't worth while taking a rod apiece, we shall have too little time," with a glance upward at the clouded sky which seemed disposed to clear every moment.

"I oughtn't to tax your self-denial so severely, dear," answered the girl, "when I know you're dying to get at the river yourself."

"Self-denial, eh? Thing the preachers strongly recommend, and — always practise. Beginning here," with a slight indicating nod.

Yseulte laughed. She knew her father's opinion of his spiritual pastor — in point of fact, shared it.

"I knew a man once who used to say that self-abnegation was a thing not far removed from the philosopher's stone. Its indulgence inspired him with absolute indifference to life and the ills thereof, and at the same time with a magnificent contempt for the poor creatures for whose benefit he practised it."

"Very good philosophy, father. But the compensation for foregoing the delights of having one's own way is not great."

"My dear girl, that depends. The key to the above exposition lies in the fact that that individual never had a chance of getting his own way. So he made a virtue of necessity — an art which, though much talked about, is seldom cultivated."

"Your friend was a humbug, father," was the laughing reply. "A doleful humbug, and no philosopher at all."

"Eh? The effrontery of the rising generation — commonly called in the vulgar tongue — nerve! A humbug! So that's your opinion, is it, young woman?"

"Yes, it is," she answered decisively, her blue eyes dancing.

"Phew-w! Nothing like having your own opinion, and sticking to it," was all he said, with a dry chuckle. Then he subsided into silence, whistling meditatively, as if pondering over the whimsicality he had just propounded, or contemplating a fresh one. These same whimsicalities, by the way, were continually cropping up in Mr Santorex' conversation, to the no small confusion of his acquaintance, who never could quite make out whether he was in jest or earnest, to the delight of his satirical soul. To the infinitesimal intellects of his neighbours—the surrounding vicars, for instance—he was a conversational nightmare. They voted him dangerous, even as their kind so votes everything which happens to be incomprehensible to its own subtle ken. What sort of training could it be for a young girl just growing to womanhood to have such a man for a father—to take in his pernicious views and ideas as part of her education, as it were? And herein the surrounding vicaresses were at one with their lords. Stop! Their what? We mean their—chattels.

But Yseulte herself laughed their horror to scorn. Her keen perceptions detected it in a moment, and she would occasionally visit its expression with a strong spice of hereditary satire. She could not remember the time when her father had treated her otherwise than as a rational and accountable being, and the time when he should cease to do so would never come—of that she was persuaded. Nor need it be inferred that she was "strong-minded," "advanced," or aspiring in any way to the "blue." Far from it. She had plenty of character, but withal she was a very sweet, lovable, even-tempered, and thoroughly sensible girl.

There were two other children besides herself—had been, rather, for one had lain in Lant churchyard this last ten years. The other, and eldest, was cattle-ranching in the Far West, and doing fairly well.

Mr Santorex was unquestionably a fine-looking man. A broad, lofty brow, straight features, and firm, clear eyes, imparted to his face a very decided expression, which his method of speech confirmed. He was of Spanish origin, a fact of which he was secretly proud; for although Anglicised, even to his name, for several generations, yet in direct lineage he could trace back to one of the very oldest and noblest families of Spain.

Though now in easy circumstances, not to say wealthy, he had not always been so. During the score of years he had lived at Lant-Hanger, about half of that period had been spent in dire poverty—a period fraught with experiences which had left a more than bitter taste in his mouth as regarded his neighbours and surroundings generally, and the Rev. Dudley Vallance in particular. Then the tide had turned—had turned just in the nick of time. A small property which he held in the north of Spain, and which had hitherto furnished him with the scantiest means of subsistence, suddenly became enormously valuable as a field of mineral wealth.

With his changed circumstances Mr Santorex did not shake off the dust of Lant-Hanger from his shoes. He had become in a way accustomed to the place, and was fond of the country, if not of the people. So he promptly leased Elmcote, a snug country box picturesquely perched on the hillside overlooking the valley of the Lant, and having moved in, sat down grimly to enjoy the impending joke.

He had not long to wait. Lant-Hanger opened wide its arms, and fairly trod on its own heels in its eagerness to make much of the new "millionaire," whom, in his indigent days, it had so consistently cold-shouldered as a disagreeable and highly undesirable sort of neighbour. Next to Lant Hall itself, Elmcote was the most important house in the parish, and its tenant had always been the most important personage. So "County Society," following the example of its head and cornerstone, the Rev. Dudley Vallance, metaphorically chucked up its hat and hoorayed over its acquisition.

Down by the river-side this warm spring morning, Yseulte, never so happy as when engaged in this, her favourite sport, was wielding her fly-rod with skill and efficiency, as many a gleaming and speckled trophy lying in her creel served to show.

The movement became her well. Every curve of her symmetrical form was brought out by the graceful exercise. Her father, standing well back from the bank, watched her with critical approval. True to his character as a man of ideas, he almost forgot the object of the present undertaking in his admiration for his beautiful daughter, and his thoughts, thus started, went off at express speed. What a lovely girl she was growing—had grown, indeed. What was to be her destiny in life? She must make a good match of course, not throw herself away upon any clodhopper in this wretched hole. That young lout, Geoffrey Vallance, was always mooning in calf-like fashion about her. Not good enough. Oh, no; nothing like. Seven thousand a year unencumbered was hardly to be sneezed at; still, she must not throw herself away on any such unlicked cub. He fancied he could do better for her in putting her through a London season—much better. And then came an uneasy and desolating stirring of even his philosophical pulses at the thought of parting with her. He was an undemonstrative man—undemonstrative even to coldness. He made at no time any great show of affection. He had long since learned that affection, like cash, was an article far too easily thrown away. But there was one living thing for which, deep down in his heart of hearts, he cherished a vivid and warm love, and that was this beautiful and companionable daughter of his.

"Never mind about me, dear. I think I won't throw a fly this morning," he said, as the girl began insisting that he should take a turn, there being only one rod between them. "Besides, it's about time to knock off altogether. The sun is coming out far too brightly for many more rises."

"Father," said the girl, as she took her fishing-rod to pieces, "I can't let you shirk that question any longer. Am I to pay that visit to George's ranche this summer or not?"

"Why, you adventurous Chickie, you will be scalped by Indians, tossed by mad buffaloes, bolted with by wild horses. Heaven knows what. Hallo! Enter Geoffry Plantagenet. He seems in a hurry."

"No! Where? Oh, what a nuisance!"

Following her father's glance, Yseulte descried a male figure crossing the stile which led into the field where they were sitting, and recognised young Vallance, who between themselves was known by the above nickname. He seemed, indeed, in a desperate hurry, judging from the alacrity wherewith he skipped over the said stile and hastened to put a goodly space of ground between it and himself before looking back. A low, rumbling noise, something between a growl and a moan, reached their ears, and thrust against the barrier was discernible from where they sat the author of it—a red, massive bovine head to wit. Struggling to repress a shout of laughter, they continued to observe the new arrival, who had not yet discovered them, and who kept turning back to make sure his enemy was not following, in a state of trepidation that was intensely diverting to the onlookers.

"Hallo, Geoffry!" shouted Mr Santorex. "Had old Muggins' bull after you?"

He addressed started as if a shot had been fired in his ear. It was bad enough to have been considerably frightened, but to awake to the fact that Yseulte Santorex had witnessed him in the said demoralised state was discouraging, to say the least of it.

"That's worse than the last infliction of Muggins you underwent, isn't it, Mr Vallance?" said the latter mischievously, referring to the idiotic game of cards of that name.

"Did he chevy you far, Geoffry?" went on Mr Santorex, in the same bantering tone.

"Er—ah—no; not very," said the victim, who was somewhat perturbed and out of breath. "He's an abominably vicious brute, and ought to be shot.

He'll certainly kill somebody one of these days. I must—er—really mention the matter to the governor."

But there was consolation in store for the ill-used Geoffry. Having thus fallen in with the Santorex's it was the most natural thing in the world that he should accompany them the greater part of the way home. Consolation? Well, have we not sufficiently emphasised the fact that Yseulte Santorex was a very beautiful girl?

It must be admitted that the future Squire of Lant did not, either in personal appearance or mental endowment, attain any higher standard than commonplace mediocrity. He was very much a reproduction of his father, though without his father's calculating and avaricious temperament, for he was a good-natured fellow enough in his way. "No harm in him, and too big a fool ever to be a knave," had been Mr Santorex' verdict on this fortunate youth as he watched him grow up. Had he been aware of it, this summing-up would sorely have distressed the young Squire, for of late during the Oxford vacation Geoffry Vallance had eagerly seized or manufactured opportunities for being a good deal at Elmcote.

Chapter Six
The Indian Village

A long, open valley, bounded on either side by flat, table-topped hills, and threaded by a broad but shallow stream, whose banks are fringed by a straggling belt of timber. Sheltered by this last stand tall conical lodges, some in irregular groups, some dotted down in twos and threes, others in an attempt at regularity and the formation of a square, but the whole extending for upwards of a mile. In the far distance, at the open end of the valley, the eye is arrested by turret-shaped buttes, showing the *bizarre* formation and variegated strata characteristic of the "Bad Lands." The stream is known as Dog Creek, and along its banks lie the winter villages of a considerable section of the Sioux and Cheyenne tribes.

The westering sun, declining in the blue frosty sky, lights up the river like a silver band, and glows upon the white picturesque lodges, throwing into prominence the quaint and savage devices emblazoned upon their skin walls. Within the straggling encampment many dark forms are moving, and the clear air rings ever and anon with the whoop of a gang of boys, already playing at warlike games; the shrill laughter of young squaws, and the cackle of old ones; an occasional neigh from the several herds of ponies feeding out around the villages and the tramp of their hoofs; or vibrates to the nasal song of a circle of jovial merrymakers. Here and there, squatted around a fire in the open, huddled up in their blankets, may be descried a group of warriors, solemnly whiffing at their long pipes, the while keeping up a drowsy hum of conversation in a guttural undertone, and from the apex of each pyramidal *"teepe"* a column of blue smoke rises in rings upon the windless atmosphere. It is a lovely day, and although the surrounding hills are powdered with snow, down here in the valley the hardened ground sparkles with merely a crisp touch of frost.

Then as the gloaming deepens the fires glow more redly, and the life and animation of the great encampment increases. Young bucks, bedaubed with paint, and arrayed in beadwork and other articles of savage finery, swagger and lounge about; the nodding eagle quill cresting their scalp-locks giving them a rakish, and at the same time martial, aspect, as they wander from tent to tent, indulging in guffaws amongst themselves, or exchanging broad "chaff" with a brace or so of coppery damsels here and there, who, for their part, can give as readily and as freely as they can take. Or a group is engaged in an impromptu dance, both sexes taking part, to a running accompaniment of combined guttural and nasal drone, varied now and again by a whoop. Wolfish curs skulk around, on the look-out to steal if allowed the chance, snarling over any stray offal that may be thrown them, or uttering a shrill yelp on receipt of an arrow or two from some mischievous urchin's toy bow; and, altogether, with the fall of night, the hum and chatter pervading this wild community seems but to increase.

Great stars blaze forth in the frosty sky, not one by one, but with a rush, for now darkness has settled upon the scene, though penetrated and scattered here and there by the red glare of some convivial or household fire. And now it becomes apparent that some event of moment is to take place shortly, for a huge fire is kindled in front of the large council-lodge, which stands in the centre of the village, and, mingling with the monotonous "tom-tom" of drums, the voices of heralds are raised, convening chiefs and warriors to debate in solemn conclave.

No second summons is needed. The unearthly howling of the dancers is hushed as if by magic, the horseplay and boisterous humour of youthful bucks is laid aside, and from far and near all who can lay claim to the rank of warrior—even the youngest aspirants to the same hanging on the outskirts of the crowd—come trooping towards the common centre.

Within the council-lodge burns a second fire, the one outside being for the accommodation of the crowd, and it is round this that the real debate will take place. As the flames shoot up crisply, the interior is vividly illumined, displaying the trophies with which the walls are decked—trophies of the chase and trophies of war, horns and rare skins, scalps and weapons; and, disposed in regular order, the mysterious "medicine bags" and "totems" of the tribal magnates, grotesque affairs mostly, birds' heads and claws, bones or grinning jaws of some animal, the whole plentifully set off with beadwork and paint and feathers.

Then the crowd outside parts decorously, giving passage to those whose weight and standing entitle them to a seat within the sacred lodge, and a voice in the council. Stately chieftains arrayed in their most brilliant war-costumes—the magnificent war-bonnets of eagles' plumes cresting their heads and flowing almost to the ground behind, adding an indescribably martial and dignified air to their splendid stature and erect carriage—advance with grave and solemn step to the council fire and take their seats, speaking not a word, and looking neither to the right nor to the left Partisans, or warriors of tried skill and daring, who, without the rank and following of chiefs, are frequently elected to lead an expedition on the war-path, these, too, in equally splendid array, have a place in the assembly; after them, lesser braves, until the lodge can hold no more. The crowd must listen to what it can of the debates from without.

From the standpoint of their compatriots, some of these warriors are very distinguished men indeed. There is Long Bull, and Mountain Cat, and Crow-Scalper, all implacable and redoubted foes of the whites. There is Burnt Wrist, and Spotted Tail, and Lone Panther, and a dozen other notable chiefs. Last, but not least, there is Red Cloud, orator, statesman, and seer, the war-chief of the Ogallalla clan, and medicine chief virtually of the whole Sioux nation.

The flames of the council fire leap and crackle, casting a lurid glow on the stern visages of the assembled warriors. Many of these wear brilliantly-coloured tunics of cloth or dressed buckskin, more or less tastefully adorned with beadwork or shining silver plates. Over this, carelessly thrown, or gracefully dangling from its wearer's shoulder, is the outer "robe" of soft buffalo hide, blazoned all over with hieroglyphics and pictures setting forth the owner's feats of arms or prowess in the chase, and among the scalp-locks fringeing tunics and leggings may be descried not a few that originally grew upon Anglo-Saxon heads. But all is in harmony, tasteful, barbarically picturesque; and the air of self-possessed dignity stamped upon the countenances of these plumed and stately warriors could not be surpassed by the most august assembly that ever swayed the affairs of old civilisation.

One more personage is there whom we have omitted to mention. Leaning against a lodge pole, as thoroughly unconcerned and at his ease among the red chieftains as ever he was in Belgravian boudoir, his splendid face as impassive as their own, sits Rupert Vipan, and if ever man lived who was thoroughly calculated to inspire respect in the breasts of these warlike savages, assuredly he was that man. That he is here at all is sufficient to show in what honour he is held among his barbarian entertainers.

And now in order to render more clearly the drift of the subsequent debate, some slight digression may here be necessary.

The Sioux, or Dahcotah, as they prefer to be called, are about the only aboriginal race in North America whose numbers and prowess entitle them to rank as a nation. They are sub-divided into clans or tribes: Ogallalla, Minneconjou, Uncpapa, Brulé, and many more, with the specification of which we need not weary the reader, but all more or less independent of each other, and acting under their own chiefs or not, as they choose. At the time of our story the whole of these, numbering about 60,000 souls, occupied a large tract comprising the south-western half of the territory of Dakota, together with the adjacent extensive range in eastern Montana and Wyoming, watered by the Yellowstone and Powder Rivers and their tributaries, and commonly called after the last-named stream. On the border-line of Dakota and Wyoming, and therefore within the Indian reservation, stand the Black Hills, a rugged mountain group rising nearly 8,000 feet above the sea level, an insight into whose wild and romantic fastnesses we have already given.

At that period popular rumour credited the Black Hills with concealed wealth to a fabulous extent. Gold had already been found there, not in any great quantities, but still it had been found, and the nature and formation of the soil pointed to its existence in vast veins, at least so said popular rumour. That was enough. Men began to flock to this new Eldorado. Parties of prospectors and miners found their way to its sequestered valleys, and soon the rocks rang to the sound of the pick, and the mountain streams which gurgled through its savage solitudes were fouled with the washing of panned dirt.

But the miners had two factors to reckon with—the Government and the Indians. The former was bound by treaty to keep white men, particularly miners, out of the Indian reservation; the latter became more and more discontented over the non-fulfilment of the agreement. The shrewd tribesmen knew that gold was even a greater enemy to their race than rum. The discovery of gold meant an incursion of whites; first a few, then thousands; cities, towns, machinery. Then good-bye to the game, whereby they largely subsisted; good-bye, indeed, to the country itself, as far as they were concerned. They threatened war.

It became necessary for something to be done. Troops were sent to patrol the Black Hills, with strict injunctions to arrest all white men and send them under guard to the settlements. This was extensively done. But the expelled miners, watching their chance, lost no time in slipping back again, and their numbers, so far from decreasing, had just the opposite tendency, arrests notwithstanding.

Then the United States Government resolved to purchase the Black Hills, and made overtures to the Sioux accordingly. The latter were divided in opinion. Some were for terms, the only question being as to their liberality; others were for rejecting the proposal at any price, and if the Government still persisted in its neglect to keep out the white intruders, why then they must take the defence of their rights into their own hands.

Pause, O philanthropic reader, ere running away with the idea that these poor savages' rights were being ruthlessly trampled on; and remember the old legal maxim about coming into court with clean hands. The Government tried to do its best, but in a vast, rugged, and lawless country the inhabitants are not to be policed as in a well-ordered city of the Old World. Men could not be hung merely for encroaching on the reservation, and the state of popular feeling precluded any sort of deterrent punishment. And then, were the Indians themselves strictly observing their side of the treaty? Let us see.

For several summers the bands roaming in the Powder River country had perpetrated not a few murders of whites, had run off stock and destroyed property to a considerable extent, in short, had taken the war-path, and this although nominally at peace. Now it was by virtue of keeping the peace that their exclusive rights over the encroached-upon territory had been conceded.

We have said that the Sioux were made up of various sub-divisions or clans. Now at that time there was not one of these which did not furnish a quota of warriors to swell the ranks of the hostiles. Nominally at peace, and drawing rations from the Government, the turbulent spirits of these tribes would slip away quietly in small parties, to join the hostile chiefs for a summer raid, returning to the agencies when they had had enough fighting and plunder, and becoming—in popular parlance—"good Indians" again. These escapades were either winked at by the tribal chiefs, who remained quietly at the agencies, "keeping in" with the Government, or were simply beyond their power to prevent. Probably both attitudes held good, for the control exercised by an Indian chief over his band or tribe seldom amounts to more than moral suasion.

Briefly, then, the Sioux and their allies, the Northern Cheyennes, might be thus classified:—

1. The hostiles, i.e., the bold and lawless faction who hardly made any secret of being on the war-path. These held the broken and rugged fastnesses of the Powder River country already referred to.

2. The Agency Indians who, sitting still on their reserves, helped their hostile brethren with information and supplies.

3. The turbulent youths on the reservation, always ready to slip away on their own account, or to join the hostiles, in search of scalps, plunder, and fun in general.

4. The whole lot, ripe for any devilment, provided it offered a safe chance of success.

Such was the state of affairs in 1873-4-5, and now apologising to the reader for this digression, let us get back to our council.

Chapter Seven
The Council

In silence the "medicine-man" prepared the great pipe, his lips moving in a magical incantation as he solemnly filled it. Then handing the stem to Vipan, who was seated on the right of Red Cloud, he applied a light to the bowl. This "medicine" or council pipe was a magnificent affair, as suited its solemn and ceremonial character. The large and massive bowl was of porous red stone, the stem, upwards of a yard in length, being profusely ornamented with beadwork and quills, and at intervals of a few inches flowed three long and carefully-dressed scalp-locks. Vipan, fully alive to the position of honour he occupied, gravely inhaled the aromatic mixture with the utmost deliberation, expelling the smoke in clouds from his mouth and nostrils. Then he passed it on to Red Cloud, who, after the same ceremony, in similar fashion passed it to the chief next him on his left, and so in dead silence it went round the circle, each warrior taking a series of long draws, and then, having handed the pipe to his neighbour, emitting a vast volume of smoke by a slow process which seemed to last several minutes, and the effect of which was not a little curious.

No word had been uttered since they entered the lodge, and not until the pipe had made the complete round of the circle was the silence broken. Then a sort of professional orator, whose mission was something similar to that of counsel for the plaintiff—viz., to "open the case"—arose and proceeded to set forth the grounds of debate. The Dahcotah, he said, were a great nation, and so were their brethren the Cheyennes, who also had an interest in the matter which had brought them together. Both were represented here by many of their most illustrious chiefs and their bravest warriors, several of whom, in passing, the orator proceeded to name, together with the boldest feat of arms of each, and at each of these panegyrics a guttural "How-how!" went forth from his listeners. The Dahcotah were not only a great people and a brave people, but they were also a long-suffering people. Who among all the red races had such good hearts as the Dahcotah? Who among them would have remained at peace under such provocation as they had received and continued to receive?

The debate was getting lively now. An emphatic exclamation of assent greeted the orator, whose tone, hitherto even, began to wax forcible.

When the Dahcotah agreed to bury the hatchet with the Mehneaska (Americans)—went on the speaker—a treaty was entered into, and under this the Great Father (the President of the United States) promised that the reservations they now occupied should be secured to them for ever—that no white men should be allowed within them, either to hunt or to settle or to search for gold, and on these conditions the Dahcotah agreed to abandon the war-path. That was seven years ago. They had abandoned it. They had "travelled on the white man's road," had sat within their reservations, molesting no one. They had made expeditions to their hunting-grounds to find food for their families and skins to build their lodges, but they had sent forth no war-parties. They had always treated the whites well. And now, how had the Great Father kept his promises? White men were swarming into the Dahcotah country. First they came by twos and threes, quietly, and begging to be admitted as friends. Then they came by twenties, armed with rifles and many cartridges, and began to lay out towns. Soon the Dahcotah country would be black with the smoke of their chimneys, and the deer and the buffalo, already scarce, would be a thing of the past. Look at Pahsapa (the Black Hills). Every valley was full of white men digging for gold. What was this gold, and whose was it? Was it not the property of the Dahcotah nation, on whose ground it lay hidden? If it was valuable, then the Great Father should make the Dahcotah nation rich with valuable things in exchange for it. But these intruding whites took the gold and gave nothing to its owners—threatened them with bullets instead. It had been suggested that they should sell Pahsapa. But these Hills were "great medicine"—sacred ground entrusted to the Dahcotah by the Good Spirit of Life. How could they sell them? What price would be equivalent to such a precious possession? There was a chief here of mighty renown—the war-chief of the Ogallalla—who had led the nation again and again to victory, whose war-whoop had scattered the whites like buffalo before the hunters, the "medicine chief" of the Dahcotah race. When the council should hear his words on this matter their path would be plain before them.

As the orator ceased an emphatic grunt went round the circle with a unanimity that spoke volumes. Red Cloud (Note 1), thus directly referred to, made, however, no sign. Motionless as a statue, there was a thoughtful, abstracted look upon his massive countenance, as though he had not heard a word of the harangue.

A few moments of silence, then another chief arose—a man of lofty stature and of grim and scowling aspect, his eyes scintillating with a cruel glitter from beneath his towering war-bonnet. After less than usual of the conventional brag as to the greatness of his nation and so forth, speaking fiercely and eagerly, as if anxious to come to the point, he went on:—

"What enemy has not felt the spring of Mountain Cat? From the far hunting-grounds of the Kiowas and the Apaches to the boundary line of the English in the North, there is not a spot of ground that Mountain Cat has not swept with his war-parties; not a village of the crawling Shoshones or skulking Pawnees that he has not taken scalps from; not a waggon train of these invading whites that he has not struck. When in the South the destroying locusts sweep down upon the land, they come not in one mighty cloud. No. They come one at a time at first, then a few more, fluttering quietly, far apart. It is nothing. But lo! in a moment there is a cloud in the air—a rush of wings, and the land is black with them—everything is devoured. So it is with these whites. One comes to trade, another comes to hunt, a third comes to visit us, two more come to search for this gold, and lo! the land is hidden beneath their devastating bands. Their stinking chimneys blacken the air, their poisonous firewater kills our young men or reduces them to the level of the whites themselves, who drink until they wallow like hogs upon the earth, and brother kills brother because he has drunk away his mind and has become a brute beast. Who would have dealings with such dogs as these?

"There was a time when our hunting-grounds shook beneath the tread of countless buffalo. Then we were great because free and feared—for who in those days dared incur the enmity of the Dahcotah? What happened? The whites built their accursed roads and the steam-horse came puffing over the plains, and where are the buffalo to-day? The land is white with their skeletons, but will skeletons feed the Dahcotah and supply skins for their winter lodges? The Great Father" (and the savage uttered the words with a contemptuous sneer) "then said, 'Let us send and kill all the buffalo, and the red races will starve.' So the white hunters came from the east and destroyed our food for ever. And where are we to-day? Are we not living like beggars? Are we not dependent on the Agencies for our daily food and clothing, instead of upon our own arrows and lances as of yore? First came the settlers, whom we treated as friends, then the steam-horse and the iron road, then the finding of the gold. Where this gold is, there the whites swarm. What do we gain, I say, by treating with these lying Mehneaska? What have we ever gained? When they sought to throw open our territory by cutting it with a broad road, did we treat? No, we fought. Where is that road to-day? Where are the forts built along it to keep it open? Gone—all gone. But the buffalo—what few are left—are there. How many would be left now had we traded away our rights? Not one. The whole Dahcotah nation went out upon the war-path.

"The whites begged for peace, and we granted it them. They agreed to respect our country, which was all we asked. Seven years have gone by, and how is that agreement kept? Go, count the white men digging in Pahsapa. Ha! There are many scalps to be had in Pahsapa."

His tone, which had hitherto been one of quick, fierce emphasis, here assumed a slow and deadly meaning. The young warriors, listening without, gripped their weapons with a murmur of delighted applause. Mountain Cat was a chieftain after their own heart. Let him but set up the war-post that very night. All the young men in the village would strike it.

"We are strong," he continued, "strong and united. Our bands are defending our hunting-grounds between this and the Yellowstone, but what shall be thought of us if we allow the whites to invade us here, to deprive us of the medicine hills without a struggle? Are we men, or have we become squaws since we began to receive doles of Government beef?"

Then the fierce savage, raising his voice, his eyes blazing like lightning, stretched forth his arm in denunciatory gesture over the assembly, and continued:

"Mountain Cat will never trust the promises of these Mehneaska. If they want Pahsapa, let them take it by right of conquest—by seizing it from the unconquerable Dahcotah. There are scalps to be taken in Pahsapa. Let the whole Dahcotah nation once more go out upon the war-path. I have said."

Vipan, listening impassively, though with keen attention, to every word that was uttered, here caught the eye of War Wolf. The young warrior's face was a study in sardonic ferocity at the words, "There are scalps to be taken in Pahsapa," and he grinned with delight over the fiendish joke shared between himself and Golden Face.

The young bucks in the background were in ecstasies of glee. They anticipated no end of fun in the near future.

Several other speakers followed, and opinions on the advisability of war varied considerably. Most of them advocated the sale, but for an enormous price. There was a white man among them to-night, they said, of a different race to these other whites, and towards him their hearts were good. He loved his red brethren; he was their brother. He had told them about other lands than that of the Mehneaska—lands as large and as rich beyond the great Salt Lake. They must listen to him, for he was wise. He understood the ways of the whites, and would teach the Dahcotah how to deal with them—so that if Pahsapa should be sold they should receive full price; and not, as in other transactions, receive payment in promises.

This, more or less plainly put, was the burden of their speeches. Vipan, listening with more than Indian composure, felt that things were tending all as he would have them. It may here be stated that he was alone among his red entertainers; Smokestack Bill, foreseeing how affairs were likely to drift, having returned to the log cabin among the mountains. For once the adventurer was glad of his comrade's absence. He could play his cards more freely; besides, the Indians trusted him as belonging to another race. Had the scout been still in the village, the two white men would not have been admitted to this council.

Then arose Spotted Tail, the head chief of the Brulé bands, and after Red Cloud, perhaps one of the most influential chiefs of the nation. He made a long oration, of considerable eloquence, but it was all in favour of peace. There was no need, he said, to reiterate that they were a great nation. Everybody knew it. As many speakers had asserted, the Dahcotah had never been conquered. Why was this? Because they were not only a brave but a prudent people. A brave man without prudence was like a grizzly bear—he might slay so many enemies more or less, but he invited his own destruction by rushing upon their rifles. As with a man, so it was with a nation. Prudence was everything. This gold which white men were now finding among the Hills—did not all experience show that wherever it was discovered, there the whites would soon appear in countless swarms? Gold was the "medicine" of the whites—they could not resist it. Not even all the warriors the Dahcotah could muster could in the long run stand between the whites and gold—no, nor all the warriors of every tribe from the Apaches in the south to the Blackfeet on the English boundary line. The last time they went upon the war-path it was to prevent the whites from making a broad road through their country—and they succeeded. If they went upon it this time it would be to keep the whites away from this gold. That was a thing which no tribe or nation had ever succeeded in doing yet, or ever would. Let the Dahcotah be prudent.

As for these Hills, it was true they were "great medicine," but the people seldom hunted in them. They were not of much use. The Mehneaska were very anxious to possess them, and the Great Father was so rich he could afford to give such a price as would make the Dahcotah rich too. Besides, it was evident that he wished to treat them fairly this time, for had he not sent troops to drive away the intruding gold-seekers? They had come back, it was true; but this only proved the difficulties besetting the whole question. Let the Dahcotah nation be prudent—prudence was the keystone to every matter of international difficulty. His counsel was for entering into negotiations at once about the purchase. He was also emphatically on the side of peace.

Very faint were the murmurs of applause from the young men outside as Spotted Tail resumed his seat. The war spirit was in the air, and the burden of his speech was unpalatable to them. Then Red Cloud said:

"Golden Face sits in an honoured place at the council fire of the Dahcotah people. They will listen to his words as to the voice of a brother."

With a slight bend of the head in acknowledgment of this graceful invitation, Vipan arose. As he stood for a few moments silently contemplating the circle of stately chiefs, the firelight glinting on the flowing masses of his beard and bringing into strong relief the herculean proportions of his towering stature, there was not an eye among the crowd of fierce and excitable savages but dilated with admiration. Here was indeed a man.

"Who am I that stand to address you to-night?" he began, speaking in their own tongue with ease and fluency. "Who knows? I will not boast. Suffice it to say that I have led men to war, in other lands beyond the great salt seas. I have struck the enemy, and that not once only. I have seen his back, but he has never seen mine. Enough. Who am I? It has been said that I am not of the race around us. That is so. There are many white races; that to which I have belonged matters nothing, for I own no race, I am akin to all the world," with a sweep of the arm that would have done credit to one of their own most finished orators.

"The people whose hearts are straight towards me, whether light or dark, white or red, that is my people. Those who deal fairly with me, I deal fairly with; those who do not, let them beware. You in council have asked my advice. I cannot give advice, but my *opinion* the chiefs before me can value or not.

"I have listened to the speeches of many valiant men. Some have advocated peace, others have been for war. It is a simple thing to go to war. Is it? When the red men strike the war-post, they muster their warriors, and go forth to battle. When the whites decide on war, they collect their dollars, and pay soldiers to go and fight for them. The red men fight with weapons, the whites with dollars. The red men would rather forego their chance of booty than lose one warrior. The whites would rather lose a thousand soldiers than five thousand dollars. But, you will say: If the whites have the dollars, and value not the lives of other people, what chance have we, for they are rich, and can pay? Wait a moment. Men are wonderfully alike, whether red or white. Is it your experience that the richest man is the man who cares least for his possessions? It is not mine.

"Now let your ears be open, for this is the point. The fear of losing men will not deter the whites from going to war; no, not for a moment, but the fear of losing dollars will. It is not the soldiers who make the war, it is the people who pay for it. These will not allow war to be made by their rulers for fun.

"Were I a councillor of the Dahcotah nation, this is what I should say: First, let the Great Father prove that he is in earnest by turning all the whites out of Pahsapa, or allowing us to do so. When this is done—but not until then—we will enter into negotiations for the purchase. Then I should ask eighty million dollars in cash. It is a large sum, but nothing compared with the value of the ground itself. The Mehneaska will gladly pay this, rather than embark in a war which they know will cost them twenty times as much, for they know the prowess of the Dahcotah nation, and respect the name of Red Cloud," turning with a graceful inclination towards the chief at his side.

"And there are many whites who will refuse to pay for a war with the red men. They love their red brethren, they say. It is no trouble to love people you have never seen. They do not really love you, but pretend to, which is more to your interest still; so that others shall say:—'What good people, to take such care of the poor red man.' They will take your part and see that you are not wronged, because sympathy gives no trouble, and is cheap, and they think it a sure and easy way to the white man's Happy Hunting-grounds.

"In short, then, were I one of themselves, these would be my words to the chiefs and warriors of the Dahcotah nation:—Be firm; fix your price, and in any attempt to beat you down, stand as immovable as the towering Inyan Kara. Having fixed it, get someone whom you can trust to see that you obtain it; and, above all, write in your hearts the warning of the great chief who has just sat down, for it contains the words of golden wisdom: 'A brave man without *prudence* is like the grizzly bear—he invites his own destruction.'

"There is one more thing to talk about. I and the warriors of the Dahcotah nation are brothers, and our hearts are the same. I who speak with you am of no race. I am akin to all the world, to all men whose hearts are good towards me. But although I am of no race I have friends of every race. When the war-parties of the Dahcotah are abroad, it may be that they will find me. Who would strike the friends of his brother? Such of the Mehneaska as may be with me are my friends, and the Dahcotah warriors will pass on, saying:—'We do not strike the friends of our brother, lest we turn him into an enemy.' Yet why should I talk of this? Only that in the days of youth the blood is hot, and young men upon the war-path strike first, and think afterwards. Enough, my words are for the ears of chiefs. My heart and the hearts of the great chiefs to whom I speak, are the same. I have spoken."

The clear ringing voice, the fluent language, the determination, even the veiled menace in the last words of the speaker, appealed straight to the most susceptible side of his savage hearers. One white man alone in their midst, and he did not shrink from threatening them with his hostility in the event of certain contingencies—threatening *them*, in their own estimation the most redoubtable warriors in the world! Assuredly he knew the way to their respect.

There were some there, however, in whom these last words aroused a feeling of rankling hostility, among them that fierce, that uncompromising abhorrer of the whole white race, Mountain Cat. This grim chieftain smiled sardonically to himself, as he inwardly promised what sort of treatment should be meted out to anyone whom his war-party should surprise, be they the friends of whom they might. Then ensued a period of silence, and every eye was turned with expectation upon Red Cloud.

But that crafty chief was not yet prepared to commit himself to a definite policy either way. Sitting motionless, he had weighed every word which had fallen from the speakers, and notably from the last. He was too far-sighted to plunge his nation into open war before the time was ripe: and his thinking out of the situation had convinced him that it was not. There were still cards to be played. So when he spoke it was briefly. Cautiously touching on the *pros* and *cons* of the speeches they had listened to, he announced that the situation must further be delayed, hinting that meanwhile such of his countrymen as felt aggressively disposed towards the common enemy had better exercise great prudence.

The council was at an end.

Note 1. This chief, over and above his skill and intrepidity as a warrior, enjoyed a high reputation among the Indians of the Northern Plains as a magician and a seer—a reputation really due to his astuteness, keen foresight, and extraordinary luck.

Chapter Eight
The Scalp-Dance

Uncas and Wingenund are very pretty creations, but they represent the savage as he really is about as accurately as the Founder of Christianity represents the average Christian of the current century. Which may be taken to mean that all preconceived and popular ideas of the "noble red man" can safely be relegated to the clouds.

Nobody was more aware of this than Vipan, consequently he knew exactly at what valuation to take all these overwhelmingly fraternal speeches of his red brethren. He knew—none better—that the wily chiefs intended to make use of him; he knew, moreover, that he could be of use to them; equally was he determined to receive a full equivalent for his services, and this equivalent he intended should be nothing less than the exclusive right of mining in the Black Hills.

His shrewd mind had grasped the sense of the council, and he realised that a sort of desultory warfare, for which no one was responsible, would be undertaken against the white men already there. These, isolated by twos and threes at their scattered mining camps, could not hope to make a successful stand against bands of savages raiding upon them incessantly. They would be driven out, and then he, Vipan, the friend and "brother" of the red possessors, would pick out all the best claims, work them with a will, and quickly make his fortune.

A daring and unscrupulous plan? Yes; but Nature had endowed the man with indomitable daring, and circumstances had combined to render him utterly unscrupulous. In advising the chiefs to ask the enormous sum named above, and to abide by their demand, he was perfectly well aware that the United States Government would not agree to it, but the larger the demand the more protracted would be the haggle, and the more protracted the haggle the more time would be his wherein to enrich himself.

There was one factor which he overlooked—or if it occurred to him he preferred to put it aside—the possibility that the yield of gold would not come up to anything like his expectations. But he was sanguine. Adventurers of his type invariably are. Give him a fair chance and his fortune was made.

Vipan was very popular in the Indian village. Apart from the consequence attaching to him as the friend and guest of the great chief—for he had taken up his quarters in Red Cloud's own lodge—he mixed freely with all the warriors, chatting with them, and treating them as friends and equals. Indians in private life are arrant gossips, and the adventurer being one of those adaptable persons at home in any society was in great request, for he was essentially "good company," and two-thirds of the night would be spent in this or that warrior's *teepe*, the structure crowded to suffocation, listening to his droll, or tragical, or romantic stories of all parts of the world. Then, too, he would accompany the young bucks on their hunting trips, in no case allowing their success to excel his; or would organise shooting matches among them. There were instances even wherein he was not above cutting out one or two of them in some—what we will call—boudoir intrigue, purely for the devilment of the thing, and if only to show them that there was nothing in which he could not surpass them—whether in love, war, or the chase. All this told. Their respect and admiration for him were unbounded, yet had they by chance the good fortune to surprise him alone on the prairie, and get him into their power, it is doubtful whether any consideration of friendship would suffice to restrain some of the young bucks from taking his scalp. And of this he himself was well aware.

It was the evening of the day after the council. Vipan, returning from a solitary hunt, to the success of which an antelope strapped behind his saddle, and several brace of sand-grouse dangling from the same, bore silent testimony, found his thoughts fully occupied weighing the position of affairs, and the more he looked at it the less he liked it. There was a hitch somewhere, and on this he had no difficulty in putting his finger. A powerful faction in the village was hostile to him altogether, and this was the uncompromising war-faction—Grey Wolf, the chief of the Cheyenne band; Mountain Cat, the Ogallalla; also War Wolf, who, although not a chief, yet aspired to this dignity, and who, his youth notwithstanding, was a warrior of such prestige among his fellows as to be no mean adversary. These especially—and there were others—he knew distrusted him and his plans. They were inveterate haters of all whites indiscriminately, and while they had hitherto treated him with grim courtesy, yet the covert hostility of their manner and words was not lost upon so shrewd an observer as himself. But it was certain that although the distrust or antipathy of these men might place obstacles in his path, yet no sort of alarm did it inspire him with. He was the proper stuff out of which adventurers are made—utterly reckless.

The crisp, frosty ground crackled beneath the hoofs of his powerful black horse; the sun had gone down, and the white conical lodges of the

Sioux village stood spectral in the grey twilight. There was a stillness and peace pervading the scene, which was very unusual in such close proximity to the savage encampment. Suddenly, shrilling forth loud and clear upon the evening air, rang out the terrible war-whoop.

To say that Vipan saw that his weapons were ready to hand would be superfluous, for they were always in a state of readiness. But he did not quite like the look of things, and more than one keen, anxious glance did he cast, without seeming to do so, into the belt of timber which he was skirting. Suddenly the semi-gloom seemed alive with dusky shapes flitting among the tree stems, and then all around him arose once more the war-whoop, which was taken up and echoed back from the village amid the frantic hammering of many drums.

"What's it all about, Three Elks?" he asked tranquilly, as a tall warrior glided past him in the twilight.

"How! Scalp!" replied the savage laconically, and then opening his mouth he once more set up the hideous shout as he rushed on.

The aspect of the Sioux village was that of the nethermost shades with all the fiends holding high revel. For the open space in front of the council-lodge was alive with excited Indians, those coming in from without whooping or shrilling their war-whistles as they rushed into the thick of the surging throng. Gangs of squaws squatted around, keeping up a wild, nasal, yelling chant, to the monotonous "tom-tom" of drums. Red fires glared upon the night; while hundreds of excited warriors, plumed and hideously painted, falling into something like a circular formation, revolved around several poles, from which dangled and flapped scalps in various stages of preservation—some dry and parchment-like, others fresh and only half cured.

Round and round circled the wild dance, the hoarse howling of the warriors, varied occasionally by a deafening war-whoop; the nasal yelling of the squaws; the hammering of drums and the screech of whistles; the lurid glare of the fires upon the fierce bounding shapes and the hideously streaked bodies and plumed heads; the gleam of weapons and the disgusting trophies flapping up aloft; all went to make up a weird and appalling pandemonium which baffles description. And yet so contagious, so insidious in its effect was this barbarous saturnalia that Vipan could with difficulty restrain himself from rushing into the maddened throng, and, brandishing his weapons, whoop and howl with the wildest of them.

One thing he observed which, in any other man as well acquainted with the Indian character as himself, would have been productive of uneasiness. The dancers consisted almost entirely of young bucks, every chief or partisan of any note being conspicuous by his absence. But although he knew that his position was precarious in the extreme there in the midst of that crowd of savages, quickly working themselves into a state of uncontrollable excitement, yet there was such an irresistible fascination about the whole thing that he felt rooted to the spot.

Suddenly War Wolf, bounding up to one of the poles, detached a couple of scalps, and, waving them aloft, uttered an ear-splitting yell. The savage, bedaubed from head to foot with yellow paint spotted all over with blotches of vermilion, brandishing a tomahawk in one hand and the ghastly trophies in the other, while with blazing eyes he yelled forth the history of his bloody exploit, looked a very fiend. Then as his eyes met those of Vipan, standing on the outside of the circle, he gave vent to a devilish laugh, flourishing the scalps ironically towards the latter.

The war-whoop pealed forth again, shriller, fiercer, and many a bloodthirsty glare was turned upon Vipan from a hundred pairs of eyes, as the maddened barbarians revolved in their frenzied rout. But he never quailed. The fascination was complete. And through it he noted two things. Both scalps were fresh. Hardly a week had passed since they grew upon the heads of their owners—and one of them was plentifully covered with a thick crop of red hair.

A voice at his side, speaking in quiet tones, broke the spell.

"Golden Face should be hungry and tired. Will he not come in, and rest and eat?"

Turning, he beheld Red Cloud. The latter's eyes wandered from his to the crowd of furious dancers with a meaning there was no mistaking. Without a word he turned and strolled away with the chief.

Chapter Nine
Some Old Correspondence

Mr Santorex and his daughter were seated in the former's own especial sanctum, busily engaged in sorting and destroying old letters and papers.

The room was a pleasant one, somewhat sombre perhaps—thanks to its panelling of dark oak—but the window commanded a lovely view of the Lant valley. Round the room stood cabinet cupboards, enclosing collections of insects, birds' eggs, plants, etc., and surmounted by a number of glass cases containing stuffed birds and animals. Fishing-rods on a rack, a few curiosities of savage weapons, and a portrait or two adorned the walls.

"Had enough of it, Chickie? Rather a sin to keep you boxed up here this lovely morning, isn't it?"

"No, father, of course it isn't. Besides, we are nearly at the end of these 'haunting memories of bygone days,' aren't we? or we shall be by lunch-time, anyhow."

It was indeed a lovely morning. The sweet spring air, wafting in at the window, floated with it the clear song of larks poised aloft in the blue ether, the bleating of young lambs disporting amid the buttercups on the upland pastures, and many another note of the pleasant country blending together in harmonious proportion.

"'Haunting memories,' eh?" replied Mr Santorex, seeming to dwell somewhat over the sheaf of yellow and timeworn papers he held in his hand. "Instructive—yes. A record of the average crop of idiocies a man sows in earlier life under the impression that he is doing the right thing. Acting under a generous impulse, I believe it is called."

Thus with that cynical half-smile of his did Mr Santorex keep up a running comment on each separate episode chronicled among the papers and letters filed away in his despatch-box. Some he merely looked at and put aside without a word; others he descanted upon in his peculiar dry and caustic fashion which always inspired the listeners with something bordering on repulsion. Yseulte herself could not but realise that there was a something rather cold-blooded, not to say ruthless, about her tranquil and philosophical parent that would have awed—almost repelled—her but that she loved him very dearly. Her nature was a concentrative one, and unsusceptible withal. She had hardly made any friends, because she had seen no one worth entertaining real friendship for, and she was a girl who would not fall in love readily.

"I wish I hadn't seen this just now, father," she said, handing him back a sheaf of letters. It was a correspondence of a lively nature, and many years back, between himself and Mr Vallance. "You see, the Vallances are all coming up here this afternoon, and I don't feel like being civil to them immediately upon it."

"Pooh! civility means nothing, not in this location at least. Why, when we first came here we were overwhelmed with it. It didn't last many months certainly, but it broke out afresh when rumour made me a millionaire. Why, what have you got there?"

For she was now scrutinising, somewhat intently, a photograph which had fallen out of a bundle of papers among the piles they had been sorting. It represented a youngish man, strikingly handsome, and with a strong, reckless stamp of countenance; and though the original must have been prematurely bald, the mouth was almost hidden by a long heavy moustache. A queer smile came into Mr Santorex's face.

"Think that's the type you could fall in love with, eh, Chickie? Well, I advise you not to, for I can't bring you face to face with the original."

"Why? Who is it?"

"Who is it? No less a personage than the disinherited heir, Ralph Vallance. The plot thickens, eh?"

"I didn't know. I thought he was dead, if I ever knew there was such a person, that is. Why was he disinherited?"

"Ah, that's something of a story. Poor Ralph! I think he was most unfairly treated, always did think so; especially when that hum—er, I mean, our spiritual guide, jumped into his shoes. No, I daresay you never heard much about it, but you are a woman now, my dear, and a deuced sensible one too, as women go, and I always hold that it is simply nonsensical and deleterious to their moral fibre to let women—sensible ones, that is—go about the world with their eyes shut. To come back to our romance. The old squire of Lant was a straight-laced, puritanical fossil, and Master Ralph was just the reverse, an extravagant, roystering young dog who chucked away ten pounds for every one that he was worth, in fact the ideal 'Plunger' as you girls estimate that article. Naturally, there were occasional breezes down at the Hall, nor were these effectually tempered by the crafty intervention of cousin Dudley, who ran the vicarage in those days. The old man used to get very mad, especially when Ralph began dabbling in *post obits*, and vowed he'd cut off that hopeful with a shilling, and leave everything to his reverend nephew. Finally, the regiment went on foreign service, and while the transport was lying at the Abraham Islands, where she had put in for coal and other supplies, that young idiot, Ralph Vallance, must needs get mixed up in a confounded domestic scandal there was no clapping an extinguisher on. The mischief of the thing was that it nearly concerned the Governor of the place, whose interest was considerable enough to get Master Ralph cashiered, in the event of his failing to send in his papers at once. Of the two evils, he chose the latter, and least; and as it could not be kept from his affectionate parent, that sturdy Pharisee duly cut him off with a shilling and departed this life forthwith. So the revered and reverend Dudley reigns in both their steads."

"I wonder Mr Vallance has the conscience to take the property at the expense of his cousin, whatever the latter might have done."

"You do, do you! Oh, Chickie, to think that you and I should have been sworn allies all through your long and illustrious career, and you still capable of propounding such a sentiment! Know then, O recreant, that our sacred friend, although he may be something of a kn— ah'm! has nothing of the fool about him, although the other was a consummate young ass, or he would never have gone the length of getting himself cut out of his patrimony."

"But didn't Mr Vallance do anything for him?"

"I have it on the best authority, that of the victim himself, that he did not. Ralph, however, was determined not to be outdone in generosity, for he came raging down here one fine day consumed with anxiety to take his reverend cousin by the scruff of the neck and give him a liberal thrashing. It was just as well, perhaps, that chance enabled me to prevent him."

"You knew him then, father?"

"Yes, we struck up acquaintance on that occasion. Poor Ralph! He was a fine fellow, whatever his faults, and, mind you, my impression is that in the last affair it was a case of clapping the saddle on the wrong horse, that he was screening somebody else, and allowed the blame to fall on himself rather than 'peach.' It was magnificent, but—stark idiotic."

"He has a very, fine face," said Yseulte, again taking up the photograph and examining it thoughtfully. The fact that he had suffered at the hands of his slippery cousin was quite enough to enlist all her sympathies in behalf of the romantic scapegrace.

"Yes, it is. You know I am not given to indiscriminate eulogium, but without hesitation I think Ralph Vallance was about the finest specimen of manhood I ever saw."

"What has become of him now?"

"I haven't the faintest notion. All this happened a good many years ago, when you were almost in your cradle. Why, Ralph, if he is alive, must be getting on in years by this time. There, that's about all the story that it's worth your while to know, my dear, and now we'll lock the correspondence away in my private safe. Let me have the portrait again when you have done with it."

Yseulte, as we have said, was not a romantically inclined girl, yet, somehow, this faded portrait of the man of whom nobody had heard anything for almost as many years as she herself had lived, made a vivid impression on her. As she sat contemplating it, a voice arose from the lawn beneath, saying in the most approved Oxford drawl:

"Ah, how do you do, Mrs Santorex? I've brought rather a queer plant that your husband may not have in his collection. It strikes me as a curious specimen." And then Mrs Santorex was heard asking the speaker in.

Father and daughter looked at each other with the most comical expression in the world. Then the former murmured, with a dry, noiseless laugh:

"He's found the four-leaved shamrock. Oh, Chickie, Chickie! have some pity on poor Geoffry Plantagenet, and put him out of his misery, once and for all!"

The girl could hardly stifle her laughter. Her father, for his part, was thinking resignedly that to the bald expedients devised by enamoured youth as pretexts for numerous and wholly unnecessary visits to the parent or lawful guardian of its idol, there is no limit.

Chapter Ten
Poor Geoffry

The clever author of "Mine is Thine" lays it down as an axiom that nothing so completely transforms the average sensible man into a consummate idiot for the time being as an *arrière pensée*; and it is an axiom the soundness of which all observation goes to prove.

Geoffry Vallance, if not passing brilliant, was endowed with average sense and more than average assurance, yet when he found himself seated opposite Yseulte at the luncheon table in accordance with that young lady's father's impromptu invitation, his wits were somewhat befogged. Not to put too fine a point upon it, he was distressingly conscious of feeling an ass, and, worse still, of looking one. His conversation, normally lucid, and, like the brook, apt to "go on for ever," was now a little incoherent, jerky, and limited in area; his demeanour, normally self-possessed, not to say a trifle assertive, was now constrained, spasmodic, and painfully apprehensive of saying or doing the wrong thing.

The poor fellow was over head and ears in love, which blissful state developed a new phase in his character—a self-consciousness and a diffidence which no one would have suspected to lie hidden there. Eager to show at his best in the eyes of Yseulte and her father, he, of course showed at his worst. It never occurred to him—it does not to most men under the circumstances—that heroic qualities are not essential to the adequate looking after of multifold dress baskets and hand luggage at the railway station or on board the Channel packet; that a Greek profile is hardly requisite to the unmurmuring liquidation of milliners' bills, or the torso of a Milo to the deft fulfilment of the *rôle* of domestic poodle. These considerations did not occur to him, but a wretched consciousness of his own deficiencies in appearance and attainments did, and now to this was added the recollection of that ridiculous position they had seen him in only a day or two ago, and which had lain heavily on his mind ever since.

"Too great a fool ever to be a knave" had been Mr Santorex's dictum, not meaning thereby that Geoffry was a dunce or a blockhead, the fact being that he was a hard reader and expected to take high honours at the end of the ensuing term. But in other matters, field sports and real *savoir vivre*, he was something of a duffer. Yet though father and daughter disliked the residue of the house of Vallance, they entertained a sort of good-humoured kindness towards Geoffry, who was at worst a muff, and good-natured, and with no harm in him. And of this feeling poor Geoffry had an inkling.

A little chaff about Muggins' bull, and Yseulte, seeing that the topic was distressful to the hero of the adventure, good-naturedly turned it; for in spite of her previously expressed disinclination for showing any civility towards the Vallances that day, she seemed quite to have forgiven them as far as Geoffry was concerned, and was as kind to him as ever. The plant, by the way, which had served as pretext for this visit, was a fraud of the first water, but Mr Santorex, while showing its worthlessness as a specimen, had not only spared, but even flattered, the feelings of the donor, for, thorough cynic as he was at heart, in his practice he was a very tolerant man where the wretched little tricks and subterfuges of mediocrity in distress were concerned, always provided that these were not intended to serve as a cloak to knavery. When they were, his merciless predilection for, and powers of, dissection had full indulgence.

The hereditary searing-iron must have found place in his daughter's composition, though untempered by the experience of years and maturity. For there was something of feline cruelty in the way in which, when luncheon was over, she lured poor Geoffry out into the garden, talking serenely in that beautifully modulated voice of hers, as, every action full of unconscious grace, she bent down to pluck a flower here, or raise a drooping plant there; or looking up into his face now and then with such a straight glance out of her grand eyes as to make the poor fellow fairly tremble with bewilderment, and stammer and stutter in his attempts to express himself, until he was pitiable to behold. But though ashamed of the impulse, Yseulte was unable wholly to resist it. This poor-spirited adorer of hers—was he not standing in another's place, smugly enjoying and thriving upon what had been reft from its rightful owner by a pitiful and underhanded trick—a trick which, though legally permissible, was morally as complete an act of deliberate fraud as any for which men were sent into penal servitude? That photograph, you see, had fired a new train of thought in the girl's adventurous mind. It was a splendid face, that which looked at her from the bit of faded cardboard. Its strong, reckless expression had seemed to haunt her ever since. She had never seen anything like it. And it was that of an injured and ill-used man; a man, too, with a vein of real heroism running through his character, and therefore unlike other men; for had not her father expressed his conviction that this man was suffering wrongfully, was a beggar for life, rather than speak the word which should inculpate someone else? She looked at her stuttering, flurried admirer there present, and turned away to hide a contemptuous curl of the lip; she thought of the defrauded and absent one—whose place he had usurped—wandering destitute over the earth, and her feelings were strangely stirred. Yet the former she knew well, his failings and his good points; the latter she had only seen in a portrait—and an old and faded portrait at that. Was she going to fall in love with an old and faded portrait? Well, it was beginning to look uncommonly as if she might.

Geoffry was on tenterhooks. They were alone, and likely so to be left for some little while longer at any rate. Should he try his fate? Anything was better than this suspense. He would.

Alas for the defeat of praiseworthy enterprise! The words would not come. He pounced upon a flower which Yseulte had been toying with and had thrown down, and while stuttering over the discarded blossom as a preliminary, a well-known and silky voice behind the pair made him start and redden like a child detected in the forbidden jam-cupboard.

"Ah, there you are, Geoffry. We thought you were being well taken care of by our good friends here, so we didn't wait lunch for you. How are you, Yseulte? My young people will be here soon. I left them on the road, or just starting."

It is doubtful whether Geoffry's feelings towards his sire were affectionate just then. Yseulte, however, felt that the latter's presence was rather welcome. Her adorer's embarrassment portended something she preferred to avoid. So she welcomed the reverend squire quite cordially.

A gleam of colour on the lawn and the sound of voices betokened the arrival of the rest of the family, and lo—Lucy and Agnes and Cecilia and Anastasia, tennis-racquet in hand and arrayed in white flannels or scarlet flannels, or blue flannels, and crowned with hats of stupendous dimensions. They were all fair, blue-eyed girls, passable-looking if somewhat expressionless, very much alike, and numbering just a year apiece between their ages.

No great cordiality existed between these young ladies and Yseulte Santorex, as we have said; still, society has its duties, and leaving the latter to fulfil the provisions of this threadbare truism on the sunny lawn at Elmcote, wave we our magic wand to transport the reader to a very different scene.

Chapter Eleven
"Hands Up!"

A dull, leaden-grey sky; a few stray feathery flakes floating upon the frosty air; an icebound stream; a dark serrated ridge rising to the heavens on the one hand; on the other a lofty peak towering away into the misty heights. The dull moaning noise of the wind through the forest, and the distant howling of wolves, for the wintry evening is rapidly closing in, renders the whole scene and surroundings indescribably desolate and dreary.

A hoof-stroke on the frost-bound earth. Who is this riding abroad in the weird wilderness at such an hour, with the snowstorm lowering overhead, darkness and the multifold perils of the great mountains in front! Phantom steed and phantom rider?

Whether visionary or material, however, the latter glances upward anxiously from time to time. Darkness and the impending storm! What he urgently needs is daylight and tranquillity. He reins in his powerful black steed, and gazes intently for a few moments at the towering peak half lost in the snow-cloud; then abruptly turning his horse, rides about forty yards at right angles, and again sits contemplating the lofty crag.

Somewhat of an extraordinary proceeding this. Why does not the man hasten upon his way? A matter of but a few hours and these desolate solitudes will be the theatre of such a strife and whirl of the elements that any human being, one would think, would strain every effort to reach a place of safety and comfort before the fury of the tempest is upon him. But this man seems in no sort of hurry; indeed, were it not for his occasional anxious glances heavenward, he might be deemed ignorant of the impending cataclysm.

"There is Ma-i-pah, the Red Peak," he muses. "There is the forked pine, and I have got them in line. So far good. The next thing is to find the scathed tree. But—oh curse the snow-cloud! It may be months before—"

"Cau-aak!"

A flap-flap of wings in the brake. A raven, rising almost under the horse's feet, wings its way to the boughs of a neighbouring oak.

So sudden is the hideous croak, echoing upon the stillness of this deathly solitude, that even the iron nerves of the horseman are not proof against a superstitious thrill. But those nerves are strung up to a pitch of suppressed excitement which is all engrossing.

"Cau-aak—Cau-aak!"

A second raven rises from the brake, and floats lazily off to join the first, resembling in its grim blackness some foul demon of the wilderness disturbed in his den of horrors. Struck with an idea, the rider turns his horse and enters the covert. Following him, we seem to have stood on this spot before.

There are the two crosses recently cut upon the huge pine-trunk, so recently that the fresh resin exuding from them is all red and sticky as though the very tree were weeping blood for the two hapless ones, victims of a deed of blood, lying beneath it. There is the mound of earth and stones. Stay! that mound has surely undergone a transformation; for it is half overthrown, and the earth is rent and burrowed, and cast up in all directions. And there, scattered around, lie the bones of the murdered men, broken and picked nearly clean by the carrion beasts and birds of the wilderness. By a ghastly coincidence, the two scalpless heads, half denuded of flesh, lay side by side grinning as if in agony, their sightless sockets, gory and half filled with earth, gaping up at the intruder. An awful, an appalling sight to come upon suddenly in the twilight gloom of that grisly forest—a sight to shake the strongest nerves, to haunt the spectator to his dying day.

But he who now looks upon it is little concerned, though even he cannot repress a slight shiver of disgust as he contemplates the horrid spectacle. He dismounts, and leading his horse away from the mournful relics, at which the animal snorts and shies in alarm, hitches him up to a sapling, and then proceeds narrowly to scrutinise the ground.

The man's figure looks gigantic in the semi-gloom, as casting his ample buffalo robe off one shoulder, he lays his rifle on the ground and extracts something from the breast of his fringed hunting-shirt. It is nothing less than a crumpled and dirty piece of paper, oblong in shape, and containing what is evidently a plan of some sort, rudely drawn, and undecipherable without the aid of a few words equally rudely written and misspelt, clearly the work of some unlettered person.

"*Forkt pine, Red Peak, Blarsted tree, the creek where half-buried rock!*"

"The plot thickens," murmurs the investigator excitedly, conning over the laconic cipher. "Having established the relationship between the forked pine and Ma-i-pah, otherwise the Red Peak, the next thing is to discover the blasted tree, which should not be difficult, unless the term represents obloquy rather than the effects of lightning. That done, the rest will be easy."

A few steps further into the brake. Suddenly the blood surges into his face. Something white and ghostlike glints athwart the gloom. A huge pine, dead, and stripped of all its lower bark, clearly by several successive strokes of lightning. This can be no other than the "blasted tree" of the cipher. Almost trembling with excitement, once more he unfolds the dirty sheet of paper and eagerly scans it.

"Hands up, stranger! Hands up! or you're a stiff 'un, by God!"

The harsh, threatening voice, cleaving the twilight solitude, where a moment before Vipan had imagined himself absolutely alone, was enough to unnerve a less resolute hearer. It proceeded from a tall, sinister-looking man, who standing on a ridge or bank some five-and-twenty yards off, and slightly above him, had him covered with a rifle-barrel. There was no disputing the grim mandate. The other held him at a complete disadvantage. Any hesitation to comply would mean a bullet through his heart that instant. But while holding both hands high above his head, his eyes were keenly on the look-out for the smallest chance.

"I don't seem to have the pleasure of your acquaintance, friend," he answered coolly. What a fool he was to have parted company with his Winchester, he thought.

"You don't?" yelled the man, amid a volley of curses. "You soon will, though, I reckon, you pesky-white Injun. I'll learn you to set the red devils on to scalp and knife my pardners. Now, you jest throw down that hunk of paper, slicker nor greased lightning—mind me."

The tone was so fierce and threatening that there was no room for delay. No man living was more keenly competent to realise the situation than he who had now the worst of it.

"All right," he answered. "I'm standing on it. You'll see it when I move my foot."

"Don't move a hair else then, or you're a stiff," was the grim uncompromising reply.

"Now," went on the fellow, having assured himself that the paper was there, "take six steps backward—six and no more. Quick march!"

With the deadly rifle-barrel still covering his heart, Vipan obeyed.

"Well! what's the next thing?" he said, and at the same time he noticed that the other carried a lariat rope dangling in loose coils from his left arm.

"The next thing, eh?" jeered the fierce aggressor. "I and some of the boys have kept our eye upon you for a good while, and the next thing is we're going to lynch you. Now—Turn round!"

The man in his eagerness had made a step forward, with the result that, the little ridge of ground whereon he was standing being slippery with the frost, he missed his footing, stumbled, staggered wildly in his efforts to recover his balance, and finally rolled headlong almost at Vipan's feet.

Crack!

The aggressor lay writhing in his death-throes. All this time warily on the look-out for the smallest chance in his favour, Vipan, quick as thought, had whipped out the little Derringer which he carried in his breast-pocket, and sent a bullet through his adversary's brain.

"I think I've turned the tables on you with effect, my hearty," he said, contemplating the dead man with a savage sneer. Now that there was no further necessity for coolness, his blood boiled at the recent humiliation this fellow had made him undergo. "Ha, ha! Go and tell your two precious 'pardners' what a sorry hash you made of it on their account, you miserable idiot, and bait a few more Tartar traps down in the nethermost shades. Ha, ha!"

The first thing he did was to pick up and secure the sheet of paper. Then he searched the dead man lest anything bearing upon the cipher might be in his possession, but without avail. He was about to leave the spot, when an idea struck him.

For a moment he stood contemplating his late enemy. Bending down, an expression of strong disgust in his face, he gripped the dead man by the hair—a couple of quick slashes, and the scalp was in his hand. Then he drew his knife across the throat of the corpse.

"The Sioux—his mark," he muttered, with grim jocosity. "Faugh! Now to stow away this beastly thing," wiping the scalp upon its late proprietor's clothing.

He removed the latter's weapons—rifle, revolver, knife—and keeping a sharp look-out against any further aggression, regained his horse. In mounting, he trod on something which crackled crisply. It was a dried and shrivelled knee-boot, from which the leg-bone still protruded. And his attention being once more attracted to these ghastly relics, it almost seemed to him that the two heads had changed their position, and were glaring at him with hideous and menacing scowl. The ravens, from a neighbouring tree, renewed their lugubrious croak, as if resentful at being so long kept away from their repulsive feast. Overhead, the sky grew blacker and blacker, and the snowflakes whirled round the horseman as he emerged from the gloom of that grisly brake.

"There's more carrion for you, you black devils," he muttered, apostrophising the ravens. "Heavens! What had I to do with the brute's unwashen 'pardners'? If I'm to be held answerable for the scalp of every idiot who goes to sleep with both eyes shut, I've got my work cut out for me. Ha, ha! The red brother comes in mighty convenient sometimes."

Thus musing, he had gained the crossing of a mountain torrent, at the entrance to a long, narrow cañon, whose sheer, overhanging walls were gloomy and forbidding, even by the light of day. Dismounting, he took out the scalp, and wrapping it round a stone, hurled it away into a deep, swirling pool, whose centre was free from ice. The dead man's weapons followed suit.

"There! Pity to throw away good serviceable arms, but—'Self-preservation, etc.' I only treated the dog as he would have treated me, but I don't want to establish a vendetta among his desperado mates with myself for its object. A lot the scoundrels care about such a plea as self-defence. No. Let them credit the reds with the job."

The rising gale shrieked wildly overhead, but within the black walls of the cañon the wayfarer was entirely protected from its force. The snowflakes, large and fleecy, now fell thickly about him. And now there was exultation in place of the former anxiety in his glance as ever and anon he studied the dark and overcast sky.

"Better and better. Nothing like snow for covering up a trail, and by the time it's open again there'll be not much left of yon carrion. Up, Satanta! We'll soon be home now."

The black steed arched his splendid neck responsive to his master's voice. And his said master, muffling himself closer in his buffalo robe, settled himself down in his saddle with every confidence in the ability of one or other, or both of them, to keep the right trail, even through the pitchy blackness which was now descending upon them. The driving snow, the shrieking of the gale, the howling of wolves in the dark forest, the grisly sight left behind, the stain of blood, were nothing to him who rode there—on—on through the night.

Chapter Twelve
"To Quit"

When Vipan narrated the events of the last chapter to his friend and partner, the latter looked grave.

"I know the chap you dropped," he said, "and he'll be no loss to this territory, nohow. He's one o' them desperate, hard-drinkin', cussin' bullies that a whole township—ay, and many a township 'll be only too glad to see laid. But then, you see, there are his mates to reckon with; bullies, all of 'em, like himself. I'm afraid if they light upon the trail we shall have some warm work along."

"But they won't light on it, Bill, thanks to this friendly blizzard. Why, the snow'll be there for the next three months, but most, if not all, of my late friend won't. He'll be pretty evenly distributed among the wolves and crows by that time," was the grim reply. And the speaker kicked the logs into a blaze, and took a long pull at his whisky-horn. "Besides," he added, "I took all precautions. If they do strike the trail, they'll credit the whole business to the red brother."

The scout puffed earnestly at his pipe for some little while, his features in no wise relaxing their gravity.

"See here, Vipan," he said, at length; "that's one side of the affair I've been cudgelling over. Most of the chaps located around have got a notion that you're too thick with the reds, and they're pretty mad. I've run against several of 'em, and have been hearin' some tall talk among 'em while you were away down there. Now, the best thing we can do is to clear out our *caches* (Note 1) as soon as the weather lifts, and git."

"No, no, Bill; that's not my line at all. It's no part of my idea to be choused out of the goose with the golden eggs just as I've brought that biped home, not to mention being obliged to sneak away from a lot of yapping curs, any one of whom I'm ready to meet, how, when, and where he chooses." And Vipan's face was a picture of contemptuous resentment.

"Whatever they are, old pard, they can shoot—they can. I don't know what's to stand in the way of a straight volley just any time we hap to be on the move, even if not when we poke our noses out of our own door. But if your mind's set on stayin' on, I'll just dry up."

The other's face softened. This staunch and loyal comrade of his was prepared, as a matter of course, to stand by him and equally share the peril in which the jealous resentment of the incensed miners placed or might place himself.

"Now, look here, old chum," he said, "I'll just tell you what sort of a prospecting I've made. I always maintained the upper bend of Burntwood Creek was worth tapping. It's my private opinion we've at last struck the real yellow, and if you don't think it worth following up after what I'm going to show you, why I'll fall in with your idea, and light out now for some where else. Look at this," and he placed in his friend's hand the paper which he had taken from the pocket of one of the dead miners whom he had helped to bury.

Smokestack Bill studied the plan thoughtfully for a few moments.

"It's tarnation vague," he said at length: "'Forkt pine, Red Peak, blarsted tree, and the creek where half-buried rock.' Why, there's parks of forked pines, and as for the blasted tree it's like enough to be some stem against which one o' them chaps was squelched by his mule, and known only to them. And the creek's just chock full of half-buried rocks."

"Ha, ha, ha! Bill, my boy, I've located them all—all but the half-buried rock, that is. The tree's a scathed pine all right, close to where the two fellows were scalped. I was just going to locate the creek part of the business, when that unhung skulker 'jumped' me. You may just bet your bottom dollar we'll light upon something rich."

"Well, well, I'll see you through it," said the other in a tone as if he began to think there might be something in it. "But seems to me we shan't be much the better for a lot of gold even if we find it. You're bent on a rush to Great Britain, Vipan, I can see that. Well, my boy, if we light on a find, you can take the bigger half, and go and pay off old scores with the party that's tricked you. I've not much use for the stuff, I reckon."

"Bill, old friend, you're an extraordinary production of your day and species—a thoroughly unselfish specimen of humanity to wit. Now, do you think it in the least likely that I should agree to any such arrangement? No, no; share and share alike is the motto between partners. If we make a good thing of it we'll take our jaunt together."

"'M, p'raps. Cities don't like me, and I don't like cities. If it were otherwise I should be jingling my tens of thousands of dollars to-day, instead of owning nought but a good rifle, a good horse, and a *cache* full of pelts. There's mighty mean tricks done in cities, and those done in a lawyer's office ain't the least mean. My old dad was in that line, and though a good chap in other ways, I saw queer things done in that office of his. I couldn't stand it, and I couldn't stand the life, so I kicked over the stool and struck out West. I got blown up in a Missouri steamboat first thing, and came down on a chunk of the smokestack into the mud on the Nebraska side—leastways, that's what the boys declared, and that's why they call me Smokestack Bill, though I reckon I must have got astride of the smokestack while I was half drowning. And now my brother Seth, who took kindly to lawyering, is the richest man in Carson County."

"But that you are thoroughly happy as a plainsman, Bill, I should say you had made a mistake," answered Vipan, in whom the other's story seemed to have touched a sympathetic chord. "Otherwise the man who sacrifices wealth—beggars himself for a principle—is a consummate ass, and deserves all he condemns himself to; that is, a lifetime spent in regretting it," he added, with an unwonted bitterness. "But never mind that," resuming his normal tone. "When the snow melts we'll go down and prospect Burntwood Creek, and as it's unlucky—deuced unlucky—to discount one's successes beforehand, we'll just dismiss the subject out of hand until then. Meanwhile, life being uncertain, we'll *cache* the cipher in some snug place in case anything should happen to me."

Three months went by. All the rigours of winter had set in upon the Black Hills. Everywhere the snow lay in an unbroken sheet, attaining in many places such prodigious depths as almost to bury the brakes and thickets of a shorter growth. The dark foliage of the great pines afforded some relief from the dazzling whiteness around, but even that was almost concealed by the huge masses of snow which had there effected lodgment. And here and there a mighty cliff of red sandstone stood forth from the surrounding snow, its face half draped with glistening icicles. But the weather was glorious, and the air as exhilarating as champagne. The peaks, shining like frosted silver, rearing their heads to the ever-cloudless blue—that marvellous combination of subtle shades of the richest azure, tempered with green, which is produced by contrast with a snow-enshrouded earth—the smooth face of each great precipice, frowning beneath its brow of dark and bristling pines; the muffled roar of the mountain torrent struggling for freedom, far down under its successively imprisoning layers of ice; the wild cry of bird or beast, even more at fault in the icebound rigours of its native waste than its artificial enemy, man—all this went to make up an engraving from the scenes of Nature in her winter magnificence, in all her savage primeval beauty, in her unsurpassable and most stately grandeur.

In the midst of it all our two friends were thoroughly comfortable. They trapped a good deal and hunted occasionally. Many a valuable fur of silver fox and marten and beaver were added to their stores, and the thick coat of the great white wolf, and the tawny one of the cougar, or mountain lion. Two grizzlies of gigantic size also bit the dust—the redoubted "Old Ephraim" standing no chance whatever before the rifles of two such dead shots—while deer, both black-tailed and red, unable to make much running in the deep snow, fell an easy prey.

The entrance to their cabin was all but buried in snow, but within it was thoroughly warm and snug. Here, before a blazing fire, they would lounge at night. Stores of every kind were plentiful—flour, coffee, and sugar, whisky, warm furs, and abundance of tobacco—and surrounded by every creature comfort they would sit and smoke their long pipes, after a day of hard and healthful exercise, while the wind shrieked without, and all the voices of the weird wilderness were abroad, and the great mountains reverberated ever and anon the thunderous boom of some mighty mass of snow which, dislodged by the wind or its own weight, roared down the slopes, perchance to plunge with a crash over a huge cliff. Now and then old Shanks would lift his shaggy head and growl as the dismal yell of a cougar would be borne upon the night, but he was well-used to the sounds of the forest, and quickly subsided again. And the ghostly hooting of owls, and the shrill barking of foxes, in the dark pine forest mingled with the ravening howl of the wolves in ceaseless chorus from the frozen and wind-swept slopes.

Sometimes an Indian, belated on his hunt, would take advantage of their hospitality, and on such occasions Vipan would delight to "draw" his savage guest, with the result that the red-skinned warrior, replete with good cheer and good humour, would lie back on his furs, puffing out huge clouds of tobacco smoke, and narrate—with that absence of reserve which characterises the savage when so engaged—many a strange tale of love and war, and among them, here and there, an instance of such fiendish and ruthless atrocity as would have caused the ordinary listener's hair to stand on end with horror and repulsion, not swerving in the smallest degree from his smiling and good-humoured imperturbability during the narration. But Vipan was wholly proof against any such ordinary weakness. The way to know Indians, he said, was first to get them to talk, and then to let them talk. *He* wanted to know Indians thoroughly, and reckoned by this time he had about succeeded. So in him the red warrior found an attentive, not to say appreciative, listener.

Thus the months went by, and when the crocuses and soldanellas began to appear from beneath the melting snow, and the torrents and creeks ran red in the first spring freshets, an impatience, a feverish longing to be up and doing came upon Vipan, rendering him moody, and at times irritable. But until the rivers should have run off the melted snows nothing could be done. In vain his comrade preached philosophy.

"I judge you'll get no good by tearing your shirt, old pard," said the honest scout. "See here, now. Did you ever set your heart on a single thing, that when you got it you wondered how the snakes you could ever have been so hot on gettin' it? No, you didn't. About this *placer*. Maybe we shall find plenty of stuff—maybe little—maybe none at all. But whatever we find or don't find, it's no part of good sense to tear our shirts a' thinkin' of it."

"No, it isn't," agreed the other. "But—'many a slip,' etc."

"'M, yes. What's the odds, though? We can always light on fresh ground. And if the reds go on the war-path soon as the grass grows, it'd do us both good to get a scouting berth with the command for a spell."

Vipan's forebodings were destined to be realised. A few mornings later the two occupants of the winter cabin were awakened by the trampling of many hoofs. With their minds full of the threats of those around them, both seized their rifles and stood ready for any emergency. But with no body of jealous and exasperated miners had they now to deal. Cautiously peering forth, their gaze fell upon the trappings and accoutrements of a cavalry patrol.

A furious curse escaped Vipan's lips. His plans were ruined.

Note 1. A *cache* is a sort of underground storeroom or place of concealment—generally jar-shaped—wherein peltries and other goods are deposited, pending their convenient removal.

Chapter Thirteen
Henniker City

Henniker City was a typical prairie township in no wise bearing out the imposing idea which its name might convey.

It might have contained some five score dwellings, mainly of the log-hut order; a few frame houses, with real glazed windows figuring as the aristocratic and advanced representatives of civilised architecture among the more primitive structures. It boasted a brace of churches, one of which, only occasionally used, having been reared through the efforts of a travelling priest attached to the nearest Catholic mission, the other representing no creed in particular, though chiefly resorted to by what our friend Smokestack Bill was wont to define as "the pizenest kind of Hard-shell Baptists," a definition we should be loth to attempt to elucidate. It boasted more stores than churches, and more drinking saloons than stores. It contained a bank, whose manager reckoned handiness at drawing, and, if necessary, using, the six-shooter at least as essential a qualification for his clerks as the footing up of figures. It boasted a sheriff, whose three predecessors had "died in their boots" within less than the same number of years. And for population, fixed and floating, it mainly comprised about as daredevil, swash-bucklering, unscrupulous a set of cut throats, as ever shot a winning adversary at euchre or "held up" (from "Hold up your hands"— the "road agent's" warning) the Pony Express.

Such was the place to which our two friends were moved by the detachment of troops which had so suddenly and unwelcomely invaded their mountain retreat. A shout of mingled mirth, derision, and resentment went up in the township at this fresh evidence of the high-handedness of Uncle Sam, and in a trice the whole population crowded around the prisoners and their escort.

"Hello, pard!" sung out a slouching-looking fellow in a frowsy shirt and cabbage-tree hat, addressing Vipan. "Don't be down on your luck, now. When the Colonel here's fightin' the Sioux, we're the boys to slide back and pouch the stuff. Hey!"

"Say, Colonel! Going after Sittin' Bull soon?" sung out another, to the officer in command of the cavalry. "'Cause Smokestack Bill's the boy to raise a mob of scouts for yer, and we're the boys to jine."

"Not till you put a hunk of lead through yon cussed white Injun, I reckon," growled a forbidding ruffian, on the outskirts of the crowd, with a scowl at Vipan.

"Snakes! Wasn't he with the Injun as scalped Rufus Charlie and Pesky Bob?" said another, taking up the suggestion. And then a knot of men, gathered in conclave, eyed the object of the discussion in a manner that boded no good.

Meanwhile the crowd, surging round the new arrivals, continued to pour forth banter and queries.

"Got the 'dust' about yer, strangers, or did yer *cache* it?"

"Say, pardners, whar did yer leave yer squaws? Or did Uncle Sam confiscate 'em as national property? Ho, ho!"

"See here, boys, am I sheriff of Henniker City, or am I not?" drawled a cool, deliberate voice, as the chaff reached its height. "'Cause if I am, jest clear a way; and if I'm not, I reckon I'd like to cotch a glimpse of the galoot as says so." A shout of mirth greeted this speech, and speedily a lane was opened through the crowd, down which advanced a tall, spare man. This worthy's sallow visage was adorned with a grizzled beard of the "door-knocker" order, above which protruded a half-chewed cigar, a pair of whimsical grey eyes, and a determined mouth. In his hand he carried a Winchester rifle, and the inevitable six-shooter peeped forth from his hip-pocket.

"How do, Colonel? Brought me some more citizens, hey? Smokestack Bill, as I'm a miserable sinner! That your pard, Bill? All right, come this way. Citizens of Henniker, the High Court is about to sit."

Without more ado, the two "prisoners" and their custodian, resuming the thread of their previous conversation, followed the whimsical sheriff into the Courthouse, as many as could crowding in until the room was full, laughing, chatting, bantering each other; kicking up an indescribable uproar. At last, raising his voice above the shindy, the whimsical sheriff succeeded in obtaining something like silence.

"Citizens!" he said, "we must proceed with the business which has brought us together. The prisoners at the bar having been handed over to me to be dealt with according to law—that is, kept in custody until able to take their trial for 'truding on Indian lands—cannot be so kept because the gaol with which this city is supplied would not hold a clerk of a dry goods store, let alone a couple of Indian fighters. That being so, the prisoners may consider themselves under bail to the tune of fifty dollars apiece, to appear when wanted; snakes, and that'll be never," he parenthesised, in an undertone. "Citizens, the court is adjourned—and now disperse—git—vamoose the ranch. Those who are not too drunk will go home peaceably, those who are, will adjourn to Murphy's saloon and get drunker. Prisoners at the bar, you will accompany me right along and take supper. I have spoken."

If any confiding reader imagines that when night settled down upon Henniker City the wearied denizens of that historic township retired to their welcome couches to recruit their toil-worn limbs in sweet and well-earned repose—why we are sorry to dispel the illusion. But in the interests of stern truth we must place it upon record that the hours of darkness usually witnessed the liveliest of scenes, for it was only then that the township began to live. The saloons drove literally a roaring trade, for the shindy that went on in them as the night wore on, and their *habitués* waxed livelier, was something indescribable. Miners in their rough shirts and cabbage-tree hats, here and there a leather-clad trapper, cowboys and ranchmen in beaded frocks and Indian leggings, and more or less "on the burst," but all talking at a great rate; all tossing for, or shouting for, or consuming drinks, and, we regret to say, a large proportion somewhat the worse for the latter. Now and then a chorus of ear-splitting whoops, a clatter of hoofs down the street, to an accompaniment of pistol-shots, while the red flashes and whistling of balls in the darkness, warning those who might be under cover not to venture forth just yet, told that a group of cowboys were engaged on the time-honoured and highly popular pastime known among their craft as "painting the town red," *i.e.*, galloping through the streets whooping and discharging their six-shooters at everything or nothing. But this was far too ordinary an occurrence to attract any attention. It all meant nothing. Here and there, however, it did mean something. Partitioned off from the bar-room was the space devoted to card-playing, and it might be that from here the ominous sound of cards vehemently banged down with a savage curse upon the table warned those who heard it to stand clear. In a twinkling the flash and crack of pistol-shots—then a lull, and amid inquiries from many voices, eager, hurried, perhaps in a lowered tone, a dead man is raised and deposited on a table or carried forth to his home if he have one.

"Who is it?"

"How did it happen?"

"Was it a fair draw?"

"Oh yes, both blazed together!" "All right—fair and square enough!" and the other players resume their gamble, and the talkers their narratives, and more drinks are ordered, and nothing further is thought of the affair.

At that time Henniker City was blessed—or the reverse—with a considerable influx on its normal population. Grouped around the outskirts of the town lay the tents of many of the dispossessed miners—who, like our two friends, had been removed from the Indian lands. All these men were more or less discontented; and suffering in addition from enforced idleness, it follows that monotony and drink rendered them ripe for any mischief which might suggest itself. Moreover, among their ranks was a sprinkling of the very scum of the frontier—horse thieves, "road agents" or highwaymen, professional assassins, and bullies of repute whose presence here was due to the fact that they had rendered every other State too hot to hold them, and where, did they venture to return, they would be lynched without fail, if not shot on sight.

Into one of these tents we must invite the reader to peep with us.

Look at those two knights of the hang-dog countenance. He who is now speaking would stand not a chance before any intelligent jury, if only on account of his aspect alone. By the dim oil-lamp in the tent we can make out two other forms lying around, but the cloud of tobacco smoke, added to the dimness aforesaid, precludes a more familiar study of their not less forbidding features.

"See now, Dan," hang-dog number one was saying. "May I be chopped in splinters by the reds if I allow this darned white Injun to get away out o' this without a carcase full o' lead. So we'd better go up and finish the job to-night."

"Can't be done, I reckon. What about his pard—eh? To say nothin' about Nat Hardroper, who seems to have kinder taken him up!"

"Darn his pard, and darn Nat Hardroper!" replied the other, furiously. "Only a set of doggoned skunks 'ud have elected Nat Hardroper sheriff, and only a set of white-livered coons 'ud have kep' him in the berth. I guess I don't fear him."

"See here, Rube," suggested the other, "why not tumble to my plan? He'll be going to Red Cloud's village in a day or two—see if he don't. Then we can ambush him at Bald Eagle Forks and plant him full of lead."

"Don't want that. Want to string him up. Shooting's too good. Didn't he set the red devils on to sculp my pardners? Didn't he wipe out my brother?

leastways, he must have, for I reckon Chinee-Knifer Abe ain't the boy to be taken playin' possum. Ef it hadn't bin for a squad of his reds, we'd have strung him up down in Burntwood Creek the day before the snow."

"Guess our scalps sat loose that day. Snakes! but they ran us hard," answered the fellow addressed as Dan. "This Vipan 'd have been buzzard-meat then but for that."

"Reckon he shall be to-night," furiously retorted the first speaker. "I've said it—and Bitter Rube ain't the boy to go back on his word. That blanked white Injun, helpin' to dance around my pardners' sculps!"

And a volley of curses drowned the speaker's utterance.

Chapter Fourteen
In a Tight Place

"Stranger—I guess I want this floor!"

The place, an inner room partitioned off from Murphy's saloon; the time, late evening; the speaker a tall, half-drunken ruffian in frowsy miner's dress; the spoken to, Vipan—who, lounging against a table was chatting with the saloon-keeper; the tone, insolent and threatening to the last degree; the attitude, that of a man sure of his advantage.

"Stranger—I guess I want this floor!"

"And I guess you've got it," came the quick reply, but not more quickly than the change of attitude which it described. For, in a twinkling, a straight "right and left" from the shoulder had sent the aggressor to earth like a felled ox, while his pistol-bullet buried itself in the wall half a yard above Vipan's head.

Then ensued a stupendous hubbub. Pistols cracked, as the stricken man's mates in the outer room hurled themselves at the partition door intent on taking up their comrade's quarrel. But the door, a solid slab one, met them in full career, pinning the foremost of their number half in, half out.

"Now, Dan Harper, back's the word!" said the quiet, but stern voice of Smokestack Bill, to whose promptitude was due this first check to the enemy.

"You move a little inch forward and you're a stiff, you bet."

"Leggo the darn door, then—F-fixed t-tight," gasped the pinned one, who, with the muzzle of the scout's six-shooter within an inch of his nose, would willingly have obeyed, but could not. Smokestack Bill, however, relaxing his pressure, the crushed one was able to draw back, considerably bruised, into the outer room, and the door was jammed to, but not before a couple of bullets fired into the room had narrowly grazed Vipan's shoulder.

"Now then, boys," called out the scout. "Anyone feel like trying an entrance? Better not, believe me."

All this had befallen within infinitely fewer minutes than it takes to chronicle. The felled bully lay prone where he had first dropped, stunned, insensible, and motionless—and disarmed, for the first act of his adversary was to put it out of his power to get the advantage of them. The room, half filled with stifling smoke from the pistol-shots; the barricaded door, against which the besieged ones had run up a couple of casks; the two determined men, fully prepared to defend themselves at the expense of any number of their adversaries' lives; the fierce, threatening summons to yield entrance from the infuriated gang without; all went to make up a strange and startling metamorphosis on the hitherto quiet evening, which the two men had reckoned upon when they retired into the private room of the saloon-keeper to be clear of any disturbance.

"Air you agoin' to open?" sung out a harsh voice, at the close of a muttered consultation. "We know you, Smokestack Bill, and we've nothin' again you. But that pizen skunk, the white Injun, we're bound to have him if we burn down the old log to do it. So you come out of it, Bill, right along, while you can."

"You be advised, Dan Harper," cried the scout in reply. "You're a dead man this very night if you don't git—mind me."

"So are a dozen of you, by God!" sung out Vipan. He knew the whole business was a deliberate plan to take his life. The ruffian whom he had felled was to pick a quarrel and shoot him on sight, while his scoundrelly mates stood ready to make sure of him if the first part of the scheme miscarried. A roar went up from the crowd. "Let's get at him! What'll we do with him, boys?"

"Tar and feather him!"

"Burn him at the stake!" "Scalp him!" "String him up!" were some of the yells that burst from the maddened throng as it surged round the building, narrowly scanning every door and window for a chance of forcing an entrance. But the defenders of the inner room knew better than to be caught that way.

"One minute before you begin any tricks," cried the scout, and his voice had the dangerous ring about it of that of an ordinarily cool and quiet man roused at last. "One minute, and just listen to me. We've molested nobody, and don't want to molest nobody. Bitter Rube in here picked a quarrel with my pardner and got knocked down. If he'd done it with any of you boys he'd have been shot dead. He'll be shot before anyone gets in here—"

"Darn Bitter Rube! Serve the bunglin' fool right! What do we care about Bitter Rube? It's the pizen white Injun we're going to lynch—and lynch him we will—by God!"

"Try it!" rejoined the scout. "There'll be a few of you dead in your boots before mornin', I reckon. And anyone who thinks Smokestack Bill the boy to go back on a pardner is makin' an almighty big error in the undertaking. So now, stand clear for squalls."

A roar and a yell was the only reply. A deafening crash, as some of the rioters in the outer saloon vented their rage in smashing all the glass they could lay hands on; then a shock, as the end of a beam, wielded as a battering ram, came full against the door. A couple of flashes and reports, mingling like a single one. The beam fell to the earth at the same time as three of its bearers, whom the fire of the besieged, discharged through a chink at such close quarters, had literally raked in line. The remainder promptly got out of the way.

"Put in the faggot. Don't give any of the skunks a further show," yelled the frantic mob, exasperated by this reverse. And a rush was made for the further end of the building.

Chapter Fifteen
Judge Lynch takes a Back Seat

It is not wonderful, all things considered, that the citizens of Henniker, together with its fortuitous and floating population, should have been moved to such lengths as to resolve upon lynching Vipan. Indeed, it would have been surprising had matters turned out otherwise. Here was a man they very much more than suspected of being in league with their barbarous and dreaded foes, at a time when the frontier was almost in a state of war. A man of known daring and unscrupulousness, and whom they knew to have been present—the only white man—at an important council, involving issues of peace or war; to have taken part in its deliberations, going even so far as to advise the chiefs, and that, if report were to be believed, by no means in the direction of peaceful results. Several of their friends and neighbours had been murdered and scalped, those who had escaped a similar fate being obliged to carry on their mining or other operations rifle in hand, even if not forced to quit altogether. Meanwhile, this man, it was well known, could move about the country perfectly unmolested, visiting the Indian encampments at will—indeed, in one instance he was known to have witnessed a scalp-dance, wherein the prime attraction of the entertainment lay in the exhibition of the scalps recently torn from the heads of two of their murdered comrades.

And then he was an alien, which was the crowning point of the whole offence; and the good citizens of Henniker were virtuously stirred that a foreigner—an Englishman—should, while dwelling on their free and sacred soil, presume to be on friendly terms with its dispossessed and original owners; even as here and there in Great Britain may still be found a misguided and hard-headed Tory moved to honest indignation at the prospect of Fenians and Invincibles and National Leaguers stirred up to dynamite and murder by Irish-American agents and American dollars.

But how came it that so much should be known of Vipan's movements, seeing that he himself was almost the only white man who could safely penetrate the semi-hostile country or venture among the roving bands who even then were raiding and murdering at their own sweet will? Well, human nature is rather alike all the world over. Gossip on that wild Western frontier was circulated through very much the same channels as, say, at Lant with Lant-Hanger in the county of Brackenshire—through the agency of the squaws to wit. Some of the miners owned red spouses, others, again, were not above open admiration for the savage beauties—and, presto!—sooner or later the gossip of the Indian villages leaked out.

Peering through the chinks, the besieged could descry a sea of threatening faces, savagely hideous in the red torchlight. Prominent among these was a man who held a noosed cord. Hither and thither he moved, stirring up the crowd, his sinister features distorted with malicious rage. Hatred, envy, disappointed greed, all were depicted there, as with blood-curdling threats the mob clamoured for the object of its resentment.

Suddenly a clatter of approaching hoofs became audible alike to besiegers and besieged. The crowd paused aghast, the first thought being that of an Indian attack. Then a score of horsemen darted into the light, and a ringing voice was heard inquiring—

"Say, boys, what in thunder's all this muss?"

"That's the sheriff," said Smokestack Bill, coolly, lowering his revolver. "We're out of this fix, anyhow."

A roar was the answer.

"The white Injun! The pizen white Injun! We're going to lynch him."

"I guess not," was the reply. "Not while Nat Hardroper's sheriff of Henniker City. When it comes to reckoning with that invaluable officer, Judge Lynch'll have to take a back seat. Eh, boys?" turning to his well-armed followers, a score of cowboys and well-disposed citizens, whom he had prudently collected in haste on receiving the first intimation of a riot.

"That's so, sheriff," was the prompt reply.

"Say, Dan Harper," called out the sheriff, "Judge Lynch's sittin' in the State you've just left. Why not go and talk to him there?"

The face of the fellow named blanched at this allusion.

Meanwhile the crowd, composed mainly as it was of ruffians and bullies, began to show a disposition to slink off, in the presence of these well-armed and determined representatives of law and order.

"Never mind, boys," shouted someone. "We'll plant him full of lead yet. Now let's git."

"How do, sheriff?" said the scout, calmly stepping forth with extended hand. "Guess you've raised the siege on us right slick in the nick of time."

"How do, Bill? How do, colonel?" to Vipan. "Now you come right along to my log and we'll talk."

"Hold hard, friends," objected Vipan. "We've got to drink first. Murphy, bring out the juice."

"Whurroo, sheriff darlint," chuckled the saloon-keeper. "Whurroo! but it's purty shootin' there's bin around here afure you came. Be jabers! and thur'll be a big inquist to-morrow, and the power of the 'crame' 'll be on hand for the jewry, I reckon. Bedad! and whur's that shuck-faced omadhaun?" he added, gazing at the corner. For Bitter Rube, having recovered his confused senses, had profited by the confusion to steal away unperceived.

"Now, boys, mind me," said Nat Hardroper to Vipan and the scout, after a substantial supper a few hours later. "This same Henniker City's a powerful survigerous place. I've got you out of one fix, but I can't go on getting you out of fixes. It's too big a contract on one man's hands, I want you to see. Now, a power of those chirruping roarers'll be on your trail first thing you show your noses out of this shebang. If I warn't sheriff this'd be my advice—to take your hosses this very night and git. But it ain't my advice, because, you see, I *am* sheriff, and you're under my charge. No, no; it ain't my advice."

Save for the faintest possible wink, he looked them straight in the face, as solemn as an owl. Vipan burst into a roar of laughter.

"Right you are, Nat. It's not your advice—we'll remember that."

"Well, good-night, boys; good-night."

They shook hands heartily. But our two friends did not go to bed; they went to the stable. By daybreak they had put a considerable number of miles between Henniker City and themselves.

Chapter Sixteen
A Conjugal Debate and its Sequel

With all his failings, the Rev. Dudley Vallance had one redeeming point—he was excessively fond of his children; but it is probable that he loved his only son more than all the rest put together. To him he could refuse nothing. Indeed, so loth was he to part with him even for a time that he could not bring himself to allow Geoffry to enter any profession. He must remain at home. There was no need for him to earn his living, since he would one day succeed to the Lant property, and meanwhile he could be learning to look after it.

Fortunately, Geoffry was something of a bookworm, and studious of temperament, or the bringing-up he had received, and the aimless life which it entailed upon him, would have sent the boy straight to the dogs. As it was, he was cut out by Nature for a college don rather than for a country squire, and during his University career he was known essentially as a reading man.

It may be imagined, then, that when he returned home at the end of the summer term, after taking a brilliant double first, the pride and delight of his reverend parent knew no bounds, and by a series of festivities, unparalleled since the distinguished youth's coming of age, was Lant-Hanger at large, and particularly its "County Society," bidden to share the parental joy.

But, alas! that the latter should be so short-lived. The object of all this fun and frolic seemed in no way to relish it at all. Instead of returning home cheerful, overflowing with spirits, thoroughly enjoying life with the zest of the average young Englishman who has just scored a signal success, and sees a congenial and rose-bestrewn future before him, poor Geoffry seemed to have parted with all capacity for enjoyment. He was pale and listless, absent, bored, and—shall we own it?—at times excessively irritable, not to say peevish. His father was deeply concerned, and his mother, who read off the symptoms as briefly as the village doctor would diagnose a case of incipient scarlet fever, felt more of anger than concern.

"I really don't know what to do about the boy," said the Rev. Dudley, dejectedly, coming into his wife's morning-room the day after the last of their house party had dispersed. "It's dreadful to see the poor fellow in such low spirits. He must have been working too hard, whatever he may say to the contrary. It's hard to part with him so soon, the dear fellow, but we positively must send him abroad to travel for the summer. Nothing like travel."

"Try him, and see if he'll go," was the short reply.

"We must insist upon it. We must get medical advice—a doctor's opinion to back us up. The boy will be ill—ill, mark me. He eats nothing. He doesn't sleep, for I hear him moving in his rooms far into the small hours. He looks pale and pulled down, and doesn't even care for his books. Then, when all the people were here, he would steal away from everybody, and wander about and mope by himself all day. We had some nice people, too; and pleasant, good-looking girls. Come, hadn't we?"

"Oh, yes; a most complete party. Only one ingredient left out."

"And that?"

"Yseulte Santorex." And Mrs Vallance shut down the envelope she was closing with a vicious bang.

"God bless my soul! you don't say so? Surely it hasn't gone so far as that?"

"It has gone just as far as that abominable girl could carry it," was the uncompromising reply. "Surely you are not simple enough to imagine that the daughter of that hybrid Spanish atheist would neglect such an opportunity? The girl has simply made a fool of him."

"You dislike her to that extent?" said Mr Vallance, vacantly, his mind full of the woeful plight into which his son was plunged. "I don't know. Sometimes I think her not a bad sort of girl considering the fallow in which her mind has been allowed to lie. And Geoffry might do worse."

"Oh, yes. He might, but not much. A forward, bold, masculine minx, tramping the countryside, fishing and shooting. And she is utterly devoid of respect for her elders, and as for principle or religion—faugh! I beg leave to think, Dudley, that he hardly could do worse."

This spitefulness on the lady's part was not wholly devoid of excuse. For her elders, as represented by Mrs Dudley Vallance, Yseulte certainly had scant respect. And then, if she became their son's wife, the day might come when Mrs Vallance would have to abdicate Lant Hall in her favour, whereas no such calamity could in the nature of things ever befall its reverend squire. Of course Geoffry must marry somebody or other one day;

but Geoffry's mother could contemplate such a contingency with far more equanimity than that of being dispossessed by a girl whom she detested, and whom she knew despised her.

"Well, well! we won't say that; we won't say quite that," rejoined Mr Vallance. "Perhaps you are a little hard on poor Yseulte. She is young, remember, and at a thoughtless age. But she is thoroughbred in the matter of birth, and will be well off. We must not expect everything at once. And the girl is very pretty, with all her faults. I am not surprised at Geoffry's infatuation."

"No more am I," was the short reply.

"Oh, but you must look at a question of this kind apart from prejudice. And then I can't bear to see poor Geoffry simply eating his heart out like this. I am becoming seriously alarmed about him; and I tell you what it is, my dear, as he really has staked his happiness on this girl, he shall have her. I'll see Santorex about it this very day."

"Oh, well, if you have quite made up your mind, the sooner you do so the better," answered his spouse, resignedly.

"Very well, then, that's settled," said the Rev. Dudley, with a sigh of relief.

There was just one thing they forgot, this worthy couple, namely, that before settling a matter of the kind so comfortably and out of hand, it might be necessary to obtain the concurrence of the party most concerned, to wit Yseulte Santorex herself. But that Yseulte might unhesitatingly decline the honour of the projected alliance never occurred to them for one moment, and any suggestion of the bare idea of such a contingency would have thrown them into a state of wild amazement.

During the above debate, the subject thereof was doing exactly as his father had said; wandering about by himself—and moping. Strolling down the cool mossy lane, shaded between its high nut-hedges, he found himself upon the river-bank. It was time to go home. They would be wondering what had become of him; perhaps sending everywhere in search of him. In his then morbid frame of mind, Geoffry shrank from being made a fuss over. Mechanically he turned to retrace his steps.

"Great events from little causes spring." The little cause in this instance was a little flock of sheep, which a farmer's lad, aided by his faithful collie, was driving into the lane from an adjacent field. The animals were kicking up a good deal of dust; Geoffry was no fonder of walking in a cloud of dust than most people. The lane was narrow, and sheep are essentially idiotic creatures; were he to try and pass these, they would, instead of making room for him, inevitably scamper on ahead as fast as their legs could carry them, thereby kicking up about ten times more dust. That decided him. He would extend his walk.

Over a rail, an unexpected flounder into a dry ditch, and he stood up to his neck in brambles and nettles. But the sting of the latter was hardly felt; for his eyes fell upon an object which set his knees trembling and his heart going like a hammer. A moment earlier and he would have missed the phenomenon which evoked this agitation, but for the sheep. What was it? Only a broad-brimmed straw hat, and beneath it a great knot of dark brown hair rippling into gold.

It needed not this, nor the supple figure in its cool light dress which became visible, as with an effort poor Geoffry staggered up from his thorny hiding-place, to reveal the identity of this new feature of the situation. She was standing with her back towards him, about fifty yards away, taking a fishing-rod to pieces, and she was alone.

At the tearing and rustling noise caused by his efforts to free himself from the clinging brambles, she turned quickly, the half-startled look upon her features giving way to a wholly amused one as she took in the situation. Geoffry, noting it, felt savage, reckless, mad with himself and all the world. Could he never appear before her but in a ridiculous light—the central figure of some absurd situation?

"Why, Mr Vallance, you seem to have fallen among thorns," she cried, adding, with a merry laugh, "and the thorns have sprung up and choked you. But never mind. Sit down and rest here in the shade, while I do up my tackle, and then we can walk home together as far as our ways lie."

The tone was kind and sympathetic, and Geoffry felt soothed. Red and perspiring, he cast himself down with a grateful sigh upon a mossy bank, in the shadow of the great oak beneath which she was standing.

"That'll be some consolation," he replied ruefully. "It was nothing, though—the tumble, I mean. I must have caught my foot in something, and came a cropper. But, it was well worth while."

Yseulte smiled, trying hard not to render the smile a mischievous one.

"Well, you're the best judge of that. And now, have all your visitors left?"

"Yes, and a good job too," was the fervent reply.

"How ungrateful! I'm sure they did their best to make themselves agreeable, especially to you. Confess; you are dreadfully bored now that they are gone."

"Not in the very least. *You* are here—and—and—" He broke off, helpless and stuttering.

"But I shall not be much longer. I am going away too."

He sprung to his feet as if he had been stung.

"What? You are going away? When?"

"Very soon. In a week or ten days; perhaps not quite so soon." Already she wished she had not told him. It would have been better, for every reason, that he should have heard the news at second hand.

"In a week or ten days!" he echoed. "But not for long—Yseulte, say it will not be for long!"

If at times the girl had been guilty of a touch of feminine spitefulness in the reflection that she had completely subjugated—and through no artful intent—the hope of this family whom, not without reason, she detested, assuredly she felt sorry and ashamed of it now, as she noted the pitiable effect which her announcement produced upon her admirer. His face was as pale as death.

"But what if it will be for long?" she answered, gently. "For months, perhaps—or a year."

"Then I'll go and hang myself."

Poor Geoffry! For weeks—for months—he had been anticipating such a moment as this; had revolved every kind of set speech; every form of the most moving entreaty; every promise to devote his life to her happiness and welfare; all in the most impassioned language that the earnestness of his love could suggest: and had shivered with apprehension lest his nervousness and misgiving should intervene to mar the effect and leave him stuttering and looking an ass; yet now that the critical moment had come, all his carefully-planned oratory had resolved itself into the brusque, passionate statement—"Then I'll go and hang myself." Yet never was declaration more exhaustive.

She understood his meaning; she did not wish him to say more; and her tone was very gentle, very pitiful, as she replied:

"Be a man."

The utterly wretched expression upon his face, showed that he had understood her. Never was proposal more terse; never refusal more prompt and decisive. It was impossible for each to misunderstand the other.

"Have I no chance, Yseulte?" he said, the eager trepidation of his former tone having given way to one of dull hopelessness, which moved her infinitely.

"No," she answered, gently. "It would be cruel to leave you in any doubt. There are many reasons against it—insuperable reasons."

"Oh, what are they? Tell me what they are," he cried, relapsing into his former tone. "They can be removed—there is nothing I will not do, or give up, for you. What are they? You don't like my people, I know; but you have always been kind and friendly with me. Surely my relations need not stand in the way?"

"You must not ask me for reasons, Geoffry. Let us talk over this rationally. If I cared for you as you wish, nothing should stand in the way. But as I do not, even you would not thank me for coming between yourself and those who do. Only think what a firebrand I should be."

"No, you would not. I tell you there is nothing I would not do for you— or would not give up for you. Only just try me."

What complication-loving fiend should have brought to her recollection then the vision of that pictured face which had made such an impression upon her—the face of the disinherited heir of Lant Hall? The leaven of her father's cynical philosophy almost moved her to experiment on this *corpus vili* ready to her hand, and ascertain whether his protestations would go the length of espousing her ideas of right and wrong as regarded that particular subject. But she restrained herself in time.

Very dejectedly and in silence he walked beside her as far as their ways lay together. He would fain have reopened his pleadings, but with a hurried farewell she left him before he could detain her.

"Well, Chickie? Been having it out with Geoffry Plantagenet?" said her father, who, from his library window, had witnessed their parting at the divergence of the roads.

"Yes; that's just what I have been doing. And—I think, dear, we oughtn't to laugh at poor Geoffry quite so much."

"Oh, that's how the land lies, is it?" answered Mr Santorex, struck by the unwonted gravity which she had brought to bear upon the subject. "All right, we won't. Not that *we* shall have much longer to laugh at anyone," he added somewhat ruefully.

Chapter Seventeen
War Wolf is "Wanted"

"Say, Vipan. Guess we'd better draw off out o' this for a bit. There's no call for us to help do police work just now, and we can't stand looking on. There'll be hair-lifting here in a minute, I reckon."

Thus Smokestack Bill to his friend and boon companion as the two lounged on the turf, a hundred yards or so from the trading store attached to the Blue Pipestone Agency. The place was alive with Indians, gathered there for the purpose of drawing the rations with which a paternal Government supplied them, contingent on their good behaviour and in consideration of their peaceably abiding on their reservation and eschewing the fiery delights of the war-path. So Uncle Sam's red nephews occupied the ground in crowds, indulging in much jollification on the strength of newly-acquired beef and flour and other commodities which should refresh and comfort both the inner and the outer man, and while the squaws were busily packing these upon their much-enduring ponies, their lords were lounging about, chatting, smoking, merry-making, and having a good time generally. Meanwhile, the trading post had been doing a brisk business.

"Police work, eh?" returned Vipan, with a glance at the detachment of U.S. Cavalry, which, encamped in the neighbourhood of the store, showed no sign that any serious undertaking was in contemplation. "Who are they after nobbling?"

"See here, old pard—if I didn't know you well enough to stake my life you'd never go back on a pardner, you and I wouldn't be here together to-day. If they can't claw hold of their man, it mustn't be through any meddlin' of ours."

"Who is it they want?"

"War Wolf."

"The devil they do! They gave out a different story."

"That's so. Joe Ballin, who's with them, 's an old pard of mine. We've done many a scout together in '67 and '68. Well, he told me all about it. This command is out after no less a chap than War Wolf. You see the pizen young skunk has been braggin' all over the section how he scalped Rufus Charley and Pesky Bob, them two fellers we buried down by Burntwood Creek. It's got to the General's ears, and now they've come to take him over to Fort Price. They've given out a lie that they're bound down the river on the trail of a Minneconjou who ran off a lot of Government beef last month, but that's just a red herring. As sure as War Wolf comes along, they'll grab him—mind me."

Vipan meditatively blew out circles of smoke into the air, without replying. This was a most untoward *contretemps*. He remembered the scalp-dance which he had witnessed; the two scalps—including the red-haired one—which War Wolf had so boastfully brandished during that barbarian orgie, and it flashed across him vividly now that, were the Indian arrested for the deed, the bulk of his clansmen and the Sioux at large would look upon himself as having betrayed their compatriot into the enemy's hand, or would for their own purposes affect to. Here were the troops, and he, Vipan, on good terms and hob-nobbing with their leaders. The capture—if it took place—would be to himself most disastrous. It was characteristic of the man that he lost sight of the grave peril in which he himself would be placed, alone here in the midst of hundreds of exasperated savages. His plans of future enrichment would be utterly broken up, and it was of this he was thinking. Unscrupulous, self-seeking as he was, Vipan had his own code of honour, and he would no more have dreamed of betraying his friend's confidence than of cutting his friend's throat. But had the information reached him through any other channel, it is more than doubtful whether Uncle Sam's cavalry would have effected their capture that day.

"You're right, Bill," he said, at length. "There'll be an almighty rumpus if that game's tried on. Why, there are enough reds here to chaw up this command twice over, and they'll do it, too, I'll bet a hat. Why the devil did they send out so few men?"

"Well, what d'you say? Hadn't we better git?"

"Not this child. You see, if we make tracks, and War Wolf gets grabbed, the reds'll certainly think I gave him away. He's an infernal young skunk, and I'd gladly see him hung; still, it nohow suits my book that he should be just now. So I'll see it out, but if you'd rather be outside it, don't stay. We can rendezvous anywhere you like afterwards."

"Oh, well; it's no great matter. I don't care if I stay," answered the scout, with his usual imperturbability. "Here's a big burst of rain coming. We'd better get inside the store, anyhow."

Great drops began to plash around them; there was a steely gleam, followed by a long, muttering roll of distant thunder. As they made their way towards the log-house, the Indians were breaking up into groups of twos and threes, and hurrying away in the direction of a cluster of *teepes* erected hard by. Failing any necessity for it, they were no more inclined for a ducking than most people. The cavalrymen, beyond taking precautions for keeping their arms and ammunition dry, seemed indifferent to the weather.

"Hello, Smokestack Bill!" cried a hearty voice, as they entered. "So that's how Nat Hardroper custodies his State prisoners, eh?"

They recognised in the speaker the officer who had arrested them in the Black Hills. With him was Joe Ballin, the scout above referred to. Vipan, especially, further noticed a sergeant and a dozen men posted, apparently by accident, within the room.

"Lord, Colonel," replied the scout, "you don't want us to foot the Henniker trail again?"

"Not I," said the other, with a laugh. "Other game afoot this journey."

Then at Vipan's suggestion, drinks were dispensed, the storekeeper—a long, lank Eastern man—participating in the round.

Suddenly the latter exclaimed:

"Snakes! here come three reds. Your man in 'em, Colonel?"

Through the open door three Indians could be descried approaching rapidly. It was raining hard, and their blankets were drawn over their heads and shoulders, leaving only a part of their faces visible. The swarthy features of Ballin the scout lit up with a momentary excitement.

"The centre one, Colonel," he whispered, hardly moving his lips. "The centre one. He's the skunk we want, and no mistake."

The Indians continued to advance with their light, springy step. When about a hundred yards from the store they were suddenly joined by a large band of fully-armed and mounted warriors, clearly a band which had just arrived upon the ground, but which had hitherto been unseen by those inside the store, owing to the limited range of vision afforded by the latter's doorway.

This untoward arrival placed a critical aspect on the state of affairs. But Captain Fisher's orders—the higher rank by which that officer was commonly addressed, was mere popular brevet—were concise. They were to the effect that he should apprehend upon sight, and convey to Fort Price an Ogallalla Sioux, known as War Wolf. This was sufficient. If that Indian were not apprehended it would only be because he had made himself remarkably scarce. As it was, however, here he stood before them, advancing confidently into the trap. But then, he had at his back a formidable force of his compatriots, outnumbering the cavalrymen three to one, not reckoning the number of warriors already on the ground, and whom the first whoop would bring upon the representatives of authority in crowds. Clearly here was a critical situation. So thought Vipan, who stood prepared to watch its *dénouement* with intense interest. So thought Smokestack Bill and the storekeeper, who, however, with characteristic phlegm, stood prepared to act as events should decide. So, especially, thought the Captain and the dozen men disposed inside the store to effect the capture.

The whole band, in delightful disorder, was now straggling around the door; the three pedestrians, who had been joined by a couple of the new arrivals, leading. All unconscious of danger, War Wolf was chattering and laughing with his companions. Then a shadow darkened the doorway, and the first Indian entered. Before his eyes became sufficiently accustomed to the sudden darkness—for the windows had been purposely shaded—the second was in the room. A rapid movement, a sudden exclamation, and two struggling bodies—all quick as lightning. Captain Fisher had seized the second Indian from behind, effectually pinioning him.

It was done in a moment. The desperate struggles of the lithe and active savage taxed all the efforts of the half-dozen men who had been told off for the purpose, while the remainder held the entrance. In a trice he was subdued, disarmed, and securely bound. His comrade, to whom Ballin the scout had hurriedly explained that no harm was intended, stood by sullen and immovable.

Then arose an indescribable hubbub. The warriors outside, who had dismounted, rushed helter-skelter for their ponies, and the loud, vibrating shout of the war-whoop rose above the clamour of angry and inquiring voices. At its sound the temporary village became as a disturbed ants' nest, Indians pouring from the *teepes* in swarms: and in less than a minute a crowd of excited savages—mounted and afoot—came surging down upon the log-store, brandishing their weapons, and fiercely clamouring for the instant release of their compatriot.

But a line of disciplined men barred their way. Drawn up in front of the store, the troopers, some fifty strong, stood with carbines levelled, awaiting the word of command; while Ballin, duly instructed, went outside and informed the Indians that, should they approach twenty paces nearer, the troops would fire.

The effect was magical. The entire mass halted dead. Then, yelling the war-whoop, a number of young bucks darted out from the main body and, putting their ponies at full speed, began circling round the tenement and its defenders. But a peremptory mandate from one of the chiefs present recalled these young-bloods, and for a moment the two rival forces stood contemplating each other—the savages with a fierce scowl of hatred, the troops, cool, determined, and not altogether anxious for a peaceful solution to the difficulty.

Then the chief who had recalled the more ardent of his followers, advanced making the peace-sign—extending his right hand above his head with the palm outwards.

What had War Wolf done, he asked, that he should be seized like a common thief in the white men's towns? Had he not come peaceably with the rest to obtain his rations, and had obtained them—a clear proof that the Government was not angry with him? He had been living on the reservation with them all, as everybody knew; why then should the Great Father send soldiers to take him?

Briefly Captain Fisher explained the charge against the young warrior. The killing of two citizens in time of peace was murder—not an act of war. The prisoner would have to answer for it before the Civil Courts of the Territory.

The chief's face was a study in admirably feigned surprise, as the above was interpreted to him. He was a warrior of tall, commanding aspect, just past middle age, and looked almost gigantic beneath his nodding eagle plumes. He was the head war-chief of the Minneconjou clan, and had the reputation of being well-disposed towards the whites. He rejoiced in the name of Mahto-sapa, or The Black Bear.

"What the white Captain had just told them contained sound sense," he replied. "But would it not do as well if War Wolf were released now, and called upon to answer to the charge against him later on, when the Great Father should want to try him. Such a course would be most gratifying to his countrymen, who were highly incensed that a warrior of his standing and repute should be seized in the way he had been. It would be best, perhaps, for all parties," the Indian explained, with just a shadow of meaning in his uniformly courteous tone—"for his young men were so hot-blooded and impatient, he feared they might not act with the prudence and moderation to be looked for in men of riper years, a contingency which would be in every way lamentable to himself and the other chiefs of the Dahcotah nation."

If the speaker expected his veiled threat to produce any effect on Captain Fisher, he must have been sadly disappointed. Concisely that officer informed him that, in the matter of a grave charge of this kind, War Wolf could not expect more lenient treatment than would be accorded to a citizen under similar circumstances. No white man would be held to bail if arrested for murder, and an Indian must look for precisely the same treatment—

no better and no worse. At the same time he guaranteed that the prisoner should receive every consideration compatible with his safe keeping until such time as the authorities should decide upon his guilt or innocence. As for the anger of the warriors he saw before him, greatly as he should regret any breach of the peace, that consideration could not in any way be suffered to interfere with him in the discharge of his duty. Were he, the speaker, the very last man left of the command they saw before them, he should still do his best to convey his prisoner whither he had been ordered, and would die rather than release him.

The chief, seeing that further parley was useless, turned and rejoined his followers. Then once more arose a wild hubbub of angry and discordant voices, and for a moment it seemed that the crowd of impulsive and exasperated barbarians would hurl itself forward and in one overwhelming rush annihilate that mere handful of troops. Suddenly a body of warriors, some hundred strong, sprang on their ponies, and, unmindful of their leader's mandate, scoured away over the plain, whooping and brandishing their weapons. The remainder having withdrawn some little distance gathered into knots, or squatted in circles on the ground, talking in eager and menacing tones.

"Thunder! Reckon that lot's gone to raise hell among the pesky varmints camped along your return trail, Colonel," said the lank storekeeper, pinning a fly to the wall with his quid at half-a-dozen paces. "You'll need to keep a bright lookout on the road if you're ever going to get this skunk to Fort Price."

And what of the captive? The first expression of rage, mingled with amazement and mortification, having rapidly glinted across his countenance, his features became as a mask of impassibility. Only once, as his glance met that of Vipan, his eyes glared as he hissed in a tone inaudible to those around:

"Golden Face! The Dahcotah's *brother*! Ha! We shall meet again!"

"War Wolf walks straight into the trap, as a silly antelope walks up to the fluttering rag upon the hunter's wand. Who is to blame but War Wolf himself?" replied Vipan, in the same almost inaudible tone. But the Captain hearing it, turned sharply round. Vipan's reputation as being on more than ordinarily friendly terms with the Sioux had already reached him. However, he made no remark, but having disposed his prisoner in such wise as to guard against all possibility of escape or rescue, he prepared to start. Just then the other Indian who had accompanied the prisoner into the store, inquired if he might go and fetch his pony. War Wolf was his brother, and he, Burnt Shoes, did not intend to leave him. He would go as a prisoner too.

"He's a fine, staunch fellow," said the Captain, kindly, as this request was interpreted. "But we can't take him. Tell him so, Ballin, and also that he can serve his brother's interests better by going back to his people and notifying them that in the event of their making any attack upon us either now or along the road, the prisoner will be shot dead."

This was interpreted, and at War Wolfs request the two Indians were allowed a few moments' conversation together. Then Burnt Shoes, having taken leave of his brother, strode away, looking straight in front of him.

The threat and the warning were by no means superfluous. As the troopers appeared outside with their prisoner, the bands of savages clustered hard by sprang to their feet with an angry shout. Many of the warriors could be seen fitting arrows to their bowstrings, and the click of locks was audible as they handled their rifles in very suggestive fashion.

Even the emphatic message which Burnt Shoes strove to deliver, concerning the fate awaiting his brother in the event of a rescue, was hardly heard. The clamour redoubled, and the attitude of the savages became menacing to the last degree. Meanwhile the cavalry escort, with its prisoner in the midst, had got under way, and was retiring cautiously, and at a foot's pace. By this time, however, the authority of Mahto-sapa, and the earnest appeals of Burnt Shoes, had availed to quell the tumult. The crowd began to melt away. By twos and threes, or in little groups of ten or twelve, the warriors began to disperse over the plain in all directions, only the chief, with comparatively few followers, remaining.

"Say, but there'll be trouble when those chaps come up with the sodgers," said the lank storekeeper, contemplating the retreating Indians. "They'll jump 'em in an overwhelming crowd somewheres about Blue Forks, and I'll risk ten dollars there'll not be a scalp left in that command."

"Well, I'm going to persuade the residue to hear reason, anyhow," said Vipan carelessly, making a step towards the door.

"Don't risk it," urged his friend, promptly. "They're plaguy mad, and it's puttin' your head into the alligator's jaws to go among 'em jes now."

"Well, you see, it's this way," was the rejoinder. "They are plaguy mad just now, as you say, but they'll be madder by-and-by. A classical authority has said, 'agree with thine adversary quickly,' and I'm going to agree with mine."

"You're a dead man if you do," said the storekeeper.

"No fear. Mahto-sapa and I are rather friends. I reckon I'm going to sleep in his village to-night, and I'll risk twenty dollars if you like, Seth Davis, that I look round here again, with all my hair on, within a month."

"Done!" said the storekeeper, shortly.

They watched him join the group of sullen and brooding savages— moving among them, alone, absolutely fearless, as among a crowd in an English market-town—addressing one here, another there. Then they saw him fetch his horse and ride away with the band, which had been preparing to take its departure.

"Gosh! I never saw such a galoot as that pard of yours," said Seth Davis, ejecting an emphatic quid. "Takes no more account of a crowd of Ingians a-bustin' with cussedness, nor though they were a lot o' darned kids. Wal, wal! Reckon that wager's on, all there; hey, Smokestack Bill?"

"That's so," was the laconic reply. "Let's liquor."

Chapter Eighteen
"Through a Glass Darkly"

About a month later than the events just detailed, a solitary individual might have been descried occupying one of the high buttes overlooking a large tract of the northern buffalo range, somewhat near the border between the territories of Montana and Wyoming. Howbeit, we must qualify the statement in some degree. Save to the keen eye of yon war-eagle, poised high aloft in the blue ether, the man was not to be descried by any living thing, for the simple reason that he took very especial care to keep his personality effectually concealed.

Beneath lay the broad rolling plains extending in bold undulation far as the eye could reach, stretching away to the foothills, and then the distant snow peaks, of the Bighorn range. No cloud was in the sky. The atmosphere in its summer stillness was wondrously clear, all objects being sharply definable up to an incredible distance. From his lofty perch the man looks down upon the surrounding country as upon a map lying outspread before his feet.

That something is occupying his attention is evident. Lying flat on his face, his gaze is riveted on the plain beneath. What object has attracted his keen vision—has sufficed to retain it?

Crawling onward, unwinding its slow length like some huge variegated centipede, comes a waggon train, and, though it is at least ten miles distant, the observer, from his vantage-ground, can with his unaided vision master every essential detail—several great lumbering waggons, veritable prairie schooners, their canvas tilts looking like sails upon that sea of rolling wilderness; a little way ahead of these a lighter waggon, drawn by a team of four horses. He can also make out a few mounted figures riding in front.

"Looks a pretty strong outfit," would run his thoughts, if put into words. "Looks a pretty strong outfit. The boss—two guides, or scouts—six or eight bullwhackers—a chap to worry the horse team—probably two or three more men thrown in—a dozen or more all told—possibly a score. But then—the family coaches—Lord knows how many women-folk and brats they hold—all down-Easters, too, most likely, who never saw a redskin, except a drunken one at the posts. A dozen men ought to be able to stand off the reds; and anyhow whether they can or not the next few hours will decide. But then they've got their women to look after, and their cattle to mind. No, no; they must be idiots to come crossing this section at this time of day."

The observer's reflections are, to say the least of it, ominous for those who belong to the waggon train. Let us see what there is to justify them.

Far away in front of him, at least as far as the waggon train itself— ahead of it, but rather off its line of route, is another object; an object which he has espied before the outfit appeared, and the sight whereof has kept him immovable on his lofty observatory for upwards of an hour. This object the inexperienced eye would hardly notice, or would pass over as an indistinct clump of scrub lying on the slope of a deep ravine. To the practised eye of the watcher, however, that object stood revealed in its true light at the very first glance, and it hardly needed the aid of the powerful double glass which he carried, and which rendered an object at ten miles almost as distinct as one at a hundred yards, to tell him that the harmless-looking clump of scrub was nothing less formidable than a strong band of Indians—a strong band of red warriors *on the war-path*.

"That'll be it," he mused. "The old game. They'll jump that outfit at yonder creek while it's unhitching just about sundown—rather over two hours from this. If those chaps are, as I suspect, down-Easters, they'll be thrown into the liveliest confusion, and while a few of the reds run off every hoof of the cattle, the rest'll rush the whole show. Their guide or guides can't be worth a damn, anyhow, to judge from the free and easy way in which the whole concern is shuffling along. There'll be fresh scalps among that war-party to-night, I'll lay long odds; but—it's rough on the women-folk, to put it mildly."

To the ordinary observer there would have been something terrible beyond words in the situation. That little handful advancing fearlessly into the vast wilderness, their every step watched by the hawk-like gaze of savage videttes lying face to the ground on more than one of the adjoining heights, advancing step by step into the trap, heedless of the awful cloud overhanging their march, even that lurking band of the fiercest and most ruthless barbarians to be found upon the earth's surface. And the radiant sun shedding the golden glories of his nearly run course upon the majestic vastness of those fair solitudes sank lower and lower to his rest, only too certain to be lulled in his far-off mountain bed by the crash and rattle of shots, the exultant yells of human fiends, the unheeded prayer for mercy, then massacre mingled with a demon orgie of sickening barbarity from the very thought of which the average mind shrinks in dismay. Well, what then? Only one more chapter of horror in the annals of the blood-stained West.

But if to the ordinary mind the situation would have been appalling, repulsive and incomprehensible to the last degree would have been the attitude of this man, who lounged there as cold-blooded a spectator of the coming struggle as a frequenter of the bull-ring awaiting his favourite entertainment, and in much the same vein; who saw those of his race and kindred advancing step by step to the most terrible form of death—for the chances in their favour were about equal to those of the bull when pitted against the *cuadrilla*—and made no effort to warn them of their peril. Yet had he delivered his mind on the subject he would coolly have justified himself by the explanation that in the first place he made a point of never interfering in other people's business; while in the next he was a man who recognised no race or kindred, and who, if anything, had a greater respect for the savage red man than for the huckstering, swindling, lying white Christian. The former was man ruthless as Nature made him, the latter a nondescript product—equally ruthless, but *plus* hypocrisy and cant wherewith to cloak his blood-sucking propensities.

And now the waggon train was well-nigh abreast of his position. Cautiously adjusting his field-glasses so that no ray of the sun glinting on the lens should betray his whereabouts, either to friend or foe, he narrowly scanned the travellers. There were, as he had conjectured, females among them, two of whom rode on horseback among the group of men in front. He scanned the ground beyond, and not a detail escaped him, even to the heads of the three Indian scouts lying *perdu*, like himself, at intervals along a high ridge overlooking the line of march. Then he closely scrutinised the lurking war-party.

The latter was astir, and he could easily make out a sea of plumed crests and painted countenances, even to the colour of the pennons floating from the lance-heads. Warriors might be seen rapidly caparisoning their ponies, while others, already prepared for action, were gathered around the little group of chiefs in the centre apparently engaged in debate. It wanted an hour to sundown.

Once more he brought his glasses to bear upon the travellers. Suddenly the blood surged in waves over the man's bronzed and sunburnt countenance, and his hand trembled to such an extent that he nearly dropped the telescope. What did he see? Pausing a moment, with an angry frown at his own weakness, again he sent a long, eager, steady look into the group riding ahead. What did the powerful lens reveal to upset the equanimity, to shake the very nerves of this cool, hardened, cynical plainsman? Among the group of advancing specks is a white one—a mere white speck. Framed within the lens, however, that speck becomes a white horse, and upon his back is a girl of extraordinary beauty. Surely this is not the disturbing factor? We shall see.

"*That's* too good for our dear red brother, anyhow," said the watcher half-aloud, shutting up his glass. Then, without arising to his feet, he slid behind the knoll. But before doing so he sent one more glance at the distant halting place of the savages. The band was on the move, riding slowly down into the ravine.

Chapter Nineteen
Winthrop's Outfit

Nearer, nearer, the sun sank down to the western peaks, and upon the wilderness rested the sweet and solemn stillness of the evening hour. Save the call of a bird at intervals within the timber belt, there was a silence that might be felt. The broad stream, tranquilly flowing around its bend, gleamed first with living fire, then red, as the last rays of the sun fell upon its surface, to lift in a moment, leaving its waters grey and cold. Then one last kiss of golden light upon the tree-tops, and the lamp of day had gone down.

One living creature moved within this solitude, however. Alone, enjoying with all her soul the spacious grandeur of the Western wilderness, stood a very lovely girl. Every now and then she would pause for a few moments to drink in that glorious sense of unfettered freedom which the vast expanding roll of hill and plain, never ending, like a sea of billowy verdance stretching from sky to sky, inspired in her, then return to her occupation. That occupation was—fishing.

She wore a riding-habit which, fitting her like a glove, revealed the undulating curves of an unrivalled figure. By some clever contrivance she had shortened its otherwise inconvenient length, and with the grace and deftness of a practised hand she was wielding a trout-rod. What a spectacle to come upon suddenly in the heart of the wild and blood-stained West! And what insane fatuity should bring her here alone in the fast falling twilight?

At this moment, however, the last thought in her mind is any fear of danger. Her cast whirls in the air; the flies drop noiselessly into a bubbling eddy. There is a rush through the water and a splash. An eager light comes into the velvety blue eyes, fading as rapidly to give place to one of vexation as the cast, suddenly released from its tension, springs high overhead, describing many a fantastic gyration.

"How sickening," she cries, with a little stamp of impatience. "How unutterably sickening! That *was* a beauty, and I shan't rise another to-night. But—it's nearly dark. I must go back."

What is that stealthy rustle in the depths of yonder scrub? For the first time the girl is conscious of a shade of nervousness as she hurriedly begins to take her rod to pieces. Her thoughts suggest the proximity of some hideous snake, or a panther perhaps.

She turns towards where she left her pony. Can the gathering dusk be playing her tricks? The animal is not there. Though securely fastened, it has disappeared.

But the sight which does meet her eyes roots her to the ground with horror. Stealing noiselessly towards her, in the dark shade of the timber, are three half-naked Indians—tall, athletic, hulking savages, hideously painted. They halt for a moment as they see themselves perceived. They are barely a dozen yards distant.

"How, lily gal!" grunts the foremost, wreathing his repulsive face into a frightful grin, and advancing with outstretched hand. "How, lily gal! No 'fraid! Me good Injun, me. Ha, ha! Me good Injun brudder."

The exultant mockery underlying this friendly address was too transparent. Her eyes dilating with horror, the girl stepped back, the consciousness that she was alone in the power of these fiends turning her limbs to stone. They, for their part, secure of their beautiful prize, were enjoying her terror.

"No run 'way," said the first speaker, who had diminished the distance between them. "No run 'way. Injun, good brudder." And he seized her left wrist in the grasp of a vice—while another, with a fierce chuckling laugh, made a movement to seize her right one.

But the brutal contact broke the spell of horror which was weaving around her. A wild cry of indignation escaped her lips, and her eyes blazed. Wrenching her right wrist free, she dashed the heavy butt end of her fishing-rod with all her force—and it was not small—full into the first assailant's face, knocking out some of his front teeth, and causing him to loosen his hold.

With the fierce growl of a wounded cougar, the savage sprang at her again, the blood streaming from his mouth, and as the unhappy girl recoiled to renew her efforts to keep her persecutors at bay, such a marvellous change came over the scene that not one of the actors in it was quite aware what had happened.

An enormous dark mass seemed to fall from the very heavens, simultaneously with a thundrous roar. The girl, now tottering on the verge of faintness, saw, as in a flash, her first assailant lying with his skull crushed to pulp, another lay gasping in the agonies of death, while the third was just vanishing in the timber! At him pointing the still smoking muzzle of a revolver, mounted on a huge black horse, was the most splendidly handsome man she had ever seen.

"Quick! Drop all that gear and mount in front of me. Give me your hand."

There was no disobeying the curt commanding tone. Resisting a deadly impulse to faint right away, she extended her hand. In a second she was swung up before the stranger on his powerful horse.

It was all done like lightning. The first appearance of the savages—the assault—the rescue—occupied barely a couple of minutes. Pale to the lips, shaky, and unnerved, she could hardly now realise it all. But often in the time to come would she look back to that strange ride, the weight of the appalling danger she had just escaped still hanging over her, the courage and promptitude of her rescuer, the struggle she was waging with her own natural terror, dreading she knew not what.

The black steed was going at a gallop now, but his rider had him well in hand. The girl noticed that they were making something of a *détour* which took them far out on the open plain, whereas her ride down to the river had led her along the very edge of the timber. She noticed, too, the anxious, alert look on the stranger's face. Though he did not turn his head, she felt assured that not a detail in the surroundings escaped him.

"There are your people," he said briefly, as they suddenly came in sight of the camp. The waggons had just unhitched, and the mules and oxen were being driven down to the water; not the river we have seen, but a small creek running into it. Already columns of smoke were rising on the evening air.

"I can never thank you enough," said the girl, suddenly and with a shudder. "But for your promptitude where should I be now?"

"Say but for your own courage and self-possession. The average idiot in petticoats would have shrieked and fainted and gone into hysterics. Meanwhile, the reds would have captured her and shot me," he rejoined, somewhat roughly. "Be advised by me now. Don't startle the rest of the women, or they'll hamper us seriously. Now we'll dismount."

He lifted her to the ground, and, without another word, turned to confront a man who had hurried up. But the girl's clear voice interrupted him before he could speak.

"This gentleman has rescued me from frightful danger, Major Winthrop. There are Indians about."

"By Jove!" said he addressed, with a start of astonishment, looking from the one to the other. He was a man below middle age, of medium height, active and well-built, and there was no mistaking him for anything other than what he was—an English gentleman.

"Boss of this outfit, I take it?" said the new arrival shortly.

"Yes. Allow me to offer you my most grateful thanks for—"

"Well, there's a big lot of Sioux preparing to 'jump' you at any moment. Corral your waggons without delay, and have your cattle brought in at once. Not a second to lose."

A frightful yell drowned his words. There was a thunder of hoofs upon the turf as a band of some fifty mounted Indians, dashing from their cover, bore down upon the herd of draught stock which was being driven back from the water in charge of three or four men. On came the savages, whooping and whistling, brandishing blankets and buffalo robes with the object of stampeding the now frantic cattle.

But among those in charge of the latter there chanced to be a couple of experienced plainsmen. In a trice there rang out three shots, and two of the assailants' ponies went riderless. Crack—crack! Another pony went down. This was more than the redskins could stand. Like a bird of prey alarmed in its swoop, the entire band swerved at a tangent and skimmed away over the plain as fast as their ponies could carry them. The herd was saved.

"There goes the first act in the drama," said the stranger coolly. "Now stand clear for the second."

The suddenness of it all—the yelling, the shots, the swoop of the painted and feathered warriors—had created a terrible panic in the camp, and had the main body of the savages charged at that moment nothing could have saved its inmates. As the stranger had at first conjectured, two of the waggons were full of women and children, the families of some of the emigrants. These at once rushed to the conclusion that their last hour had come, and shrieks and wailings tended to render confusion worse confounded. But Major Winthrop, with military promptitude, had got the men well in hand, and a very few minutes sufficed to corral the waggons, bring in the cattle, and put the whole camp into a creditable state of defence. It was now nearly dark.

"Will they attack us to-night?" enquired Major Winthrop, as, having completed his arrangements, he returned to where the stranger was seated smoking a pipe and gazing narrowly out into the gloomy waste.

"I should be inclined to say not. Their surprise has fallen through, you see, and then Indians don't like fighting at night. But it's at the hour before dawn, when we're all infernally sleepy and more or less shivery with being up all night—it's then we shall have to keep a very bright look-out indeed. I should keep about half your men at a time on guard all night through if I were in your place."

"Who air you, stranger?" said a not very friendly voice.

He addressed turned, and beheld a lank, dried-up individual who might have been any age between thirty and fifty. His hawk-like face was the colour of mahogany, and, but for a small moustache, was devoid of hirsute adornment. His deep-set grey eyes, however, were those of a man prompt and keen to act in the moment of difficulty or danger. His dress consisted of a rather dirty blue shirt and fringed breeches.

"Who am I? Why just who I look—neither more nor less," was the rejoinder, given with provoking tranquillity.

"And what might your name be—if it's a fair question?"

"It might be Jones, or it might not. The question is a fair one, however. That being so, I don't mind telling you my name is Vipan. What's yours?"

"I'm Oregon Dave, champion bronco-buster (ranch term for a professional horse-breaker) of Wyoming. I'm boss-guide of this hyar outfit, and the chap who reckons he knows Injuns and their little ways better nor I had best just step out and say so."

"If I were boss-guide of any outfit, I'm damned if I'd let a young lady belonging to that same start off by herself to go fishing among a Sioux war-party," said Vipan, with a quiet satire in his tone that was maddening to the last degree. He resented the other's truculent bearing, and intended to let him know it.

"Eh! Say that again," said the first speaker, flushing with anger.

"We mustn't quarrel my friends, we mustn't quarrel," put in Major Winthrop, earnestly. "It was mainly owing to your pluck and promptitude, Dave, that we haven't lost every hoof of our cattle. And but for Mr Vipan, here, Miss Santorex would at this moment be a prisoner among the Sioux. I was to blame in that matter, and I bitterly acknowledge it." Then he told him the circumstances of Vipan's unexpected and opportune appearance among them. Before its conclusion Oregon Dave turned to the latter with outstretched palm:

"Shake, stranger, shake. You're all there, and I'm only fit to be kicked into a kennel to yelp. Guide? No, I ain't no guide, only a tenderfoot—a doggoned professor. Scalp me if I don't go and hunt bugs upon the perairie with a brace o' gig-lamps stuck across my nose. I'll go now and ask the reds to tar and roast me. Good-bye, Kurnel; good-bye, stranger, I ain't no guide, I ain't. Thunder, no!"

"Nonsense, man," said Winthrop, clapping him on the shoulder. "We were all to blame. We were informed along the road that the Indians were peaceable, and that all chance of war was at an end, for this summer, at any rate," he explained, for Vipan's benefit. "That being so, we have travelled much too carelessly, although in camp we've been on the alert for horse or cattle thieves."

"I've been watching your outfit, and I've been watching the reds for nearly two hours," said Vipan. "They mean't jumping you yonder at the creek, and would have done so before this if you had not changed your plan, and camped here. As near as I can count, there are about three hundred of them. See that butte away up there? That's where I've been located. Came down to warn you—none too soon, either."

"No, indeed. We owe you a debt of gratitude we can never repay, myself especially. Good God, if harm had befallen Miss Santorex! I can't even stand the idea of it."

"Relative of yours?" said the other shortly.

"*No*. She's the sister of a neighbour of ours—man who runs the adjoining ranch. She's come out from England to stay with her brother for a bit, and took the opportunity of travelling with us. And—if anything had happened—good God, if anything had happened! It's an awful responsibility, and I devoutly wish we were safe through it. Now, I think, we may go and get some supper."

Major Winthrop, as we have said, was English. He had retired early from the service, and being an energetic fellow had soon found an unoccupied life pall upon him. Accordingly he had migrated to the Far West and started ranching—a life that suited him thoroughly. His wife, a pretty little vivacious brunette, was American. She was considerably his junior, and they had not been long married; and at the time we make their acquaintance were returning from a visit to her home in the Eastern States.

"My! what a fine-looking fellow!" she whispered to her friend, as she watched the approach of her husband's guest. "Why, Yseulte, it was worth while getting into a fix to be rescued by such a knight-errant as that."

To her surprise the colour came to the girl's face—visible in the moonlight—as she answered:

"What nonsense, Hettie! Do be quiet, or they'll hear you."

"I ought to scold you severely, Miss Santorex, for running such an awful risk," said Winthrop, as they sat down to supper, picnic fashion, beside the horse waggon which served as the ladies' bedroom, saloon, and boudoir—and in bad weather, dining-room—all run into one.

"Please don't, for I assure you I'm very penitent," she answered.

"And then just think what an adventure she'll have to tell about when she gets home again," put in Mrs Winthrop. "Well, now, Yseulte, what do you think of our Indians, now you have seen them—real ones—at last?"

"Oh, don't ask me!" answered the girl, who was still rather pale and shaky, in spite of her plucky efforts to recover her self-possession. "That last charge was all over so quickly. But aren't they rather cowardly?"

"Why?" said the Major.

"Well, a number of them like that to be turned back by three men."

"I trust you may have no practical occasion to alter your opinion," put in Vipan, speaking for the first time. "That was a small surprise party bent on running off the stock—not fighting. As it was, they lost two killed and wounded at the first fire, and one pony, which is enough to turn any Indian charge of that strength."

"Killed! Were there any killed?" asked Mrs Winthrop, in a horrified tone. "They seemed only frightened."

"H'm, perhaps that was all, or they may have been only wounded," said Vipan, inventing a pious fraud for the occasion. These two delicately nurtured women would require all their resolution on the morrow; there was no need to unnerve them with an instalment of horrors to-night. So both men affected an unconcern which one of them at any rate was far from feeling, and little by little the contagion spread, and the emigrants' families began to forget their first fears, and the spell of brooding horror which had first lain upon them began to pass away, and the terrible danger with which they were threatened seemed more remote, yet, the night through, men sat together in groups, chatting in an undertone, as, rifle in hand, they never entirely took their gaze off the moonlit waste, lest the ferocious and lurking foe should creep upon them in his strength and strike them unawares.

Chapter Twenty
The War-Path

"Steady, boys. Here they come!" whispered Vipan, his eyes strained upon the point of a long narrow spit of scrub looming dark and indistinct in the heavy morning mist. Within the waggons, whose sides were securely padded with sacks of flour and other protective material, the women and children, worn out with anxiety and apprehension, were slumbering hard. It was the gloomy hour of early dawn.

A moment's aim, and he discharged his Winchester. The report rolled out like thunder upon the heavy mist-enshrouded atmosphere. Then a moment of dead silence.

Suddenly a line of fire darted along the ground. Then whirling down like lightning upon the corral came what resembled a number of wavy balls of flame. There was a roar and thunder of hoofs, the loud, horrible, quavering war-whoop rent the air, and a plunging sea of hideously painted centaurs, streaming with feathers and tags and scalp-locks, and bathed as it were, in a ring of flame, surged around the corral, enfolding it in a mighty moving mass of demon riders and phantom steeds. A shower of blazing torches came whizzing right into the midst of the camp, followed by another. Thick and fast they fell, lying sputtering and flaring everywhere. The encampment and its defenders were in a sheet of flame, and amid the clouds of sulphurous smoke, even the crash and rattle of volleys was well-nigh drowned in the demoniacal and stunning yells of the attacking savages, who, pressing the advantage afforded them by this unlooked-for panic, saw success already theirs.

In the excitement of this sudden surprise the shooting on both sides was wild in the extreme. Amid the whirling, plunging mass, a warrior was seen to leap convulsively in his saddle, and, throwing up his arms, sink beneath the pounding hoofs. More than one pony rolled upon the ground, but still the flying horde circled in nearer and nearer, full half its strength preparing for a final and decisive charge. It seemed that the doom of every man, woman, and child in that camp was sealed.

Maddened by the terrific yells, by the flames of the burning missiles scorching their legs, the frantic animals picketed within the corral plunged and kicked, and strained wildly at their picket ropes. It only needed for them to break loose to render the general demoralisation complete.

But amid the indescribable tumult, the yelling of the Indians, the plunging of the frenzied cattle, the crash and rattle of volleys, the fiery peril which threatened to wrap the whole camp in flames, the on-rushing squadrons of demon centaurs, and the piteous shrieks of terrified women and children, three or four men there kept their heads, and well indeed was it for the rest that they did so.

"Keep cool, boys! Don't fire too quick," thundered Vipan, deliberately picking up one of the blazing torches and hurling it with good aim full against the striped countenance of a too daring assailant. Winthrop, whose trained eye took in the weakness, the frightful jeopardy of the situation, had his hands full at the side of the corral which he had elected to attend to.

"Jee-hoshaphat!" exclaimed Oregon Dave, between his set teeth. "Now for it, boys! They mean hair this time."

For the Indians, who, wheeling and turning on their quick active little steeds in such wise as to render themselves difficult targets in the uncertain light, as well as to bewilder the eye of their enemy, were now seen to mass together with marvellous celerity. Then, with a long, thrilling whoop, they charged like lightning upon the weakest point in the defences.

Never more deadly cool in their lives, half-a-dozen men, among them Vipan and Oregon Dave, stand in readiness.

"Now let drive," whispers the latter.

A raking volley at barely a hundred yards. Several saddles are emptied, but it does not stop the charge. Led by a chief of gigantic stature and wildly ferocious aspect, the whole band hurls itself forward, as a stone from a catapult. Then the fighting is desperate indeed, for it is hand-to-hand. A score of warriors slide from their horses and leap within the enclosure, their grim and savage countenances aglow with the triumph of victory, only, however, to retreat helter-skelter as several of their number drop dead or wounded before the terrible six-shooters of that determined half-dozen. In the confusion the gigantic chief, watching his opportunity, puts forth his lance and spears one of the unfortunate emigrants through the heart. Then bending forward he drags out the still quivering body, and with amazing strength throws it across his horse.

"That's that devil Crow-Scalper," cries Vipan, amid the roar of rage which goes up at this feat. But the chief, flinging the body to the earth again, wheels his horse and utters his piercing rallying *cry*, brandishing aloft the bleeding scalp he has just taken. More than one bullet ploughs through the eagle plumes of his war-bonnet; his horse is shot under him; but he seems to bear a charmed life. Leaping on the pony of a warrior at that moment shot dead at his side, again he utters his shrilling, piercing whoop and strives to rally his band.

But the latter have had about enough. The deadly precision of those unceasing close-quarter shots is more than Indian flesh and blood can stand up to.

"They're off, by th' Etarnal, they're off!" roared one of the emigrants, a tall Kentuckian who boasted a strain of the blood of the Boones. "Give 'em another volley, boys!"

"Guess so, Elias," yelled his spouse, a raw-boned masculine virago, who throughout had been wielding a rifle with good effect. But the Indians showed no desire to wait for this parting attention. They kept up a show of fight just long enough to enable them to bear away their dead, always an important feature in their military drill. Then with a final whoop of defiance they vanished into the mist.

Suddenly they returned, but only a handful. One of their fallen comrades had been overlooked. Darting from among the rest a couple of warriors, riding abreast, skimmed rapidly along towards the corral. Suddenly they were seen to bend over, and seizing an inert corpse by the neck and heels, raise it and fling it across the pommel in front of one of them. Then, almost without abating speed, they wheeled their ponies and disappeared.

"By the Lord! but that was well done," cried Winthrop.

Throughout this desperate affray, which had not occupied many minutes, the weaker members of the community, frozen with fear, crouched shudderingly within their shelters. These helpless women knew what terrible fate awaited them in the event of the savages proving victorious, and to their appalled senses the hideous war-whoop, the thunder of charging hoofs, the shouts and the wild crashing of shots seemed as a very hell opening before them.

Shivering in her well-padded waggon, poor little Mrs Winthrop was in a pitiable state of terror and anxiety.

"Oh, Yseulte, I wish I could be as brave as you," she moaned, clinging to her friend as to a final refuge. "How do you manage it? Tell me."

"I don't know," answered the girl, with something of a warrior-light shining in her eyes. "Only I'm sure we shall win."

The calm, steadfast tones conveyed to the distracted, terrified creature, as she herself phrased it, "tons of comfort." Then the tumult had ceased.

The mist was rolling back, unfolding heaven's vault of brilliant blue, and in less than half an hour the whole country-side stood revealed. Not an Indian was in sight. Slain ponies lay around, and here and there a dark clot of gore showed where a warrior had fallen.

"Will they come again?" said Winthrop, turning to Vipan. Many an ear hung upon the answer.

"No," replied the latter, tranquilly, beginning to sponge out his rifle. "I never saw a finer charge than that last, and they know perfectly that if it wouldn't carry the corral nothing will. They intended a surprise, you see, but it broke down completely, and unless they try the palaver trick we shall see no more of them just yet. But we shall have to keep a bright lookout, for depend upon it, they won't let us be out of sight long—for some time at any rate."

"Waal, boys," drawled the tall Kentuckian, "I reckon we'll jest squat around a bit, and be darn thankful."

"That's so, Elias," assented his martial spouse, diving into the waggon to lug out her brood by the ears, as if nothing had happened.

Chapter Twenty One
Truce

It was afternoon, and quiet had settled down upon the emigrants' camp once more. While its inmates were despatching their much-needed breakfasts Vipan and Oregon Dave had sallied forth upon a scout. They soon returned, reporting the whole party of Indians to be retiring over a distant range of hills some twelve miles to the eastward. So, pickets being posted to give warning should they think better of it and return, the cattle were driven down to the water and were now enjoying a graze under the watchful supervision of half-a-dozen men.

It was afternoon. Most of the inmates of the camp were recruiting themselves after their night of watching and the exciting events of the morning's conflict. A few drowsy snores, or now and then the puling cry of some child within the waggons, or perchance the clatter of pots and pans, as one or two of the women were cleaning up the culinary implements which had served for the morning meal; these were the only sounds which broke the slumbrous stillness.

Stretched upon the turf about fifty yards outside the corral, puffing lazily at an Indian pipe, lay Vipan. He alone of all there present seemed to feel no need of slumber. The dash and excitement of the conflict over, a strange reaction had set in. There was a look upon his face as of a man who, turning back upon the chapters of his own history, finds the reminiscences therein recorded the reverse of pleasant. It was also the look of one who is undergoing a new experience, and a disquieting one.

A light step on the grass behind him.

"Are you really made of cast-iron, Mr Vipan?"

"H'm, why so, Miss Santorex?"

"Because everyone else is snoring like the Seven Sleepers, and you, who have had as trying a time of it as any three of the rest put together, are still wide awake."

"I might say the same of you. You, too, have been awake all night."

"Oh, dear no; nothing like it. And now—and now we are alone, I want really to thank you as I ought, but—but—I don't know how," broke off the girl, with a comic ruefulness that was inexpressibly bewitching. "Really, though, I never was further from joking in my life. Now that I have seen what those dreadful savages are like, I seem to realise what a frightful fate you saved me from," she added earnestly, with a lovely flush.

"Let us talk of something else," he answered, somewhat abruptly. "You showed extraordinary grit during the recent little unpleasantness between us and our red brothers. May I ask where, when, and how you served your apprenticeship as an Indian fighter?"

She laughed and gave a slight shiver. Now that they were over, the appalling experiences of the early morning could not but tell upon her. She was rather pale, and dark circles round her eyes told of an apprehensive and restless night.

"Poor Mrs Winthrop is quite ill this morning, and no wonder. I hope we shall have no more of those frightful experiences. And yet, to look round the camp no one would suspect that anything out of the way had happened."

Vipan followed her glance. He was glad that all traces of the bloody struggle had been removed—the dead bodies, including that of the unfortunate emigrant who had been scalped, had been buried while the terrified and worn-out women were sleeping the slumber of exhaustion.

"No, it was all horrible—horrible," Yseulte went on, speaking gravely and sadly. "If I was not half-dead with fear it was thanks to my father's teaching. He always used to say that panic was fatal to self-respect, and still more fatal to self-preservation. Child as I was, the idea took root, and I was able to conquer my fears of bulls or savage dogs, or mysterious noises at night, or at any rate very nearly so."

"Quite, I should say. Your father must be a somewhat rare type of man."

"He is. Wait till you see him. Then you will think so."

"Is he coming out here, then?"

"Coming out here!" she echoed, wonderingly. "Oh, no. I am going back in a few months' time. I mean when you come to see us and give him the opportunity of thanking you as I never can."

Vipan looked curiously at her. They had been strolling all this while, and were now well out of earshot of the camp.

"When I come and see you," he repeated. "To begin with, it is extremely unlikely I shall ever leave these festive plains, let alone go back to England."

"Ah, you *are* English. I guessed that much from the very first. But I thought—we all thought—you were only out here on a trip."

He did not even smile.

"Do you think, Miss Santorex, that a man out here 'on a trip' would be up to every move of a Sioux war-party? No; I have been out here a good many years. There are those in the settlements who speak of me as the white Indian, who have more than once attempted my life because I happen to feel more respect for the savage as he is than for that vilest of all scum of humanity the 'mean white.' Why, not many weeks ago I was in a far tighter place than this last little shindy of ours, and narrowly escaped with my life at the hands of the latter."

"Bang!"

The picket posted on an eminence a mile distant had discharged his piece.

"We must cut short our walk," went on the adventurer. "That shot means Indians in sight."

A few minutes and the pickets could be seen riding in. As arranged, the cattle, which had been brought near on the first alarm, were now quickly driven into the corral.

The man who had fired the shot reported a large party of warriors approaching rapidly from the direction in which the assailants had retired. He reckoned it was the same lot coming back.

"Hoorar! Guess we'll lick 'em into pounded snakes again," drawled the long Kentuckian, on hearing this news.

"They don't want to fight," said Vipan, "or they wouldn't have drawn off so kindly to let us water and graze the stock. This time they're coming to talk."

"Well, that's better, anyhow," said the Major. A sentiment which his wife, who was standing at his side looking very pale and scared, thoroughly echoed.

Mounted figures now began to appear on the ridge about a mile away, and presently the entire band was halted upon the eminence. Then a couple of warriors rode out from the main body, and advancing a little distance, made the peace-sign. By way of answer a white towel was run up on a pole and waved above the waggon corral.

"I want you to see this, Miss Santorex," said Vipan. "It's a sight you may not see again in a lifetime."

The band had now left its halting place and was riding slowly down towards the camp. If in the wild fury of their swooping charge the Indians had worn a savagely picturesque aspect, with their waving plumes, and flowing tags and scalp-locks on weapon and garment, none the less now was the appearance of the warrior phalanx stately and striking to the last degree. So thought Yseulte Santorex, as she gazed with more admiration than fear upon this array of the barbaric chivalry of the Western plains.

The Indians approached in crescent formation, some half-dozen chiefs riding a little in advance. All were in their war-paint—the dresses of some being, moreover, exceeding rich with colour and embroidery—the eagle-plumed crest of many a noted brave streaming to the ground as he rode. Not a warrior but showed some bit of gorgeous colour. Even the ponies' manes were adorned with feathers and vermilion, and the lance-heads and floating pennants gleaming above the sea of fierce stern faces put the finishing touch to a battle array as martial and gallant-looking as it was redoubtable and ruthlessly unsparing.

"It is magnificent!" said Yseulte, as from the coign of vantage which the other had secured for her she surveyed the approaching band. "What tribe are they, Mr Vipan?"

"Sioux. There may be a few Cheyennes among them, but the war-party is a Sioux one. Take the glass, and I'll tell you who some of them are. The chief there most to the right is Crow-Scalper, of the Uncpapa clan, a record of whose atrocities would keep you awake at night for a week."

"He's a splendid-looking fellow," commented the girl, gazing withal at the gigantic warrior who had led the last and most persistent charge upon the camp.

"Oh, yes; I know him well. Many's the hour I've spent in his lodge making him talk. Now, look again. The middle one is Mountain Cat—the trappers call him Catamount, but the other's the real rendering of his name. He hates the whites more than any Indian on this continent, and would willingly put a bullet into me if he got the chance. He's an Ogallalla, and a good big chief too."

"He looks an awful savage," answered Yseulte, with the glass still at her eyes. "I never saw a more diabolical expression. Who is the man who has just joined them?"

"Lone Panther—a half-bred Cheyenne—a small chief in standing, but a fiend when he heads a war-party. And now I must leave you for a little, and go and hear what they have to say. It may interest you to watch the progress of our conference through the glass."

"That it will. But, oh, Mr Vipan, do try and persuade them to leave us in peace. You know them so well, I am sure you can."

"I'll try, anyhow, if only for your sake," he answered, with a queer smile.

The three chiefs named had halted their band, and, attended by a couple of warriors displaying dingy white rags on their lance-points, were cantering down towards the corral. Arrived within two hundred yards, they halted. There went forth to meet them Vipan, Major Winthrop, and one of the latter's cowboys, who rejoiced in the name of Sam Sharp; also two of the teamsters to hold their horses.

When within a hundred yards of each other, both parties dismounted. The three chiefs, giving their horses to their attendants, advanced with slow and stately gait to where the three white men awaited them.

"Do we meet in peace, or do we meet in war?" began Vipan, as both parties having surveyed each other for a few moments the Indians showed no inclination to break the silence. No answer followed this straight question. Then Lone Panther, breaking into a broad grin, said:

"Injun brother Goddam hungry. White Colonel gib him heap 'chuck.'" (Food.)

Of this flippant remark Winthrop, to whom it was addressed, took no notice beyond a signal to Vipan to carry the negotiations further.

The latter explained to the chiefs that the "white Colonel" entertained his friends, not his enemies. They had attacked his outfit, tried to run off his stock, and had made themselves a dangerous nuisance. But that the camp had been vigorously defended they would have killed every one in it. They could not do this, and now they came and asked to be feasted as if they were friends.

To this Crow-Scalper, putting on his most jovial smile and manner, replied that the whole affair had been a mistake. Young men, especially when on the war-path, would not always be restrained; that being so, the chiefs were obliged to humour them. Beside, the warriors had no idea that these whites were among the friends of Golden Face, or that Golden Face was in the camp at all. Otherwise they would never have attempted to run off even a single hoof.

Vipan could hardly keep from roaring with laughter at the twinkle which lurked in the speaker's eye, as he delivered himself of this statement. Both he and the red man knew each other well—knew the futility of trying to humbug each other. Hence the joke underlying the whole thing.

What himself and his warriors most ardently desired now, went on Crow-Scalper, was to show themselves friends of the friends of Golden Face. To this end they proposed to accompany the waggon train as an escort. There were, he feared, bands of very bad Indians roaming the country, who would leave them unmolested if they had for escort a Dahcotah war-party. This course would wipe out all bad blood between them, and atone for the mistake they had made in attacking their dear friends the whites. So having settled this to his own satisfaction, Crow-Scalper suggested that a proper and most harmonious way of cementing their new friendship would be for the white men to join camp with their red brothers and to invite the latter to participate in a feast.

Vipan managed to preserve his gravity while translating these proposals for the benefit of his companions. The chiefs meanwhile watched every expression of their faces with steady and scrutinising gaze.

"They must take us for born idiots," said Winthrop.

"Thunder! I guess there's no end to the sass of a redskin," said Sam Sharp, the cowboy. "Travel with a war-party of pesky Sioux! Haw-haw-haw!"

"Better conciliate them to a small extent, though I never did believe in buying off your Danes," said Winthrop. "I'll give them an order for coffee and sugar and tobacco on the post we last quitted; but I'll see them hanged before they'll get anything out of us here."

This resolve Vipan communicated to the chiefs. The white Colonel felt quite strong enough to protect his own camp and did not need the escort so kindly offered. At the same time his red brothers could best show their friendship by retiring altogether and leaving him quite alone. The chiefs had admitted their inability to control their young men under all circumstances, and this being so, it would be best to part good friends. They could proceed to Fort Jervis and obtain the supplies, for which he would give them an order.

The emissaries saw that the game was up. They might eventually wear out the patience and watchfulness of the whites, and obtain the scalps and plunder they so ardently desired, but they would have to fight. No safe and easy way of treachery lay open to the coveted spoil, and this they recognised.

Then Mountain Cat, who up till now had preserved a stern and contemptuous silence, said:

"Golden Face, the friend and brother of the Dahcotah! Should he not rather be called Double Face?"

The sneering and vindictive tone was not lost upon the other two whites, although they understood not a word of its burden. Glancing at Vipan, they noticed that he was as unconcerned as though the other had never spoken.

"Does one friend kill another?" went on the savage, his eyes flashing with hatred. "Ha! More than one of our young men has been shot this day. Who was their slayer? Golden Face—the friend and brother of the Dahcotah nation!"

"What were my words to the great Council at Dog Creek?" was the calm rejoinder. "'Those who strike my friends strike me, and turn me into an enemy.' Were there not enough whites abroad upon the plains for your war-party to strike without attacking my friends whom I accompany? Enough. My words stand. I never go back from them."

For a moment things seemed to have come to a crisis. The chief made a step backward and cast a half-involuntary glance in the direction of his party. A threatening scowl came over his grim countenance, and his hand made a movement towards the revolver in his belt. But Vipan never moved a muscle, beyond carelessly dropping his rifle so as to cover the Indian in a manner apparently accidental.

"The Dahcotah have entertained a false friend in their midst," went on Mountain Cat, darting forth his hand with a menacing gesture, "one who smokes in their council and then betrays them. Where is War Wolf?"

"Is War Wolf my horse or my dog that it is my business to take care of him?" was the coldly contemptuous reply.

"Who witnessed the scalp-dance in our village at Dog Creek, when War Wolf showed his scalps? Who delivered him into the hands of the soldiers?" said the other, meaningly.

"I know who did not—and that was myself. We may as well speak plainly. War Wolf appears to have gone about the country bragging how he took the scalps of two white men, when he ought to have kept his mouth shut. If he was seized by the soldiers he has himself to thank for it, and nobody else—certainly not me, any more than yourself. I would even have warned him if I had been able, but it was impossible. That is enough about the matter."

"Good," repeated the savage chieftain, in a tone full of grim meaning. "Golden Face talks well, but in future our war-parties will know an enemy from a friend."

"So be it," replied Vipan, wholly unmoved by the threat. "If your party attacks our outfit again, we shall fight, as we did before."

"Excuse me," put in Winthrop, who was waxing impatient during this protracted conversation. "Excuse me—but our friend there does not seem to enter into the situation in a right spirit. Here is the order. It is made available only up till three days hence. So if you will kindly inform him accordingly, no doubt we shall get rid of the whole crew."

On the principle of "half a loaf," the other two chiefs grasped the bit of paper eagerly. They were beaming with smiles, and brimming over with affection for their dear white brothers. Only Mountain Cat held scowlingly aloof. Then they returned to their men.

It was uncertain now how matters would turn. Watching them, the occupants of the corral could see that an animated conference was being held. Would there be another battle? Even if not, a large war-party like this, determined to annoy them, could soon reduce their position to one of imminent peril. By closely investing the camp they could render it nearly an impossibility for the stock to obtain proper grazing—let alone bringing all progress forward to an utter standstill. They could even make it a matter of extreme difficulty to replenish the water supply—and then, too, there would be the constant strain and fatigue of ever being on the watch against surprise—whether by day or night. So that when their conference ended, the whole party mounted their ponies and retreated in the same way as they had come, the feeling evoked in the minds of the spectators was one of entire and undiluted relief.

Chapter Twenty Two
A Peril of the Plains

"A 'tenderfoot,' and—'turned round'!" (Lost.) And the speaker hands his field-glass to his companion. The latter brings it to bear and gazes with interest upon the object under observation.

The said object is a horseman, now between three and four miles distant. The observers from their point of vantage and concealment, a little belt of scrub and timber cresting a knoll, have been watching this object ever since it appeared on the skyline.

Thanks to the powerful glass they can make out every movement of the solitary horseman, and very irresolute his movements are. Now he reins in, and looks anxiously around; now he spurs his nag to the brow of some slight eminence, only to encounter disappointment, for the broad rolling plains lie around in unbroken monotony, affording no sort of landmark for the guidance of this inexperienced traveller. There is weariness and disappointment in his every movement. In his countenance there is more— an expression of strong apprehension, not to say alarm. This, too, thanks to the developments of science, is clear to the observers.

"A 'tenderfoot,' and turned round," repeats Vipan. "Now, what the deuce can he be doing here, alone, and away from his outfit? Why—what's the matter, Miss Santorex?"

"Look—look!"'is the hurried reply. "There—to the right—down in the hollow! What—who are they?"

In her eagerness she has seized his arm, and her face has gone pale as death. But Vipan has seen at the same time what she herself has. His reply is grave and in one word.

For a new factor has appeared on the scene. Stealing around the slope of the hill, out of sight of the horseman, but so that a few minutes will bring them suddenly upon him, come nearly a score of mounted figures. Their plumed heads and long lances show them to be Indians, their painted faces and the fantastic trappings of their ponies show them to be warriors on the war-path. Their stealthy glide, as nearer and nearer they advance upon their wholly unconscious victim, leaves no doubt whatever as to their present intentions. Indeed, the observers can plainly distinguish the exultant grin on each cruel countenance as the warriors exchange glances or signals. A few moments, and the solitary horseman will ride right into their midst.

"Oh, can nothing be done to save him?" cried Yseulte Santorex, clasping her hands in the intensity of the situation.

"I'm afraid, under present circumstances—nothing," was the reply, given with a calmness that outraged and exasperated her.

"What! I should never have believed it of you, Mr Vipan," she cried, her eyes flashing with indignation. "I should never have believed that you—you of all men—would stand by and see a fellow-creature barbarously done to death, and make no effort to save him, or even to warn him."

There was a strange look in Vipan's eyes as he met her scornful and angry glance—full and unflinchingly.

"Should you not!" he replied. "Well, then, I would stand by and see a hetacomb of 'fellow-creatures' done to death, if the alternative lay in exposing you to serious danger."

"Forgive me," she said, hurriedly, and in a softer tone. "But leave me out of the question, and let us try and save him. See! There are not many Indians; we can surely do something. Oh! It is too late!"

The stranger's horse was seen suddenly to stop short, pause, swerve, then start forward with a bound that nearly left his rider rolling on the plain. He had scented the Indians, who at the same moment appeared within a few hundred yards of the white man. Feigning astonishment at the suddenness of the meeting, one of the foremost warriors called out in broken English:

"How! White brother not run away. We good Injun—damn good Injun! Stop!—say 'how.' Smoke pipe—eat heap 'chuck'! Damn good Injun, we! White brother—stop!"

But the "white brother," though obviously a greenhorn, was not quite so soft as that. For all answer he dug the spurs into the sides of his nag in such wise as materially to increase the distance between himself and the savages. The latter, baulked of an easy and bloodless capture, together with the rare sport of putting a prisoner to death amid all manner of slow and ingenious tortures, cast all pretence to the winds, as they darted in pursuit.

Then began a race for life, which the spectators could not but watch with thrilling interest. Fortunately for the fugitive, his horse was an animal of blood and mettle, and seemed likely to show a good lead to the fleet war-ponies. But on the other hand the fugitive himself was an indifferent rider, and more than once, wholly unaccustomed to the tremendous pace, he would sway in the saddle, and only save himself by a hurried clutch at his steed's mane from being cast headlong to the earth. The whoops and yells of the savage pursuers sounded nearer and nearer in his ears, and the expression of his countenance, livid as with the dews of death, and eyeballs starting from their sockets, was that of such despairing horror as to turn one of the two spectators sick and faint.

"There's just a chance for him," muttered Vipan, more to himself than to his companion. "If he takes the right fork of the valley he's a dead man — nothing can save him. If he takes the left, it'll bring him close under us, and I'll give him a hail."

"Do, for the love of Heaven!" gasped the girl through her ashy lips. "God will help us, if we try and save this stranger."

Along the valley-bottom swept this most engrossing of all hunts — a man-hunt. Whatever advantage the superiority of his horse afforded him the fugitive was throwing away by his own clumsiness; for wildly gripping the bridle to steady himself in his seat, he was checking and worrying his steed to a perilous extent. Bent low on the necks of their ponies, the savages were urging the latter to their utmost speed. Slowly but surely now they were gaining. But a minute more and the fugitive must choose — the right fork of the valley, away into certain death — the left, succour, possible safety.

Suddenly a warrior, urging his steed in advance of the rest, literally flying over the ground, comes within fifty yards of the fugitive. Five — ten — another effort and he will be within striking distance. Then rising upright in his saddle the savage whirls a lasso in the air. Another moment and the fatal coil will have settled around the doomed man's shoulders.

But it is not to be. A crack and a puff of smoke from the spectators' hiding-place. The distance is too great for accuracy of aim — six hundred yards if an inch — but the ball ploughs up the ground under the pony's feet, causing the animal to swerve and the rider to miss his cast. The warriors, disconcerted by this wholly unlooked-for danger, halt for a moment, gazing in the direction of the report. At the same time a stentorian voice calls out:

"This way, stranger. This way, for your blessed soul, or you're a dead man!"

The fugitive needs no second invitation. His horse's head is turned towards the never-so-welcome refuge. Amid a shower of bullets and arrows from his discomfited pursuers he gallops up the gradual slope which lies between himself and safety, and, fainting, exhausted, speechless, more dead than alive, at length flings himself upon the ground at his rescuers' feet.

Vipan's attention is for the moment more taken up with the red warriors than with the man he has saved from their ruthless clutches. The whole party has now withdrawn beyond range, and is busily discussing the sudden turn affairs have taken. Then turning to the panting and exhausted man stretched at full length upon the ground with closed eyes, he remarks drily:

"You've had a narrow squeak for it, friend. I don't think your scalp could sit much more lightly than it has done within the last few minutes short of coming off altogether."

But the fugitive seemed not to hear. His whole attention was fixed—riveted—upon the beautiful face bending over him in alarm—solicitude—then unbounded surprise.

"Yseulte!" he stammered. "Yseulte! Is it really you, or am I dead or dreaming?"

"Why it's Geoffry. Geoffry Vallance! Why, Geoffry, where on earth *have* you dropped from?"

"Er—I was trying to catch up your—er—Major Winthrop's party—and lost my way," hé answered stupidly—rubbing his eyes in sheer bewilderment.

Chapter Twenty Three
The "Tenderfoot"

If Yseulte Santorex stood lost in amazement at this wholly unlooked-for meeting, there was really considerable excuse for some upsetting of her mental poise. Beyond a brief and formal farewell in the presence of her family, she had not seen her former admirer since that passionate and despairing declaration of his in the summer meadows which skirted the pleasant Lant, and neither at that time nor since had the faintest idea crossed her mind that he contemplated any such undertaking as Western or any other travel. And now here he was, flung, so to say, by Fate at her very feet, escaping by the narrowest chance from the hands of hostile savages, the most ruthless in the world. And she had been mainly instrumental in saving him.

But Geoffry had the advantage of her, in that his surprise was mainly confined to the circumstances and place of their meeting. When he had quarrelled with and separated from the rather worthless guide whom he had engaged at the nearest frontier post, he had reckoned on pushing on so as to overtake Major Winthrop's outfit in a day at the outside, and having found it, the first part of his object would be accomplished. Then he had lost himself, as we have seen, and but for the present opportune meeting his fate was sealed. And now here was the object of his search, more winsome, more beautiful than ever, her loveliness enhanced tenfold by the glorious open-air life she had been leading. But who on earth was her companion? Not her brother. George Santorex could never have altered beyond recognition within three or four years; besides, he was dark-haired — darker than Yseulte herself — and had not the herculean build of this stranger. Thus ran Geoffry's thoughts as, with half-closed eyes, he lay on the sward, thoroughly done up with fright and exhaustion.

Vipan, for his part, took no notice of the man whose life he had saved. He saw before him a loosely hung, shambling sort of youth, commonplace of aspect, and in no wise over-burdened with practical intelligence. Beyond the first half-bantering, half-contemptuous remark, he hardly seemed to think his new acquaintance worth addressing. Nor did he seem to think the unexpected recognition between him and Yseulte Santorex worthy of notice.

"Will they attack us, Mr Vipan?" asked the latter, with a shade of anxiety. For the Indians, having finished their consultation, were riding just beyond range, so as to make a wide circuit of the position.

"I doubt it. They are going to find our trail leading in here, so as to discover the extent of our force. They will find the trail of two horses, and not having seen you will take for granted that represents two men, instead of one man and a non-combatant. That, with our friend here, makes three. Three men with rifles, snugly fixed in a strong position, constitute far too tough a nut for a small force like that to try and crack, and they are only sixteen. No. They will conclude to go away and leave us alone."

Yseulte gave a sigh of relief. A skirmish would mean bloodshed, and, brave as she was, the idea of seeing men shot down, even in self-defence, could not be otherwise than abhorrent to her.

"Look," went on Vipan, "they have picked up our trail, and—there goes the inevitable white rag."

The warriors had stopped, clustered together, and having briefly scrutinised the ground, one of their number rode out, waving a dirty rag on a lance-point.

"Flourish away, friend," remarked Vipan, drily; "I guess we're not going to be drawn by any such childish device."

"Don't they want to make terms?" said Yseulte.

"No doubt. But we don't. They know our number. What they want now is to find out our strength—who we are, in short. Now there isn't a red on the Northern Plains who doesn't know me, by sight or intuition, and this time I'm going to let them entertain a Tartar unawares; if they try fighting, that is."

Finding no notice whatever was taken of their signals, the savages again gathered in consultation. Then the warrior who had hoisted the white flag advanced from among the rest, and yelled out in broken English:

"Ha-yah, ha-yah! Golden Face Injun's brudder! Good hoss, ole debbil Satanta—make big trail. Golden Face bring out lily white gal. Good squaw for Injun brudder! Ha-yah!"

The whole band screamed with laughter, but the insolent buck grinned rather too soon. Long as the range was, a ball from Vipan's rifle crashed through his shin-bone, and both he and his pony rolled upon the ground; the latter in the throes of death. Their mirth changed into a yell of rage; the band scattered, and withdrawing to a more respectful distance, began circling frantically around the position, waving their weapons and bawling out such expletives and coarse expressions as their limited knowledge of Anglo-Saxon allowed. Finally, their vocabulary having given out, they once more collected together, and with a parting jeer rode leisurely away.

"There go sixteen as disgusted reds as are to be met on the Plains this day," said Vipan as the last of the warriors disappeared over the far rise. "And now, Miss Santorex, sorry as I am to disappoint you, we must put off our picnic *à deux*, or rather *à trois*, and get back to camp as soon as possible. Those chaps might fall in with a lot more of their tribe, and double back on us sharp, or half-a-hundred things might happen. So we've no time to lose."

Vipan was not the man to leave anything to chance, but although no square foot of the surrounding country escaped his keen glance, as they cantered merrily away from the scene of the late *fracas*, not a sign of their recent foes was visible. The vast rolling plains shimmering in the afternoon heat lay silent and deserted, and save that a film of smoke in the far distance, marking the site of the emigrants' camp, was faintly discernible, might have been untrodden by human foot.

"By the way, Mr—er?" began Vipan.

"—Vallance."

"Well, Mr Balance."

"Er—Vallance."

"Oh, Vallance, I beg your pardon. Well, Mr Vallance, I was going to say, what do you think of Indian fighting? Never saw 'Mr Lo' (Note 1) on the war-path before, I take it?"

"No, never. And I don't particularly care if I never see him again," answered Geoffry, flurriedly. "Er—you have saved my life, Mr—er—?"

"Vipan."

"—Mr Vipan," he stuttered; "and but for you I should be a dead man at this moment."

"Not strictly accurate, and that in two particulars," was the quiet reply. "In the first place, you should have said 'But for Miss Santorex'; in the second, you would not have had the luck to be a dead man at this moment. You would be squirming a good deal nearer to a slow fire than is either pleasant or salubrious."

Geoffry turned pale, nor could he repress a slight shudder as he thought of the ghastly fate from which he had escaped, as it were, by the skin of his teeth. Then the sight of his enslaver—so unexpectedly met with, and, like himself, dependent for aid and protection amid the grisly perils of these Western wilds, upon this mysterious stranger, who treated him, Geoffry, with a patronising and tolerant air which under any other circumstances would have been galling in the extreme—roused a wave of jealousy and distrust in the young man's breast. What the deuce was she doing here, careering about the country with this splendidly handsome desperado? But the latter's next words seemed to solve the enigma.

"I reckon you'll follow the crowd next time you feel like running buffalo, Miss Santorex. I ought not to have exposed you to even this small risk."

"A delicate way of reminding me that I've only myself to thank for risking being scalped," she replied demurely, but with a mischievous smile struggling not to break forth. "Well, it's perfectly true. I made you take me, and you all agreed it was quite safe. But we killed our buffalo after all—though I didn't like the killing part of it—and I shall never get the chance of a buffalo hunt again. Besides," with a glance at Geoffry and a serious ring in her voice, "it looks as if we had been sent here on purpose."

"I say," sputtered Geoffry, staring at Vipan, as though bursting with a new idea. "I say, w-were you ever at the 'Varsity?"

"Which 'Varsity?"

"Why, Oxford or Cambridge, don't cher know. You give me the idea of a man who has been there."

"Do I? If I was there at all, it must have been rather before you were born," replied the other, imperturbably.

"Hang the fellow, he needn't be so close!" thought Geoffry, with a sullen sense of having been "shut up." But he was glad enough to see safety and comfort in the shape of Major Winthrop's camp, which lay about a mile distant, between them and the setting sun, although he was conscious of a profound feeling of jealousy and distrust towards the man to whom he owed that safety and comfort.

"My partner will show up this evening," said Vipan, tranquilly. "In fact I shouldn't wonder if we found him in camp when we arrive, and what's more, he'll know exactly what we've been doing since I joined you."

"How on earth will he know?" asked Yseulte, wonderingly.

"That's just how he will know," was the amused reply. "By looking on the earth. We have a code of our own. But, you'll see, anyhow."

Note 1. A Western joke, from the passage in Pope's Essay on Man which runs: "Lo, the poor Indian, whose untutored mind."

Chapter Twenty Four
A Bomb for the Rev. Dudley

The Rev. Dudley Vallance sat in his library sorting out the contents of the post-bag.

There was his usual correspondence, all of which he knew at a glance, and tossed impatiently aside, and two or three missives in an unknown hand, which met with no greater attention. But that which he sought was not there. Not a line from his absent son.

More than a month had elapsed since Geoffry had started on his travels. To the surprise of his parents, he had as suddenly come round to their plans, and was as ardently ready to go abroad as he had been formerly opposed to the idea. Still more to their surprise, he had expressed a firm determination to travel in the United States and nowhere else; and, with an energy wholly foreign to his limp nature, had extorted from them a promise to reveal no word of his intention until after his departure. Of course, the reason of this was soon made manifest; yet his indulgent father would not oppose him. And now, for nearly a fortnight, no news of him had been received. To be sure, he had been on the eve of quitting the furthest limits of Western civilisation when he last wrote—probably opportunities of communication were few and far between. Yet the Rev. Dudley felt very anxious, very disappointed.

Mechanically he opened his letters, one after another, but hardly glanced at the contents. Even the announcement that a couple of farms would shortly be thrown on his hands—a notice which at any other time would have disturbed his rest for a week—passed unheeded now. Suddenly his face paled, and a quick gasp escaped his white lips. He had come to the last letter of all, and it was from his solicitors.

We know of nothing more calculated to knock a man out of all time than a wholly unexpected and equally unwelcome communication imparted through the agency of the post. If imparted by word of mouth, he can find some relief in questioning his informant, but when coming through the medium of a letter, especially a lawyer's letter, there is that in the cold, stiff paper, in the precise, hateful characters, as unbending, as inexorable as the very finality of Fate. The communication which, even in the midst of his paternal anxiety, had knocked Mr Vallance so thoroughly out of time, conveyed nothing less than the news that a claimant had come forward to dispossess him of the Lant estates, to contest the late squire's will on several grounds, including that of fraud. And the said claimant was no less a personage than the late squire's son.

And really it is not surprising that he should have been knocked out of time. In a lightning-flash there passed before him a vision of years of litigation, draining his resources and impoverishing his estate—and that even should things not come to the worst. The tone of his lawyers' letter was not reassuring. This meant that, in their opinion, the claimant had a good case. How good that case might be was a consideration which turned the reverend squire's features a trifle paler.

Then came a ray of hope. Ralph Vallance had not been heard of for years, nearer twenty than ten. He had probably gone to the dogs long ago, had joined the ranks of the "shady," and, in keeping with his umbrageous character, was now trying to extort a compromise, or, failing that, a sum of money not to make himself troublesome. But to this happy idea succeeded a darker one, dousing the first as in a rush of ink. Probably with the extraordinary luck which now and then befalls the thorough adventurer, Ralph was returning a rich man, prepared, out of sheer vindictiveness, to devote a large portion of his wealth to plunging his cousin into protracted litigation, with all its harassing and impoverishing results. This would be about as disastrous, in the long run, as the actual establishment of the claim.

Again and again he read the hateful missive, until every word of it was burnt into his brain, but he gleaned no comfort. From whatever point he thought it over, the outlook was about as gloomy as it could be. The summer air came into the room in soft and balmy puffs, laden with the scent of roses. He could hear his children's voices on the terrace below, and away over many a mile of rolling down his eye wandered over pleasant pastures alternating with velvety woodland, and yellow corn-fields awaiting the sickle; to the river flashing like a silver streak through the shade of the beeches, where the deer lay in antlered and dappled groups, lazily chewing the cud in the soft and sensuous forenoon. All this was his own, and his son's after him— an hour ago, that is. But now? He saw himself adrift in his old age, and his idolised son drudging miserably for daily bread. He saw the kinsman, in whose place he had for so long stood, ejecting him pitilessly, vindictively; exacting, it might be, all arrears to the uttermost farthing. Even after this lapse of years (nearer twenty than ten) he cowered beneath the bitter and burning home-truths which that kinsman had hurled at him, here, in this very room, and his heart quaked and his blood curdled at the promise of a terrible and unlooked-for vengeance with which his kinsman had left him. Time had gone by; year had succeeded year; his children growing up, and he himself in undisturbed possession, and the force of these denunciations and threats had become dulled. He had long since come to categorise them in his own mind as the furious vapourings of a desperate and disappointed man. And now they were to bear fruit, to strike him down in his old age, to turn him and his homeless and helpless on the world. The wretched man dropped his head into his hands and groaned aloud.

But, the reader will ask, what was the man made of to start by discounting the worst; to throw up the sponge so abjectly at the very first threat of battle? Well, there may be something in the adage that conscience makes cowards—of certain temperaments, or there may have been a something underlying the whole affair unknown even to Mr Vallance's own lawyers, or, possibly, a good deal of both. We can only say: Reader, persevere, and discover for yourself.

Suddenly there floated in upon the summer air a mellow peal of church bells. Mr Vallance aroused himself. He had forgotten it was Sunday, forgotten his anxiety about Geoffry, forgotten everything in this new and terrible blow that threatened him. The turning of the door-handle made him fairly start from his chair, so overwrought were his nerves.

"The girls have gone on, Dudley," said his wife, entering, a sumptuous presence in her church-going attire.

"All right, my dear. Kindly overtake them, will you? I'll follow you when I'm ready."

"But you'll be very late. Why, what is the matter?" she broke off, alarmed by his appearance and the huskiness of his tone. Then glancing at the pile of newly-opened letters—"Is it bad news? Not—not about Geoffry?"

"*No*, not about Geoffry; thank Heaven for that. There is no word of the boy or his movements. It is—er—merely a very unfortunate and perplexing matter of business. Please don't wait for me."

Those who caught a glimpse of their pastor's face that morning as he swept up the church behind his little procession of choir-boys were startled at the grey, set expression it wore; and when, after several mistakes and omissions in the performance of the service, he brought it to a close without a sermon, the parish—such of it as was present, at least—came to the conclusion that something must have gone very wrong indeed. Had Mr Vallance heard bad news about his son? No, for when the retired jerry-builder, who was also churchwarden, meeting the parson after service, made the enquiry in a sepulchral and sympathising stage-whisper, he met with a very unconcerned answer in the negative.

"Parson do look main sick, surely" was the verdict of the village, as, represented by its choicest louts, it hung around the churchyard gate, and subsequently at the corners of the roads and lanes, previous to its afternoon Sunday loaf among the same. "Parson, he be agein', he be."

Thus the village verdict.

"Poor Mr Vallance was looking very ill this morning," remarked Mrs Santorex at dinner that day. "He could hardly get through the service. Everybody thought at first that he had heard bad news of Geoffry, but it appears not. In fact, he had heard no news of him at all."

"Likely enough he has been hard hit in the pocket department," rejoined her lord. "Probably, 'poor Mr Vallance' has been dabbling in bubble investments; and his particular bubble has—gone the way of all bubbles. Rather rough that he should hear about it on Sunday, though, the day of all others when he has to show up in public. So he blundered over the service, did he? Well, our shepherd ought to know by this time that he can't serve two masters—ha—ha!"

But when later in the afternoon Mr and Mrs Vallance, with a brace of daughters, dropped in, Mr Santorex felt persuaded that at least one of the quartet had come there with further intent than that of making a mere friendly call, and accordingly he awaited events in a kind of mental ambush congenial to his cynical soul.

"Any news of Yseulte?" asked Mrs Vallance, rising to depart.

"Yes. She has fallen in with a Major Winthrop and his wife. They seem very good sort of people, and the little girl is going to travel under their charge. They are neighbours of my boy George, and are returning to their ranche."

"Can I have a word with you, Santorex?" said the Rev. Dudley, lingering at the gate, having told his wife and daughters to go on without him. "Er— the fact is," he continued, lowering his voice, as the other nodded assent, "the fact is—er—something rather troublesome—a mere trifle that is to say—has occurred to worry me. Have you any idea of the whereabouts of Ralph Vallance?"

"Not the faintest."

"Oh. I thought perhaps you might know something about him. I believe you and he were—er—on friendly terms at one time?"

"Yes, we were. Why? Have *you* heard anything about him?"

"Er—well, I may say this much. I fancy the poor fellow is in need of assistance—if only I knew where he was."

"Afraid I can't help you to learn. Stay. It was only lately I was turning out a lot of old correspondence, and there was a whole bundle of Ralph's letters. It was just before Chickie went away. I'll hunt them up and see if they afford any clue."

The other started. A scared, anxious look came into his face at the mention of the correspondence.

"Might I—might I just look over those letters?" he asked, eagerly.

"H'm. I'm afraid I can hardly agree to that. But if I find anything in them likely to be of service to you I won't fail to let you know."

With this, Mr Vallance was forced to be content. His late host stood shaking his head softly as he looked after his retreating figure, and that cynical half-smile played about the corners of his mouth.

Chapter Twenty Five
Poor Geoffry Again

True to Vipan's prediction, the first person they met on their return to camp was Smokestack Bill.

Leaning against a waggon-wheel, lazily puffing at his pipe, his faithful Winchester ever ready to hand, the scout watched their approach as imperturbably as though he had parted with his friend but half-an-hour back, instead of nearly a month ago, when he had watched the latter ride off with Mahto-sapa's band into what looked perilously like the very jaws of death. But he could not restrain a covert guffaw as he marked in what company he now met his friend again.

"Hello, Bill! Any news?" cried the latter, as they rode up to the waggon corral. "By the way, I must call round and collect that twenty dollars from Seth Davis."

"Guess you'll have to trade his scalp to raise it," was the grim reply. "And you'll find it drying in the smoke of an Ogallalla *teepe*."

"That so?"

"It is. Couple o' nights after War Wolf was run off, a crowd of 'em came along and shot Seth in the doorway of his store. Then they cleared out all the goods and burnt down the whole shebang. They couldn't nohow get rid of the idea that he'd had a hand in giving War Wolf away."

"Well, we've just stood off a handful of reds."

"Sho! With the young lady too! Say, stranger"—he broke off, turning to Geoffry—"are you the 'tenderfoot' them reds was after?"

"Er—yes. But—how did you know?" answered Geoffry, staring with astonishment.

"Struck your trail. But jest before, I'd struck the trail o' them painted varmints. Knew they'd jump you, but reckoned you'd make camp 'fore they got within shootin' distance."

"You're out of it this time, Bill," said Vipan. "He'd have been roast beef by now if we hadn't happened along. It was a very pretty chase, though," he added, with a laugh. "Our friend here covered the ground in fine style."

"Bless your heart, stranger, that's just nothing," laughed the scout, noting the offended look which came into the young man's face at this apparently unfeeling comment on the frightful peril from which he had barely escaped. "Why, me and Vipan there have had many and many such a narrow squeak when we've been out scoutin' alone—ay, and narrower. Haven't we scooted for a whole day with a yellin' war-party close on our heels, and no snug corral like this handy to stand 'em off in!"

"Really!" exclaimed Geoffry, open-mouthed. "You bet. Them devils were just a lot of young Cheyenne bucks out in search of any devilment that might come handy. But you were in luck's way, stranger, this time."

Smokestack Bill was the bearer of news which tended not a little to relieve the travellers' minds. He had thoroughly scouted the country ahead and pronounced it free from Indians. He was of opinion that no further trouble need be feared. The Sioux, he declared, had quite enough to occupy their attention at home, for they were mustering every available warrior to resist an expected invasion of the troops, and to this end all raiding parties then abroad on the Plains had been called in. A council of war on a large scale, together with a grand medicine dance, was to be held at the villages of Sitting Bull, Mad Horse, and other chiefs of the hostiles, and it was expected that from twelve to fifteen thousand warriors would assemble. Red Cloud, Spotted Tail, and some few other chiefs still remained on their reservations, but the bulk of their followers had deserted and joined the hostiles. The scout was of opinion that they would encounter no considerable body of Indians, though their stock might be exposed to the risk of stampede at the hands of a few adventurous young bucks, such as those who had so nearly captured Geoffry Vallance.

The latter's arrival in the camp, or rather the manner of it, was productive of no slight sensation among the more inexperienced of the emigrants. The seasoned Western men, however, characteristically viewed the incident as of no great importance, and after one glance at the new comer, tacitly agreed that the advent of a "tenderfoot" more or less constituted but a sorry addition to their fighting force. However, with the consideration and tact so frequently to be found among even the roughest of the pioneers of civilisation, no sign of this was suffered to escape them, and beyond a little good-humoured chaff, and an occasional endeavour—generally successful—to "cram" the "Britisher," Geoffry had no reason to complain of lack of kindliness or hospitable feeling on the part of the travellers, who, while amusing themselves at the expense of his "greenness," were ever ready and willing to give him the benefit of their experience or lend him a helping hand.

By the Winthrops the young man was made warmly welcome. The Major, glad of such an acquisition as an educated fellow-countryman, pressed him to remain with them until they arrived at their destination, and see something of the West under his own auspices, and his kind-hearted little wife, very much impressed by his tragic escape from such a terrible fate, took the young stranger completely under her wing, and was disposed to make a hero of him.

Thus the days went by, and the waggon train pursued its slow course over the Western plains; now winding around the spur of some high foothill of a loftier range; now emerging from the timber belt fringing some swiftly-flowing river, upon a level tableland carpeted with the greenest of prairie-grass, bespangled with many a strange and delicate-hued flower. The exhilarating air, the unclouded blue of the heavens, the danger lately threatening them removed—removed, too, by the sturdy might of their own right hands—infused a cheerfulness into the wanderers. And when the camp was pitched and the waggons securely corralled for the night, many a song and jest and stirring anecdote enlivened the gathering round the red watch-fires. By day the more enterprising spirits would diverge from the route to track the red deer or the scarcer blacktail in the wooded fastnesses of some neighbouring ravine, while the waggons creaked on their slow and ponderous course.

To this strange new life Geoffry Vallance took with a readiness which was surprising to himself. Indeed, he would have been thoroughly happy but for one thing. From the moment they had recognised each other, when he reeled panting and exhausted to the ground at her feet, Yseulte's demeanour towards him had been one of studied coldness and reserve. She would never address him of her own initiative, and deftly defeated any attempt on his part to be with her alone. The poor fellow was beside himself with mortification; and when he recalled the circumstances of that first recognition, how he had found her alone with the splendidly handsome scout, to his mortification was added a perfect paroxysm of jealous rage.

Mrs Winthrop took in the situation at a glance—indeed, it would have been manifest to a far less clearsighted observer, so transparent were the symptoms in so simple a subject as poor Geoffry—and it annoyed her.

"I can't think why," she began one day, when the latter was away on some hunting expedition with most of the men, and the two ladies were alone together, "I can't think why you treat the poor fellow so standoffishly, Yseulte. I'm sure he worships the very ground you walk on, and you might be a little kinder to him."

"Really, I don't see that the fact entails upon me a corresponding reciprocity," was the reply, given a little coldly.

"There you go with your long words, Yseulte. And now you turn the stand-offishness upon me. I only mean, dear, that I want everyone to be friendly and on good terms around. Let him say what he wants to say. Then give him an answer. That'll fix him one way or another right along, and put everything on a friendly footing again."

"Would it? Supposing I were to tell you, Hettie, that Geoffry Vallance can't take No for an answer, you would retort that you thought the more of him for it. But there is more than that. He should not have followed me out here. It was not right—it was even ungentlemanly. He has taken an unfair advantage in besieging me like this. In fact, he has placed me in a thoroughly false position."

"But, dear," mischievously, "so far from following you, it was you who brought him here."

"Say Mr Vipan, rather. *I* am not an Indian fighter."

Then spake Hettie Winthrop unadvisedly.

"Well, Mr Vipan, then. But, Yseulte dear, you are always pleasant and cordial enough with Mr Vipan. Naturally the other poor fellow notices it."

Yseulte turned her grand eyes full upon the speaker, and there was an angry flash in them. These two friends were as near a quarrel as they would ever be likely to arrive.

"I don't know what you mean, Hettie. Mr Vipan saved me from the most horrible of fates. Am I to show my appreciation by keeping him at arm's length to please Geoffry Vallance?"

"Tut-tut! You needn't be so fiery about it," said the other, laughing mischievously. "I didn't mean anything in particular that I know of, and I guess I don't hold a brief for any Geoffry Vallance."

That evening, for the first time since her rescue just alluded to, Yseulte was strolling by herself. She had been strangely reserved and silent all day, and now had stolen quietly away to be alone and think. A stream flowed between its fringe of fig and wild plum trees, about two hundred yards off the camp, and now she stood meditatively gazing into the current and thinking with a pang over the loss of her trout-rod. The evening air was lively with many a sound, the screech of myriad crickets, the shout of the teamsters driving in the animals for the night, the occasional cry of a fretful infant, and the wash and bubble of the water flowing at her feet. Suddenly the utterance of her own name broke in upon her meditations. There stood

Geoffry Vallance, the expression of his face that of eagerness to make the most of his opportunity.

"Why do you always avoid me now?" he began, with a quick glance around, as if fearful of interruption, "What have I done that you will hardly speak to me now?"

A flush of anger mounted to her face.

"Have they come back from hunting?" she said, ignoring the question.

"No, I came back by myself. I couldn't go on any longer till I knew what I had done to offend you. Have I not followed you to the end of another world? And this is how you treat me."

She could have struck him. "What an idiot the boy is!" she thought. "Father was right. A witless idiot!"

"That is just what you have done," she flashed forth. "Who gave you any sort of encouragement to follow me to what you are pleased to call 'the end of another world'? Why did you come here to render me thoroughly ridiculous, to place me in a false position? By what right do you presume to call me to account? Answer me that, and then kindly leave me at once."

For a moment he seemed thunderstruck, and stood staring at her in blank dismay. Then a light seemed to dawn upon him.

"I thought, at any rate, that one more to protect you—to stand between you and harm—in this wild country, counted for something. But it seems to constitute an offence. Well, I will leave, this very night if you wish it."

"Nonsense!" was the angry retort. "Have you so soon forgotten the result of trying to cross the plains alone? You know perfectly well I don't want you to run any such foolish risk. But you should not have followed me here at all. I thought I had given you a final answer once and for all at Lant—"

"Good evening, Miss Santorex!" struck in a voice behind them. And Vipan raised his hat as he rode by at a foot's pace within a dozen yards of them. So engrossed had they been that they had not heard the hoof-strokes of his horse. A flush came over Yseulte's face. Could he have heard? she thought. Surely he must have. The evening air was so still, and Geoffry's voice was of the high "carrying" order. Oh, that unlucky Geoffry! And for the moment she found it in her heart to wish that he had been left to the tender mercies of the red men.

"I can't think how it is," said Geoffry, moodily, bringing his glance back from Vipan's retreating form to the flushed face of his companion. "I've a dim recollection of having seen that fellow before—how, when, and where is just what puzzles me."

Yseulte started. If she was thinking the same thing she was not going to say so. She suggested a return to the camp.

"And it's my belief," pursued Geoffry, with a dash of venom—"my firm belief, that he's a bad hat."

"Is it?"

"Yes. I've heard one or two queer whispers about him in the camp. It's said that he's too friendly with the Indians."

"Especially the other day when you and I had the pleasure of meeting. Where would you be now but for him, or where should I? I don't think we ought to go out of our way to cultivate a bad opinion of a man who has saved both our lives, do you?"

She left him, for they had now reached the camp—left him standing there feeling very sore, very resentful, and thoroughly foolish. Yseulte Santorex could be very scornful, very cutting, when she chose.

Chapter Twenty Six
"At his Time of Life"

"Something not quite right there—not quite right. No, sir," said the scout to himself, shaking his head softly as he furtively watched his companion. "And I reckon I can fix it," he added. "Lord! Lord! To think what we may come to—the most sensible of us as well as the most downright foolishest."

Vipan, stretched at full length beside the camp fire, smoking his long Indian pipe, looked the very picture of languid repose. Yet his thoughts were in a whirl. Why had he come there?—why the devil had he stayed?

The hour was late—late, that is, for those destined to rise at the first glimmer which should tell of the rising dawn—and sundry shapes rolled in blankets, whence emanated snores, betokened that most of the denizens of the encampment were sleeping the sleep of the healthy and the just. The murmur of voices, however, with now and then an airy feminine laugh from the Winthrops' side of the corral, told that some at any rate were keeping late hours.

"Say, Bill, I conclude I'll git from here."

No change of expression came into the speaker's face. Nor did he even glance at him addressed. The words seem to escape him as the natural and logical outcome of a train of thought.

"Right, old pard. I'm with you there. Where'll you light out for?"

"I think I'll go to Red Cloud's village and see what's on. Perhaps look in upon Sitting Bull or Mahto-sapa on the way."

"There I ain't with you," answered the scout decisively. "Better leave the reds alone just now. Haven't you been shooting 'em down like jackrabbits around here, and won't they now be bustin' with murderation to take your hair? No, no."

"May be. But I want a change, anyway. So I'm for looking up that *placer* on upper Burntwood Creek. The troops won't molest us this time, because all the miners'll have left. Besides all available cavalry will be told off against Sitting Bull."

"It's strange that Mr Vipan hasn't been near us all day," Mrs Winthrop was saying. "But I suppose he'll clear out as suddenly as he came. These Western men are queer folks, and that's a fact."

"Vipan isn't a Western man," answered the Major, thoughtfully. "And it's my private opinion he could give a queer account of himself if he chose. Sometimes I could swear he had been in the Service. However that's his business, not ours."

"Well, he might be a little more open with us, anyway, considering the time we have been together."

"Just over a week."

"That's as long as a year out here. But I shall be sorry when he does leave us—very sorry."

"May I hope that remark will apply to me, Mrs Winthrop?" said a voice out of the gloom, as its owner stepped within the firelight circle. "It's odd how things dovetail, for as a matter of fact I strolled across for the purpose of taking leave."

"Oh, how you startled me!" she cried. "Of taking leave? Surely you are not going to leave us yet, Mr Vipan? Why, we hoped you would accompany us home, and stay awhile, and have a good time generally. You really can't go yet. Fred—Yseulte—tell him we won't allow it."

"Why, most certainly, we won't," began the former, heartily. "Come, Vipan—your time's your own, you know, and you may just as well do some hunting out our way as anywhere else."

"Of course," assented his wife. "But—I know what it is. We have offended him in some way. Yseulte, what have you done to offend Mr Vipan? I'm sure I can't call to mind anything."

"There is no question of offence," protested Vipan. "I am a confirmed wanderer, you see, Mrs Winthrop—here to-day, away to-morrow. The country is clear of reds now, and you will no longer need our additional rifles. If we have rendered you some slight service, I can answer for it, my partner is as glad as I am myself."

No man living was less liable to be swayed by caprice than the speaker. Yet suddenly he became as resolved to remain a little longer, as he had been a moment before to leave. And this change was brought about by the most trivial circumstance in the world. While he was speaking, his eyes had met those of Yseulte Santorex.

Only for a moment, however.

When Vipan, in his usual laconic manner, informed his comrade that he concluded to wait a bit longer, the latter merely remarked, "Right, pard. Jest as you fancy." But as he rolled over to go to sleep, he nodded off to the unspoken soliloquy—

"It's a rum start—a darn rum start. At his time of life, too! Yes, sir."

Chapter Twenty Seven
In the "Dug-Out"

Yseulte Santorex was conscious of a new and unwonted sensation. She felt nervous.

Yet why should she have felt so, seeing that this was by no means the first time she had undertaken an expedition *à deux* under her present escort? But somehow it seemed to her that his tone had conveyed a peculiar significance when he suggested this early morning antelope-stalk at the time of making up his mind to remain.

It was a lovely morning. The sun was not an hour high, and the air was delicious. But their success had been *nil*. To account for the absolute lack of game was a puzzle to Vipan, but it could hardly be the cause of his constrained taciturnity.

Yseulte felt nervous. Why had he induced her to come out like this to-day? Instinctively she felt that he was on the eve of making some revelation. Was he about to confide to her the history of his past? Her nervousness deepened as it began to dawn upon her what an extraordinary fascination this adventurer of the Western Plains, with his splendid stature and magnificent face, was capable of exercising over her. A silence had fallen between them.

"I want you to see this," said Vipan suddenly as they came upon the ruins of what had once been a strong and substantial building. "It's an old stage-station which was burnt by the reds in '67."

There was eloquence in the ruins of the thick and solid walls which even now stood as high as ten or twelve feet in places, and which were still spanned by a few charred and blackened beams, like the gaping ribs of a wrecked ship. The floor was covered with coarse herbage, sprouting through a layer of *débris*, whence arose that damp, earthy smell which seems inseparable from ancient buildings of whatever kind. Standing within this relic of a terrible epoch, Yseulte could not repress a shudder. What mutilated human remains might they not actually be walking over? Even in the cheerful daylight the flap of ghostly wings seemed to waft past her.

"If these old walls could speak they'd tell a few queer yarns," said her companion. "Look at these loop-holes. Many a leaden pill have they sent forth to carry 'Mr Lo' to the Happy Hunting-Grounds. I don't know the exact history of this station, but it's probably that of most others of the time. A surprise—a stiff fight—along siege in the 'dug-out' when the reds had set the building on fire—then either relief from outside, or the defenders, reduced by famine or failure of ammunition, shooting each other to avoid capture and the stake."

"Horrible!" she answered, with a shiver. "But what is a 'dug-out'?"

"Let's get outside, and I'll tell you all about it. Look—you see that mound of earth over there," pointing to a round hump about a score of yards from the building, and rising three or four feet above the ground. "Well, that is a roof made of earth and stones, and therefore bullet and fire proof. It is loop-holed on a level with the ground, though it's so overgrown with buffalo-grass that the holes'll be choked up, I reckon. This roof covers a circular hole about ten or twelve feet in diameter, and just high enough for a man to stand up in. It is reached by a covered way from the main building, and its object was this:—When the reds were numerous and daring enough they had not much difficulty in setting the building on fire by throwing torches and blazing arrows on the roof, just as they threw them into our camp the other day. Then the stage people got into the 'dug-out,' and with plenty of rations and ammunition could hold their own indefinitely against all comers. The 'dug-out' was pretty nearly an essential adjunct to every stage-station, and a good many ranches had them as well. And now, if you feel so disposed, we will try and explore this one, and then it will be time to start camp-wards."

She assented eagerly. First going to the mound, the removal of the overgrowth of grass revealed the loop-holes.

"It is like looking into the *oubliettes* of a mediaeval castle," said Yseulte, striving to peer through the apertures into the blackness beneath.

"Now come this way," said her companion, leading the way into the building once more.

A moment's scrutiny—then advancing to a corner of the building he wrenched away great armfuls of the thick overgrowth. A hole stood revealed—a dark passage slanting down into the earth.

"Wait here a moment," he said. "I'll go in first and see that the way is clear."

The tunnel was straight and smooth. Once inside there was not much difficulty in getting along. But it suddenly occurred to Vipan that he might be acting like a fool. What if he were to encounter a snake in this long-closed-up *oubliette*, or foul air? Well, for the latter, the matches that he lighted from time to time burnt brightly and clear. For the former—he was already within the "dug-out" when the thought struck him.

He glanced around in the subterranean gloom. It was not unlikely that the floor of the tomb-like retreat might be strewn with the remains of its former owners, who had perished miserably by their own hands rather than fall into the power of their savage foe. But no grim death's-head glowered at him in the darkness. The place was empty. Quickly he returned to his companion.

"It's pretty dark in there," he said. "Think you'd care to undertake it? It may try your nerves."

But Yseulte laughingly disclaimed the proprietorship of any such inconvenient attributes. She was resolved to see as much wild adventure as she could, she declared. Nevertheless, when she found herself buried in the earthy darkness as she crawled at her companion's heels, she could not feel free from an inclination to turn back there and then.

But when she stood upright within the underground fortress, and her eyes became accustomed to the half-light, she forgot her misgivings.

"How ingenious!" she cried, looking first around the earthy cell and then out through the loop-holes. "Now, let's imagine we are beleaguered here, and that the savages are wheeling and circling around us. We could 'stand them off'—isn't that the expression?—till next week."

"And then if nobody came to get us out of our fix next week?"

"Oh, then we could hold out until the week after."

"You think that would be fun, eh?"

"Of course," she answered, her eyes dancing with glee in response to his queer half-smile.

"H'm. Well I'm very glad there's no chance of your undergoing the actual experience," he answered drily, turning away to gaze out on the surrounding country, but really that she should not see the expression that swept across his face. For it had come to this. Rupert Vipan—adventurer, renegade, freebooter—a stranger, for many a year, to any softening or tender feeling—a man, too, who had already attained middle age—thought, as he listened to her words, how willingly he would give the remainder of his life for just that experience. To be besieged here for days with this girl—only they two, all alone together—himself her sole protector, with a violent and horrible death at the end of it, he admitted at that moment would be to him

Paradise. Yet a consciousness of the absurdity of the idea struck him even then. Who was he in her eyes, in the eyes of those around her, her friends and protectors? An unknown adventurer—a mere commonplace border ruffian. And—at his time of life, too!

"Were you ever besieged in one of these places?" asked Yseulte.

Her voice recalled him to himself.

"Once," he answered. "In '67, on the Smoky Hill route, four stagemen and myself. The reds burnt us out the first night, and we got into the dug-out. It was wearisome work, for they preserved a most respectful distance once we were down there. They wouldn't haul off, though. So one man kept a look-out at the loop-holes, while the rest of us played poker or varied the tedium by swapping lies."

"Doing what?"

"Oh, exchanging 'experiences.' Tall twisters some of them were, too. Well, by the third night we got so sick of it that we made up our minds to try and quit. The reds were still hanging around. We needn't have, for we had plenty of rations and ammunition, but the business was becoming so intolerably monotonous. Well, we started, and the upshot was that out of the five, three of us fell in with a cavalry patrol the next evening, having dodged the reds all day, each of us with an arrow or two stuck more or less badly into him, and the Cheyennes went home with a brace of new scalps. Otherwise the affair was tame enough."

"Tame, indeed? But you tell it rather tamely. Now, how did the Indians first come to attack you? You left that out."

"Did I? Oh, well, I happened to discover their propinquity, and concluded to warn the stage people. The red brother divined my intention afar off, and came for me—and them."

"You ought to be called the Providence of the Plains," she said, with a laugh that belied the seriousness of her face. "There, I christen you that on the spot."

"That would be a good joke to tell them over in Henniker City! But to be serious, in these latter days I never go out of my way to spoil the red brother's fun. None of my business, any way."

"But you made an exception in favour of us. I don't believe you are talking seriously at all."

"You don't?" he echoed, turning suddenly upon her, and there was that in his tones which awed her into wonder and silence. "You don't? Well, let me tell you all about it. It was you, and you alone, who saved every soul in that outfit from the scalping-knife and the stake. I sighted your party straggling along just anyhow, and I'd already been watching the Sioux preparing to ambush it. Then while promising my self a good time lying up there on the butte, and looking on at the fun, I chanced to catch sight of—you. That decided the business. Instead of assisting at a grand pitched battle in the novel character of a spectator, I elected to warn your people. Otherwise—ambling along haphazard as they were—they'd have lost their head-coverings to a dead certainty. That is how you saved them."

"What! You would have done nothing to warn them? I cannot believe it."

"Wouldn't have lifted a finger. Why should I?" he broke off, almost angrily. "What interest had I in a few ranchmen and bullwhackers more or less? They were no more to me than the painted savages lying in wait to scalp them. Stop, you were going to say something about colour, religion, and all that sort of thing. But a white skin as often as not covers as vile a nature as a red one, and for the other consideration look at its accredited teachers. About as good Christians as the average Sioux medicine-man, neither better nor worse. It was a blessed good thing, though, that I had a first rate field-glass on that occasion."

She raised her eyes to his as if expecting him to continue, and they seemed to grow soft and velvety. But he did not continue. Instead, he had taken a rigid attitude, and appeared to be listening intently.

"What can you hear?" she began, wonderingly.

But the words died away on her lips, and she grew ashy pale as her dilated glance read her companion's face in the gloomy half-light of the "dug-out." No need to pursue her enquiry now.

For, audible to both, came a dull muffled roar, distant, faint, but of unmistakable import. Even Yseulte did not require her companion to explain the sound. Even she recognised in the long, dropping roll the heavy discharge of firearms.

Chapter Twenty Eight
A Terrible Drama

The waggon train had just pulled out.

Winding along over the wide prairie came the string of great cumbrous vehicles, their white tilts gleaming in the morning sunshine, the monotonous creaking of their axles mingling with the cheery shout of the "bullwhackers" and the crack of whips. Here and there along the line rode horsemen in twos and threes, some leading spare horses, others giving a general eye to the progress of the train. Squads of children chattered and squabbled in the waggons, a shrill feminine voice now and again rising high in remonstration. Women sat placidly sewing or knitting—indulging too in gossip—of which perhaps Yseulte Santorex was the subject more frequently than she would have guessed or approved. All were in good spirits, for their journey was nearing its end. No room was there for apprehension either, for they had now reached the extreme limits of the Sioux range. So far from all minds was any thought of danger that even scouting precautions had been of late very much relaxed.

Thus they journeyed.

"There's something moving away there on the bluff, Dave," said Winthrop, suddenly, shading his eyes.

"D'you say so, Colonel?" answered the cowboy, who with his employer and mate was riding some little way ahead of the train. "Likely enough it's Smokestack Bill coming back. He started off in that direction before daybreak to hunt."

They were skirting a range of low round-topped bluffs, on one of which had appeared the object which attracted Winthrop's attention.

"It's gone now," said the latter, still gazing intently. "I could have sworn it was somebody's head."

"Oh, thunder! Look!" said the cowboy, quickly reining in his horse with a jerk.

Well might even his stout heart—the heart of every soul in that company—die away. For the crest of the bluff was by magic alive with mounted figures. A great sheet of flame burst forth, and amid the deafening crash of the volley a storm of leaden missiles whizzed and hummed around the ears of the party. Oregon Dave had uttered his last words. He threw up his arms with a stiffening jerk, and toppled heavily from his saddle.

Then followed a scene of indescribable terror and confusion. Rending the air with their shrill, vibrating war-whoop, a vast crowd of painted horsemen swooped down in full charge upon the doomed and demoralised whites. Flinging themselves behind their trained steeds, the Sioux delivered their fire with deadly effect, then, recovering themselves in the saddle with cat-like agility, they rode in among their writhing, shrieking victims, spearing and tomahawking right and left. Perfectly mad with terror, the draught animals stampeded. Waggons were overturned, and their inmates flung screaming to the ground, or crushed and mangled beneath the wreckage.

The surprise was complete; the demoralisation perfect. Utterly panic-stricken, helpless with dismay, men allowed themselves to be cut down without offering a shadow of resistance. Apart from the terror inspired by the suddenness of the onslaught, there was literally not a minute of time wherein to mass together and strike a blow in defence. Even the privilege of selling their lives dearly was denied these doomed ones.

The waggon train, pulled out at its full length, offered an easy prey, and along this line, after the first and fatal charge, the warriors, breaking up into groups, urged their fleet ponies; shooting down the wretched emigrants with their revolvers, and ruthlessly spearing such few who, being wounded, instinctively tried to crawl away. Whooping, yelling, whistling, brandishing their weapons, they strove to increase the terror of the maddened teams, who, unable to break loose, upset the vehicles wholesale. They goaded the frenzied animals with their lance-points, laughing like fiends if the wheels passed over the bodies of any of the inmates thrown out or trying to escape; and once when a whole family, driven wild with terror, instinctively flung themselves from the creaking, swaying vehicle, which, upsetting at that moment, crushed mother and children alike in a horrible mangled heap beneath the splintering wreckage, the glee of the savages knew no bounds.

It was all over in a moment. Not a man was left standing—not a man with power in him to strike another blow. All had been slain or were lying wounded unto death. All? Stay! All save one.

Winthrop, alone out of all that outfit, was untouched. But he had better have been dead. His wife! Oh, good God! For her to fall into the power of these fiends!

There was the light horse waggon; but between himself and it already surged a crowd of skimming warriors. Many a piece was aimed at him—many a bullet sang about his ears, but still he went unscathed.

Spurring his horse, straight for the waggon he went—straight into the thick of the yelling, whirling crowd. Already, searing his ears like molten lead, rose the piercing shrieks of miserable women writhing beneath the scalping-knife, or struggling in the outraging grasp of the victorious barbarians. He sees a number of small bodies flung high into the air—even marks the piteous terror in the faces of the wretched little infants as they fall, to be caught dexterously on the bright lance-points extended to receive them, and the laughing yells of the painted fiends as the warm blood spurts forth and falls in jets upon their hands and persons. All this passes before his eyes and ears as a vision of hell, and more than one of those fierce and ruthless assailants deftly turns his horse away rather than face the awful fury of despair blazing from his livid countenance. One after another falls before his revolver. A moment more and he will reach his wife. Then they will both die together by his own hand.

The crowd of whirling centaurs seems to give way before him, and with his eye upon his goal he spurs between their ranks. But a roar of mocking laughter greets his ears.

The canvas curtains of the waggon-tilt part, and a great savage, hideously painted, springs forth, uttering an exultant whoop as he brandishes something in the air. It is a scalp—the blood trickling freely down the long, shining, silky tress.

The whoop dies in the Indian's throat. Winthrop's ball has sped true. His wife's slayer falls heavily, still grasping in the locked grip of death the relic of the murdered victim. Yet, grim as it may seem, the murderer really deserves the gratitude of both. Then a thumping blow on the arm sends his pistol flying out of his hand.

"How! white Colonel," says a gruff voice at his side. "How! Crow-Scalper big chief. White scalp damn better nor 'chuck.' How?"

Grinning with delight, the gigantic warrior extended his hand in the most friendly fashion; with difficulty curbing the plunges of his excited steed. He felt sure of his prey now.

Not yet.

Quick as thought, Winthrop had whipped out another pistol—a Derringer.

But for a timely swerve, Crow-Scalper would have been sent straight to his fathers. Then thinking things had gone far enough, the chief pointed his revolver and shot the unfortunate Englishman dead.

It was all over in a moment—the firing and the din, the shrieks of tortured women, the dying groans of mortally-wounded men—over in an infinitely shorter time than it takes to narrate. Not a man was left alive; and already many a corpse lay where it had fallen, stripped and gory, a hideous mangled object in the barbarous mutilation which it had undergone. Some of the Indians were busy looting the waggons. Others, scattered far and wide over the plain, were in pursuit of the fleeing animals, which had stampeded in every direction. All were in the wildest degree of excitement and exultation. They had mastered the outfit at a stroke, with the loss of only three warriors. They had wiped out their former defeat, and had reaped a rich harvest of scalps. They accordingly set to work to make merry over their plunder.

Over the worst of what followed we will draw a veil. There were females in that doomed waggon train. Where these are concerned the red man, in his hour of victory, is the most brutal, the most ungovernable fiend in the world.

Singing, dancing, feasting, whooping, the barbarians kept up their hideous orgie. Then in furtherance of a new amusement a number of them began to pile together the beams and planks of the wrecked waggons until a huge heap was formed, in shape something like a rough kiln. Up to this structure were dragged about a dozen bodies.

Dead bodies? No; living.

Men wounded unto helplessness and death, yet still with just the spark of life in them. Women, two or three, too elderly or unattractive to fulfil the terrible fate invariably befalling the female captive of the ruthless red man. Some of the elder children who had not been speared were also there. All these, bound and helpless, were first deliberately scalped, then flung inside the improvised kiln. Fire was applied.

Drowning the appalling shrieks of their miserable victims in shrill peals of laughter, the whole array of painted and feathered fiends danced and circled around the blazing pyre in an ecstasy of glee. For upwards of an hour this frightful scene continued. Then when the anguish of the tortured victims had sunk in death, the savages gathered up their spoils and departed, refraining from setting fire to any more of the wreckage lest the too conspicuous sign of their bloody work should by its volume be visible at a greater distance than they desired.

One more tragedy of the wild and blood-stained West. A pack of coyotes, snapping and snarling over their meal of mangled and defaced corpses, whose scalpless skulls shone red and clotted in the sunlight. A cloud of wheeling, soaring vultures, a few piles of charred and shattered wreckage, and many an oozy, shining pool of gore. One more frightful massacre. One more complete and ruthless holocaust to the unquenchable vendetta ever burning between the unsparing red man and his hated and despised foe, the invading white.

Chapter Twenty Nine
Thermopylae

"The camp is attacked," said Yseulte, not even pausing to brush off the dust which had gathered upon her clothing during her passage into and out of the "dug-out."

"I'm afraid so."

Both stood eagerly listening. Again came the long, crackling roll, this time more dropping and desultory, also more distinct than when they first heard it underground.

"How will it end?" she asked.

Their glances met. In the grave and serious expression of her companion's face Yseulte read the worst.

"We must hope for the best. Meanwhile, my first care must be for your safety, so we must leave this spot at once. See what comes of allowing oneself to get careless. As a matter of fact, we are off the Sioux range, and reckoning on that we haven't been scouting so carefully as we ought."

"When can we return to the camp?"

"Not a moment before dark," he replied, wondering if she knew that the chances were a hundred to one against there being any camp to return to. For to his experienced mind the situation was patent. That sudden and heavy fusillade meant a numerous war-party. It also meant a surprise. Further, and worst of all, he realised that at the time it took place the waggon train would have pulled out, in which event the Indians would not allow it time to corral. Again, the firing had completely ceased, which meant that one of two things had happened. Either the assailants had been beaten off; which was hardly likely within such a short space of time. Or they had carried the whole outfit at the first surprise; and this he decided was almost certain. But there was no need to break the terrible news to his companion.

"Can we not wait here?" said the latter. "We could retire into the 'dug-out' if they discovered us."

"How very near your ideal of fun has come to being realised!" was the reply, with a shadow of a smile. "No, we should stand no chance."

It did not escape Yseulte that, previous to starting, her escort gave a quick, careful look to her saddlery and girths, pausing to tighten the latter, and her heart sank with a chill and direful foreboding.

"You see, it's this way," continued Vipan. "It is almost certain that the war-party is a Sioux one, probably our old friends Crow-Scalper and Mountain Cat. This is the extreme western edge of the Sioux range, consequently when the reds quit the scrimmage they are bound to travel north or north-east. So we must put as much space as we can between us and them in the contrary direction. For the same reason, if your friends have whipped them—"

He paused abruptly, but it was too late. She turned to him, her eyes dilating with horror.

"*If!* Oh, tell me the truth. You think they have no chance?"

"One can but hope for the best." She turned her face away, and the tears fell thick and fast. She could hardly realise it. Her dear friends, under whose protection she had travelled many and many a day, in whose companionship she had been initiated into the delights of this wild new land, and also its perils, now massacred; even at that moment, perhaps, falling beneath the merciless blows of these bloodthirsty savages. She could hardly realise it. Her mind felt numb. Even the sense of her own peril failed to come home to her.

But her companion realised it to the full. This was no time to think of anything but how to neglect no possible means of effecting her safety, yet he could not banish the thrill of triumph which the thought inspired in him that her fate, her very life, was absolutely in his hands. Suddenly she turned to him. The black drop of suspicion was corroding her mind.

"Why did you bring me away from them all this morning?" she said, speaking quickly and in a hard tone. "Did you *know* what was going to happen?"

The adventurer's face went ashy white. Even she could entertain such suspicions!

"You forget, Miss Santorex. My tried and trusted friend of years is in that outfit. Should I be likely to sell his scalp, even if I sold those of *your* friends?"

There was a savour of contempt in the cold incisiveness of his tone that went to her heart. What is baser than the sin of ingratitude? Did she not owe her life—and more than her life—to this man already, and now to be flinging her pitiable and unworthy suspicions at him! Would she ever recover his good opinion again?

"Forgive me!" she cried. "Forgive me! I hardly knew what I was saying." And she burst into tears. Even yet she would hardly believe but that her fellow-travellers would succeed in holding their own.

Young though the day was, the torrid rays of the sun blazed fiercely down upon the great plains. Some distance in front rose a rugged ridge, almost precipitous. The only passage through this for many miles was a narrow cañon—a mere cleft. Beyond lay miles and miles of heavily-timbered ravines, and for this welcome shelter Vipan was making. This plan he explained to his companion.

"Look! What are those?" she cried, growing suddenly eager. "Indians? No. Wild horses? I didn't know there were any wild horses in these parts."

Save for a scattered line of brush here and there, the great plains until they should reach the defile above referred to were treeless, and presented a succession of gentle undulations. Nearly a mile distant, seeming to emerge from one of these belts of brush, careering along in a straggling, irregular line converging obliquely with the path of the two riders, came a large herd of ponies. It almost looked as if the latter were bent on joining them.

Yseulte did not see the change in her companion's face, so intent was she on watching the ponies.

"Get your horse into a gallop at once, but keep him well in hand," he said. But before she could turn to him, startled, alarmed by the significance of his tone, the sudden and appalling metamorphosis which came over the scene nearly caused her to fall unnerved from her saddle. By magic, upon the back of each riderless steed there started an upright figure, and, splitting the stillness of the morning air with its loud fiendish quaver, the hideous war-whoop went up from the throats of half a hundred painted and feathered warriors, who, brandishing their weapons and keeping up one long, unbroken, and exultant yell, skimmed over the plain, sure of their prey.

"Keep quite cool, and don't look back," he said. "We've got to reach that cañon before they do—and we shall. The war-pony that can overhaul old Satanta when he's in average working order has yet to be built."

So far good, so far true. But the same would not precisely hold good of Yseulte's palfrey, which steed, though showy, was not much above the average in pace or staying power.

The race was literally one for life, and the pace was terrific. To the girl it seemed like some fearful dream. Sky and earth, the great mountain rampart reared up in front, all blended together in rocking confusion during that mad race. The yells of the pursuing barbarians sounded horribly nearer, and the pursued could almost hear the whistle of their uncouth trappings as they streamed out on the breeze.

Vipan, reaching over, lashed her horse with a thong which he detached from his saddle. The animal sprang forward, but the spurt was only momentary. And the war-ponies were horribly fresh.

Nearer, nearer. The great rock walls dominating the entrance to the pass loomed up large and distinct. Again he glanced back at the pursuers. Yes, they were gaining. It was more a race than a pursuit—the goal that grim rock-bound pass. Even should the fugitives reach it, what then? Their chances would still be of the slenderest.

Ah, the horror of it! Yseulte, white to the lips, kept her seat by an effort of will, her heart melting with deadly fear. Her companion, fully determined she should never fall alive into the hands of the savages, held his pistol ready, first for them, then for her, his heart burning with bitter curses on his own blind and besotted negligence. It was too late now. They were to founder in sight of land. Ah, the bitterness of it!

Bang!

The whiz of a bullet, simultaneously with a puff of blue smoke—this time in front. Vipan ground his teeth. There was no escape, they were between two fires.

But the regular thunder of the pursuing hoofs seemed to undergo a change. What did it mean?

Bang!

Then a glance over his shoulder told him that as the second ball came whizzing into their midst, the painted warriors had swerved, throwing themselves on the further side of their horses.

Only for a moment, though. Realising that this new enemy represented but a single unit, they hurled themselves forward with redoubled ardour, yelling hideously.

"The gulch, pardner! Streak for the gulch!" sung out a stentorian voice; and sending another bullet among the on-rushing redskins, this time with effect, Smokestack Bill kicked up his horse, which had been lying prone, and in half a minute was flying side by side with his friend.

Short though this check had been, yet it had given them a momentary advantage. But, now, as they neared the mouth of the pass, it became clear to these two experienced Indian fighters that one of them must give his life for the rest.

"Take the young lady on," said the scout. "You're in it together, and must get out of it together. Reckon I'll stand them back long enough for you to strike cover."

Here was a temptation. Vipan knew well that it was so. A short ten minutes would save her—would save them both. His friend could hold the bloodthirsty savages in check for more than that. A struggle raged within him—a bitter struggle—but he conquered.

"No, no, old pard. I'm the man to stay," he answered, slipping from his saddle, for they were now at the entrance of the pass. "Good-bye. Take her in safe."

It was no time for talking. The pursuers, rendered tenfold more daring by the prospect of the most coveted prize of all—a white woman—were almost on their heels, the rocks re-echoing their exultant yells. Yseulte's horse, maddened with terror and stimulated by a shower of blows from the scout, bounded forward at a tearing gallop.

"Wait, wait! We cannot leave him like this! We must turn back!" she cried, breathless, but unable to control her steed, which was stampeding as though all the Sioux in the North-West were setting fire to its tail.

"Help me! Help me to turn back!" she cried, in a perfect frenzy of despair. "We have deserted him—left him to die!"

Left alone, the bold adventurer felt no longer any hope, but in its stead he was conscious of a wild elation. His death would purchase *her* safety, and death was nothing in itself, but every moment gained was of paramount importance. Carefully he drew a bead on the charging warriors and fired. A pony fell. Another rapid shot. This time a human victim. This stopped their headlong rush, and still wheeling in circles they hesitated to come nearer.

He glanced around. Overhead, the slopes, almost precipitous, offered many a possible hiding-place. He might even escape—but he was not there for that. He was there to hold back the enemy—till night, if necessary.

The day wore on. The Sioux, who had drawn off to a distance, seemed in no mood to renew the attack. They were resting their ponies.

Suddenly he saw a score of them leap on horseback again and ride rapidly away. What could this mean?

A shadow fell between him and the light. There was a hurtling sound—a crash—and before he could turn or look up, the whole world was blotted out in a stunning, roaring, heaving sea of space. Then faintness, oblivion, death.

Chapter Thirty
"I would rather have died with him"

Not till they had covered at least two miles could Yseulte Santorex regain the slightest control over her recalcitrant steed. In fact, in her fatigue and nervousness it was as much as ever she could do to keep her seat at all. At length, panting and breathless, she reined in and turned round upon the scout, who had kept close upon her pony's heels.

"I am going back," she cried, her great eyes flashing with anger and contempt. "I would sooner die than desert a—a friend."

"Not to be done, miss," was the quiet answer. "Vipan said to me the last thing—'Bill, on your life take her safe in.' And on my life I will. You bet."

Yseulte looked at him again. A thought struck her and she seemed to waver.

"See here, miss," went on the scout. "Vipan and I have hunted and trapped and prospected together and stood off the reds a goodish number of years. We are pardners, we are, and if he entrusts me with an undertaking of this kind, I've got to see it through. Same thing with him. So the sooner we reach Fort Vigilance, where I'm going to take you, and you're safe among the people there, the sooner I shall be able to double back and try what can be done for Vipan."

"Oh, I never thought of that. Pray do not let us lose a moment."

"So. That's reasonable. You see, miss, it's this way. Women are terrible dead-weights when it comes to fightin' Indians. The varmints'll risk more for a white woman than for all the scalps and plunder in this Territory rolled together. No. Like enough, now that you're snug away, they'll turn round and give up my pard as 'bad medicine.' I reckon there ain't a man between Texas and the British line knows Indians better than my pardner. One day he's fighting 'em, another day he's smokin' in their lodges. He knows 'em, he does."

With this she was forced to be content.

Loyalty to his friend thus moved him to reassure her, but, as a matter of fact, the honest scout felt rather bitter towards this girl. He blamed her entirely for his comrade's peril. He had narrowly watched that comrade of late, and accurately gauged the state of the latter's feelings. Why had this fine lady come out there and played the fool with his comrade—the man with whom he had hunted and trapped for years—with whom he had fought shoulder to shoulder in many a fierce scrimmage with white or red enemies? They had stood by each other through thick and thin, and now this English girl had come in the way, and to satisfy her vanity had sent Vipan to his death—his death, possibly, amid the ghastly torments of the Indian stake. She would probably go home again and brag of her "conquest" with a kind of patronising pity.

In silence they kept on their way—the scout's watchful glance ever on the alert. Suddenly his companion's voice aroused him from the intensity of his vigilance. He started.

"Tell me," she said. "What chance is there of rescuing your friend?"

Her tone was so calm, so self-possessed, that in spite of the deathly pallor of her face it deceived the worthy scout. He felt hard as iron towards her.

"About as much chance, I judge, as I have of being elected President," he replied, gruffly. "And now I want you to know this—If you hadn't troubled your dainty head about my pard, he wouldn't be where he is now. And mind me, if it hadn't been for him, where d'you think you'd be to-day? You'd be wishing you were dead. You'd be doin' scavenger work in a Sioux village, leading a dog's life at the hands of every sooty squaw in the camp— if it hadn't been for Vipan. And now if the Lord works an almighty miracle and I get my pard clear of the red devils, maybe you won't say overmuch to him if you meet him—won't be over-anxious to say you're glad to see him safe and sound again—"

The speaker pulled up short, staring blankly at her. She had burst into a wild storm of sobs.

"You are unjust. Oh, God! Oh, God! send him back to me!" Then turning to the dumbfoundered scout, and controlling herself to speak firmly: "Listen. If it would save his life I would cheerfully undergo death at this moment. I would suffer the slow fire or anything. Think what you like of me—God knows I speak the truth."

"Say that again, miss," stammered the other. "Well, I ask your pardon. I allow I don't know shucks of the ways of women. If it's to be done, my pard'll be brought out. What shall I tell him if so be I find him?" he added, as if struck with a bright idea.

"Tell him," and her voice shook with a tenderness she now no longer cared to conceal, "tell him to come straight to me wherever I am. And if— ah, I cannot think of it—I would rather have died with him!"

Thus the secret of her tortured heart escaped her in that cry of anguish; not to a sister woman, but to the rough and weather-beaten frontiersman who was piloting her across that grim and peril-haunted wilderness.

Again she relapsed into silence, and her escort noted that her tears were falling thick and fast. Suddenly she asked about the attack upon the waggon train.

Smokestack Bill felt in a quandary. She had gone through so much already, she still had need of all her strength, all her nerve, before she should reach the distant frontier post to which he was guiding her. What would happen if he were to tell her the horrible news that they two were the sole survivors of the ill-fated caravan; that he owed his escape from the hideous massacre to the same cause as she did her own—accidental absence? He felt unequal to the task, and evaded the necessity of replying by the invention of a somewhat cowardly pretext, to wit, the imperative advisability of preserving silence as far as possible.

Chapter Thirty One
A Race for—Death

When Vipan recovered consciousness he found himself unable to stir. A lariat rope was tightly coiled around him from head to foot, binding his arms to his sides, and rendering him as helpless as a log.

He tried to move, but an acute pain shooting through his head seemed to crush him again, and he half closed his eyes, stunned and confused.

A dark face peered into his. A tall Indian was bending over him. In the grim painted lineaments he recognised, to his astonishment, the countenance of War Wolf.

"Ha, Golden Face. You feel better now? Good! We will start."

He made no reply. Glancing around him, he noted that the warriors were making their preparations to move. The ponies, which had been grazing all ready saddled, were caught; and at a sign from War Wolf two of the Indians proceeded to loosen the lariat rope in such wise as to allow him the use of his legs.

"Now, mount," said one of them, as his fellow led a pony alongside of the captive, who surveyed his steed designate with a dubious air.

"That sheep isn't up to my weight," he said.

"He will carry you as far as needful," was the reply, ominous in its grim brevity. "Quick, mount."

As he turned to obey a wild thought rushed through the adventurer's mind. Could he not seize the opportunity to make a dash for it? His wily guards must have read his thoughts, for, catching his eye, they shook their heads with a ferocious grin. Then with a raw hide thong they secured their prisoner's feet beneath the horse's belly, and one of them winding the end of the lariat rope which served as a bridle round his hand, the band started.

Ever with a keen eye to opportunity, Vipan noted two things—one that the band had undergone diminution by at least half its original number, the other that they were travelling almost due north-east. The halt had been made not many miles from the fatal gorge, whose frowning entrance he could just see as he turned his head.

No one could be more thoroughly aware than himself of the desperate strait into which he had fallen. He had witnessed more than one instance of men taking their own lives at the last critical moment to avoid capture and its inevitable sequel, a lingering death amid tortures too horrible to name. And now even that alternative was denied to him. The opportunity was past and gone.

"Ha, Golden Face," said War Wolf, ranging his horse alongside his prisoner. "You thought I should have been hung before this."

"Well, yes, I did. How did you manage to get clear?"

Then the savage, in fits of laughter, narrated all that had befallen him at Fort Price; how, after a time, he had been allowed a certain amount of guarded liberty, and how he had deftly managed to disarm the sentry and make his escape. It was a bold exploit, and so his listener candidly told him.

"Ha!" cried the warrior, chuckling and swelling with inflated vanity, "I am a man. Even the stone walls of the Mehneaska cannot hold me. I laugh, and down they go!"

Several of the Indians gathered around, and the conversation became lively. No one would have thought that this white man in their midst, with whom they were chatting and laughing so gaily was a prisoner, doomed to the most barbarous of deaths at their hands. The conversation turned on his own capture, and, in a nonchalant way, Vipan asked for particulars of that feat.

"Ha! Burnt Shoes is not a fool," said War Wolf. "He is my brother."

The warrior named grinned, and at a word from the chief he narrated how he had slipped away from the main body, and, unobserved by the prisoner, had gained the rocks over the latter's head. When he was ready he had signalled to his fellows, who had made that unexpected move in order to fix the prisoner's attention. He could easily have shot his enemy, but the temptation to take him alive was great. Therefore, seeing a convenient boulder handy, he had hurled it upon his enemy's head, with the most satisfactory result to himself and his tribesmen.

"But," added this candid young barbarian, "your scalp will be mine, anyhow."

Vipan took no notice of this remark. He knew the speaker by sight apart from having recognised him as War Wolfs brother. Then he asked what had become of Satanta.

Here the Indians looked foolish, at least most of them did, while those who did not, unmercifully chaffed their companions. It came out that the black steed objected to the new ownership which it was purposed to assert over him, and watching his opportunity, which occurred while his saddle was being changed during the recent halt, had concluded to part company with the band. In a word, he had started off as fast as his legs could carry him. But several warriors had gone after him, added the speaker.

"They are after a shooting star, then," said Satanta's lawful owner. "They had the best horse in the North-West, and they have let him slip through their hands."

The party had been travelling at a rapid pace, and now the day was merging into twilight. Despatching pickets to neighbouring heights, the savages prepared for a good long halt.

Vipan was released from his steed, and allowed to seat himself upon the ground by the side of a fire that had been built. His captors crowded round him, laughing and talking in the friendliest fashion, and, noting it, his heart sank within him.

And who shall blame him? Bound and helpless, he knew the moment had come for putting him to the most hellish tortures. He read it in the grim, painted visages closing him in on every side. And between those ruthless demon-faces he beheld in the background a sight whose meaning he knew but too well.

Two Indians were busy driving strong pegs into the ground at intervals of several feet apart.

Then he did a strange thing. Quick as thought, and without any warning, he spat full into War Wolfs face.

With a yell of rage, the young chief, starting back, swung his tomahawk in the air. In another instant the prisoner would have gained his wish. He intended to exasperate the Indian into killing him on the spot.

But the others were wider awake. Seizing their chiefs arm, a couple of bystanders succeeded in arresting the blow. Then half-a-dozen sinewy warriors flinging themselves upon Vipan began to drag him towards the pegs aforesaid.

A barbarity popular among the Plains' tribes is that known as "staking out." The wretched captive is stripped and thrown on his back. Each hand and foot is then fastened to a peg driven firmly into the ground at the necessary distance apart. Thus spread-eagled, he is powerless to stir, beyond a limited wriggle. Then the fun begins, and when is remembered the hideous agony that a handful of live coals stacked against the soles of a man's feet alone is warranted to produce, it follows that the amount of burning at the disposal of the red demons before death mercifully delivers the victim from their power is practically unlimited. In fact, their hellish sport may be bounded not by hours, but even by days. They generally begin by roasting the tenderest parts of the body, finally piling up the fire all over the stomach and chest of the sufferer.

Vipan, aware of the fate in store for him, seized his opportunity. While the savages were slightly relaxing their grasp in order to pull off his clothes, he made one stupendous effort. Cramped as he was, his herculean strength stood him in good stead. A couple of violent kicks in the stomach sent as many warriors to the earth gasping, and dragging others with them in their fall. Like a thunderbolt he dashed through the group, and before his enemies had recovered from their confusion he was many rods away, speeding down the hillside like a deer.

A frightful yell went up from the startled redskins. A score of rifles covered the flying fugitive, but a peremptory word from War Wolf knocked them up. Their prisoner was safe enough, no need to spoil sport by killing him. Though his legs where free, his arms were bound. A rush was made for the ponies. The plain was open for miles and miles. In five minutes they would retake him with ease.

Of this Vipan was only too well aware. The chances of escape had never entered into his calculations when he made his wild attempt. On foot and unbound he might have distanced the savages, but what chance had he against their ponies? A water-hole lay in the bottom, a mile away. He would strive to reach this, and, bound as he was, an easy death by drowning would be the alternative to hours of fiery torment.

And as he ran it seemed to the hunted man that this was no real occurrence—only a horrid nightmare. The events of a lifetime shot through his mind. Then the thunder of flying hoofs behind.

He glanced over his shoulder. Would he reach the water? Ah, never did hunted man strain every nerve and muscle for life as did this one with death before him as the prize.

Nearer! The water-hole gleams cool and inviting. A hundred yards— then fifty. The roar and thunder of hoofs is in his ears. It stuns him. Now for the final leap. Then death! Twenty steps more. He poises himself for the final spring. But it is not to be. The coil of a lazo has settled around him; he is jerked from his feet, dragged back a dozen yards—stunned, half senseless.

Then, as he wearily opens his eyes, doubtful whether he is dead or alive, he finds himself in the midst of a crowd of Indians, all mounted save the half-dozen who have run forward to secure him. With a sensation of surprise, his glance wanders amid the sea of painted visages—of surprise because many of them are known to him, and were certainly not among the band that effected his capture. And—can he believe his ears?—the chief of the party, a fine martial-looking warrior, is giving instructions that his bonds shall be cut.

"Wagh!" ejaculated the latter, with the ghost of a smile. "You have fallen upon rough times, Golden Face."

Then the prisoner, once more a free man, looked up at the speaker and knew that he was safe. He recognised Mahto-sapa.

And now a great hubbub arose as War Wolf and his party rode up, and angrily demanded their prisoner, emphasising their request by making a dash at the latter. But at a sign from the chief a dozen warriors placed themselves in front of Vipan.

Then the debate began to wax very breezy, and small wonder. By every right of immemorial custom and usage, the late prisoner was absolutely their property, and had they not been "choused" out of a rare and exquisitely enjoyable form of sport? Vipan, though too far off to hear all that was being said, caught the name "Tatanka-yotanka" as mentioned pretty frequently, and it seemed to have the effect of a damper on War Wolf. That impulsive savage, having indulged in a good deal of swagger, ended by sullenly accepting the situation. There is not much hard-and-fast law among Indians in a matter of this kind. If the redoubted war-chief of the Minneconjou clan, surrounded by a large armed force, chose to retain half-a-dozen prisoners, War Wolf, who was not, properly speaking, a chief at all, had no redress, save such as he might attain by force of arms. But his following numbered barely thirty warriors, whereas Mahto-sapa was at the head of fully five times that number.

Dismounting, the Minneconjou chief gravely sat down upon the ground. Then filling his pipe, and applying a light to the bowl, he handed it to Vipan without a word. In silence the latter received it, and after a few puffs handed it back.

"What was said just now about Sitting Bull?" he enquired at length.

"This. I have come out to look for you, Golden Face. Sitting Bull is anxious that you should visit him."

"Oho, I begin to see," said the adventurer to himself, as he lazily watched his late captors draw their ponies out of the crowd and ride sullenly away.

Now, in the debate just held, his rescuer had justified his action on twofold ground. War Wolf having allowed his prisoner to escape had forfeited all claim to him; secondly, the said prisoner, being an Englishman, his presence was required by Sitting Bull, the renowned chief of the hostiles, for political purposes.

Chapter Thirty Two
The Village of the Hostiles

All night long—with a brief halt towards morning—the war-party, with Vipan in its midst, pushed forward at a rapid pace.

The sun rose. They had passed the intricate defiles of the Bad Lands, and were now threading the rugged and broken country beyond. Piled in chaotic confusion, the great peaks leaning towards each other, or split and riven as by a titanic wedge, caught the first red glow upon their iron faces. Dark pinnacles soaring aloft, huge and forbidding, stood in the first delicate flush like graceful minarets; and here and there through a vista of falling slopes, the striped and fantastic face of a *mesa* would come into view, seamed with blue and black and red, according to the varying strata of its soft and ever-crumbling formation. A hundred bizarre shapes reared their heads around. Here a clean rock shaft, so even and perpendicular in its towering symmetry that it seemed impossible to have been planned by the hand of Nature alone, standing side by side with some hugely grotesque representation of a head, changing from animal to human with every fresh point of view, so distorted yet so real, so hideous and repelling as to suggest involuntary thoughts of a demon-guarded land. There a black and yawning fissure whose polished sides would hardly seem to afford resting-place for the eyrie of yon great war-eagle soaring high above, his plumage gleaming in the lustre of the new-born day. Dark, cedar-clad gorges rent the mountain sides, and on the nearer slopes the flash of something white through the tall, straight stems of the spruce firs showed where a deer, alarmed by this redoubtable inroad on his early grazing ground, had darted away, with a whisk of his white "flag."

And in thorough keeping with its surroundings was the aspect of the wild host, threading its way through these solitudes. A clear, dashing mountain brook curved and sparkled along a level bottom carpeted with the greenest of sweet grass, and along this, strung out to the distance of a mile, cantered group after group of mounted savages, the fantastic adornments of themselves and their steeds streaming out to the morning breeze; their waving plumes, and painted faces, their shining weapons and brilliantly-coloured accoutrements, and the easy grace with which they sat their steeds as they defiled along the ever-winding gorge, forming about as striking and wildly picturesque a sight as would be happened upon, travel we the whole world over.

All fear of pursuit being now over, the warriors rode anyhow, broken up into groups or couples as the humour possessed them. Most of them were chatting and laughing with that ease and light-heartedness which in their hours of relaxation is characteristic of most savage peoples, a light-heartedness and freedom from care which renders them akin to children. Near the rear of the party rode Mahto-sapa and his prisoner, together with three or four warriors of high rank.

For that he was such, Vipan himself was not left in any doubt, nor was there room for any. Though relieved from the indignity of bonds, yet his arms had not been returned to him, not even a knife. Moreover, the steed he bestrode was far from being the best in the party. All of which he had hinted as delicately as possible to the chief. The latter's reply was characteristic.

"Patience—Golden Face. It is not we who have taken your weapons; it is War Wolf and his party. As for horses, my young men are none of them too well mounted. Besides," added the Indian, a humorous gleam lighting up his fine face as he noted the other's deprecatory shake of the head, "besides—Golden Face has shamefully neglected his red brothers since the Mehneaska waggons came along. Why do they bring beautiful white girls into a country where the ground is too rough for their tender feet? No. Have patience. My young men would be more than angry did you leave them now to go and look after a white woman. She is safe now, but both she and the Brown Beaver would have fallen into the hands of War Wolf had you not acted as you did," he continued. "Wagh! Golden Face, it is not like you to throw away your life for a squaw!"

The adventurer made no reply, but the other's remark set him thinking. It left, so to say, an unpleasant taste. He was at an age when most men have parted with their illusions, and he himself certainly was no exception. To his keen, cynical nature absolute trust was well-nigh impossible. Would he ever see Yseulte Santorex again, and even if he did, would he not be in the same position as before—a king in these Western wilds, in civilisation a pauper? He knew the world—none better. It was one thing for this beautiful and refined girl to feel drawn towards a companion and protector in the midst of the perilous vicissitudes of Western travel, but that after months of reflection on her return to safety and comfort she should still continue to think of a man whose antecedents were doubtful, of whose very identity she was ignorant, in the face, too, of the opposition of friends and relatives, was quite another. For long he rode in silence, and his thoughts were very bitter.

All day the march continued. That night the Indians, being comparatively beyond fear of pursuit, camped for a long rest, and resuming their progress at dawn, towards nightfall reached the bank of a river. This was immediately forded, and then halting on the opposite bank the whole band collected together. Then, after a word of instruction from their chief, the warriors formed into line, and with a loud and prolonged whoop dashed forward at a brisk canter.

The shout was answered from some distance ahead, and lo! as by magic, there sprang up the red glow of many a fire, and among the thinly-scattered timber bordering the stream tall lodges might be descried, standing in groups or in long irregular lines, hundreds and hundreds of them. Then in the gloaming the whole village swarmed with dusky shapes. Squaws flung down their burdens, or abruptly quitted their household employments, and, dancing and singing, crowded around to welcome the returning war-party. Young bucks, eager to know what had been done in scalps and plunder, turned out by the dozen. Children yelled and curs barked and howled, and still the ever-increasing crowd gathered about the returned warriors.

Suddenly the latter, reining in their ponies, burst into a wild war-song. It was taken up by the motley crowd following upon their ponies' heels, and as the savage horsemen, in all the trappings of their martial bravery, paced at length into the centre of the village, the shrill, weird chorus echoing from many thousand throats, while the red light danced and glowed upon plumed crests and burnished weapons rising above the sea of fierce painted visages, the bold mind of the white adventurer was filled with admiration as he gazed upon this stirring picture which for grandeur and awesomeness left nothing to be desired.

Thus they entered the camp of the hostiles.

"Listen, Golden Face," said Mahto-sapa, as he spread a buffalo robe for his guest. "It will not be well to wander in the camp alone."

"No, I am a prisoner, and unarmed."

The other smiled slightly, with a significant glance at an old leathern wallet hanging to the pole. Then he left the lodge.

The adventurer, following his glance, promptly explored the receptacle. He found an old single-barrelled pistol and a scalping-knife. The pistol was capped and loaded.

Chapter Thirty Three
Sitting Bull

The morning after his arrival in the village of the hostiles Vipan was seated eating his breakfast in the lodge of his host, in company with the latter and one of his brothers, when the door of the *teepe* was darkened, and an Indian entered.

Now there was nothing in the appearance of this warrior to denote special rank. His dress was strikingly plain, the beaded blanket thrown around his shoulders was considerably the worse for wear, not to say shabby, and his head was adorned with a single eagle quill stuck in the back of his hair. Yet a glance at the powerful, thickly-built frame, the deep-set, though penetrating eyes, the square jaw and slightly pock-marked countenance, and Vipan felt instinctively that this was none other than the redoubtable war-chief of the hostiles himself.

With a grunt of salutation, the new arrival sat himself down among the inmates of the *teepe*, then, without a word, and as a matter of course, proceeded to help himself out of the three-legged pot containing the smoking and savoury stew which constituted the repast. Not a word was spoken, not a question asked, and the four men proceeded with their meal in silence.

Tatanka-yotanka, or Sitting Bull, was at that time in the very zenith of his pride and influence. He represented the fearless and implacable war-faction in the nation, and in his persistent and uncompromising hostility to the Americans and the United States Government he differed from the more diplomatic Red Cloud. As in the case of the latter, however, Sitting Bull was not born to hereditary chieftainship, yet at that time the influence he had achieved among his countrymen by his personal prowess and skilful generalship was so solid and far-reaching that sagacious and powerful war-chiefs such as Mahto-sapa deemed it sound policy to co-operate with him; for the authority of a chief among the Plains tribes, in addition to his prowess in war, depends not a little on his conformity with the sense and wishes of his tribesmen, and he who should commit himself unreservedly to a peace policy in opposition to the desires of his people would soon find himself in the position of a chief without any adherents. Yet as savages rarely do things by halves, it followed that however inclined for peace they might be at first, such chiefs and warriors once they stood committed to war threw themselves into the prosecution of hostilities with all the ardour and aggressiveness of their more bloodthirstily disposed brethren.

Sitting Bull—like many another savage leader—was a shrewd thinker. The experience of the last campaign had inspired him with profound contempt for the United States Government. The latter's demands had then been successfully resisted, and after a sharp and sanguinary struggle, culminating in the Fort Phil Kearney massacre, the Government had retired, almost precipitately. The Sioux nation had never been conquered. The Sioux warriors were as daring and warlike to-day as then, and were better armed, for they could obtain, and had obtained, from unscrupulous traders as many weapons of the latest improved patterns and as much ammunition as they could afford to purchase. The Government, he reasoned, had not kept faith with them in the matter of the Black Hills and other sections of their country, then full of white men; therefore, let the Government look to itself. That the Indian leader's reasoning was sound according to his lights, was proved by subsequent events, among them the calamitous massacre of nearly three hundred brave soldiers, together with one of the most dashing cavalry officers and successful Indian fighters the United States army has ever possessed. (Note 1.) But no savage of his race and instincts could be expected to take into his reckoning the steady tide of immigration pouring into the American continent from the Old World, for the simple reason that his conception of the very existence of an Old World was of so shadowy a nature as to be practically legendary.

The meal over, each of the three Indians wiped his knife upon his leggings or the soles of his moccasins with a grunt of satisfaction. Then the inevitable pipe was filled, lighted, and duly passed round.

Vipan, thoroughly restored by a good night's rest, and with perfect confidence in himself, looked forward to the keen skirmish of wits which was at hand, and in which the slightest failure in coolness and wariness might cost him his life, with feelings not far short of downright enjoyment.

After the pipe had gone round in silence, Sitting Bull spoke. He had often heard of Golden Face, the friend of the Dahcotah nation, he said. Now he was glad to have an opportunity of smoking with him, and learning from his lips.

The speaker paused, and Vipan merely acknowledged the compliment by a grave bend of the head. The chief continued:

Golden Face, he had been given to understand, had been a great fighting man among his own people, and a leader of warriors. He was not of the Mehneaska, the nation with whom no faith could be kept. Why, then, had he fought for the Mehneaska against his Dahcotah brethren?

Vipan, with due deliberation, replied that those for whom he fought *were* his own countrymen—not Americans. They were subjects of the Great White Queen, whose dominions lay to the north (Canada). Why had the Dahcotah attacked them and run off their stock?

"Were they all King George men?" asked the shrewd chief, half closing his eyes and looking into space.

This was a staggerer, but Vipan was equal to it.

"They were not," he said. "Only the leader and his household. For the rest, they bore me as little love as they do the Dahcotah warriors who ran off their horses and cattle. Listen now, and mark." Then he graphically narrated the circumstances under which he had warned Winthrop's outfit of the lurking war-party, making it appear that his warning had been due simply and solely to his recognition of his fellow-countrymen among the travellers.

Not a muscle of Sitting Bull's crafty countenance moved as he listened.

"How!" he said, quietly, when the speaker ceased. "Did not Golden Face declare that he owned no nationality?"

This was another staggerer, and a more serious one than before. But Vipan's imperturbability was of a quality warranted to stand shocks. Inwardly he laughed over the other's shrewdness in bringing up his own words in judgment against him.

That was true, he replied. But apart from the fact of that particular white man being his fellow-countryman, and therefore one against whom the Dahcotah nation had no quarrel, he was the son of a man who had once rendered him a most important service. Who worthy of the name and dignity of a warrior ever forgot to requite a good turn once rendered, even at the peril of his life?

This answer, if not altogether received as gospel by his hearers, sent him up ten per cent, in their estimation. Nowhere is diplomatic talent and readiness in debate held in such high respect as among savage races.

"The white girl who hunted with Golden Face is very beautiful," went on Sitting Bull. "Was it for her he lifted his rifle against his Dahcotah brethren?"

"Who would not fight for a beautiful woman, be she white or red?" answered Vipan, with a burst of well-timed frankness. "Sitting Bull is a great chief, let him judge if my words are straight. Did War Wolf and his followers come to me as to a friend? No; they attacked me as enemies. Then when they treated me as an enemy and an ordinary prisoner of war, did I complain? Sitting Bull is a great chief, a warrior of renown, but who is War Wolf? Who is he, I say? Enough: I have smoked in council with Red Cloud and the chiefs of the Dahcotah nation. My words are for the ears of chiefs, not for those of boys, who passed the Sun-dance but yesterday."

The ghost of a smile flitted across Sitting Bull's grim features at this reply, while a murmur of approbation escaped the other two auditors. No one understood better than the speaker the advantage of making the most of himself among these people, nor was the dexterous compliment to his own eminence thrown away upon the bold and sagacious warrior who had, so to say, risen from the ranks.

"But," rejoined the latter, "if the white girl was of the race of King George, with whom we have no quarrel, why did not Golden Face bring her among his Dahcotah brethren, where he might have lived with her in peace and safety?"

Vipan explained that a white girl such as her of whom they were speaking would never consent to accompany him unless as his wife, and even then she must be married according to the customs of her people. To this the wily chief quoted the case of his friend and brother, Mahto-sapa, who had a white wife. She had been taken to wife according to Dahcotah custom; and whose lodge was more comfortable than hers; who was cared for better than she?

Now Vipan was aware of the existence of this personage, yet strange to say, bearing in mind his friendship with the Minneconjou chief, had never seen her. He was aware, too, that she was originally a white captive, seized by the Indians during one of their dreaded raids upon a settlement or waggon train some years previously, but that was the extent of his knowledge. It must be confessed he felt a good deal of curiosity on the subject, but he was not the man to allow any sign of it to appear. His answer, however, was ready and to the point.

That might be true, he replied; but it was a matter of which he, Vipan, knew nothing, nor did it concern him in any way. What he did know was this: The white girl in question was of very considerable account in her own country. True, most of the warriors in Sitting Bull's village were his—the speaker's—brethren. But some were not. There were some in it at that moment who looked upon him as an enemy, who had treated him as one.

What if he had brought this white girl with him, and she had met—with harm at the hands of any of these? Would not her people require a heavy reckoning? The Dahcotah hunting-grounds were bounded on the north by the British line. Would it be the act of a friend to do anything which should embroil the Dahcotah nation with two strong Powers instead of one, in such wise too that they should be surrounded with enemies on every side?

He had played a very trump card in making this reply, and he knew it. For he had seen through Sitting Bull's motives in requiring his presence in the camp of the hostiles, and was resolved to make the most of it; and upon the extent of his success he was well aware that his very life depended.

"Wagh!" exclaimed the chief, with well-feigned indifference. "The Dahcotah people fear the enmity of no one. Yet they seek no quarrel with the countrymen of Golden Face. They have always heard that the King George men have straight tongues, and that the Great White Queen keeps her promises, and fulfils her treaties with the red tribes within her territory."

Then followed a good deal of what, for want of a better word, we will call "dark" talking. Sitting Bull in a series of highly diplomatic hints, and using much figurative language, strove to sound his prisoner as to the probability of the British being induced to espouse his people's cause in the event of the coming campaign ending disastrously to them. Vipan, ever mindful of his precarious position as in fact a prisoner, though treated outwardly as a guest, answered cautiously, and to the effect that although the British would be to the last degree unlikely actively to interfere in their favour, yet it would be fatally imprudent to commit any act tending to incur the hostility of the great and mighty Power who occupied the northern boundary line of their country, and whose territory, indeed, might yet serve them as a refuge in time of need, for who could foretell the chances of war? At the same time he threw out more than one dexterous hint as to the services he himself might be able to render his Dahcotah brethren in the event of any such lamentable contingency.

Judging that enough had been said for the present, Sitting Bull arose.

"It is well," he said, throwing his blanket round his shoulders, as he prepared to depart. "The counsels of Golden Face are always good to listen to. His presence is very welcome to his red brethren."

Judging the moment a favourable one, Vipan delicately hinted that so welcome a guest should not be treated in a manner unworthy the dignity of a warrior—in a word, that his weapons should be restored to him.

Again that ghost of a smile crossed the face of the wily chieftain.

"No one could mistake Golden Face for anything but a warrior," he said, sweetly. "Is he not surrounded by his friends, his brothers? Who requires to go armed among his friends?"

There was nothing for it but to accept the position, and, moreover, to accept it with a good grace. Suddenly there arose a terrific din outside— shrieks and yells, shouts of demoniac laughter, and the trampling of many feet.

Note 1. General George A. Custer, who fell into an ambuscade on the Little Bighorn river, and perished with his entire command at the hands of the hostile Sioux, under Sitting Bull, on the 25th June, 1876.

Chapter Thirty Four
The Two Victims

If ever a spectacle of hell let loose was vouchsafed to mortal eye, assuredly it must have borne a strong family likeness to that presented by the Indian village, as Vipan and the three chiefs stepped gravely outside the *teepe* to see what was going on.

A wild, roaring, yelling crowd came surging into the open space where stood the council-lodge. Bucks and squaws, children and dogs, all mingled together in a motley mass, whooping, laughing, chattering and grinning. A sea of wild excited faces, the crowd poured onward, gathering as it rolled. Then the cause of all this excitement became discernible. In the front of the throng, in the centre of a group of yelling squaws, hustled, beaten, kicked, dragged along by the bloodthirsty harpies, were two white men. Their arms were tightly bound behind their backs, but their feet were tied so as to enable them to make short steps. They had been stripped naked, and their bodies, already lacerated with many a weal, and bruised from the switches and clubs of their tormentors, were plentifully besmeared with their own blood.

"Wagh, Golden Face!" exclaimed Sitting Bull, with grim humour. "Our squaws seem to handle your countrymen very tenderly."

The adventurer made no reply. Even he felt his heart sicken within him at the thought of the hideous fate these two wretched men were about to undergo. Yet drawn by an uncontrollable impulse, he found himself moving beside the three Indians, who were strolling leisurely in the direction taken by the crowd. Not that his red friends manifested any interest in the proceedings. The torture of helpless prisoners was sport for boys and squaws, and unworthy of the attention of great chiefs or warriors of renown. Still, with the characteristic weakness of their race to witness anything unusual, they followed the crowd.

As the latter thundered along the open space, the inmates of the clustering groups of *teepes* on either side poured forth to swell its ranks. Young bucks would dart out in front, and execute a series of leaps in the air, uttering shrill whoops, and even the river was dotted with bull-boats, as the inhabitants of the villages on the opposite bank crowded over in hundreds to see the fun. Knives were flourished in the prisoners' faces, kicks and slaps were their portion at every step; indeed, it almost seemed that the ill-usage of the infuriated mob would mercifully end their sufferings before they should reach the terrible stake. Something of this seemed to strike their tormentors themselves, for all of a sudden a compact band of young bucks charged into the mass, drove back the yelling squaws, and seizing the two unhappy wretches, dragged them forward at a smart run.

Just outside the village was a clear space. Here a couple of stout posts, eight or nine feet high, had been driven into the ground about a dozen yards apart.

And now Vipan had an opportunity of estimating the strength of the band or bands into whose midst he had so involuntarily penetrated. Far along the river-banks on either side, extending a distance of five or six miles, the tall lodges stood in lines and clusters among the thin belt of timber which lined the stream. These and the village behind him, roughly reckoning, he estimated to represent some four or five thousand warriors. Overhead the great mountains shot up their craggy heads, blasted into a score of fantastic shapes, frowning down upon the barbarous scene like grim tutelaries of destruction.

The two miserable men were backed against the posts and firmly secured, their arms being drawn up high above their heads and stretched to the utmost. Powerless to move a limb, they were ready for the torturers.

Suddenly a piercing cry for help burst from one of them. In it Vipan recognised his own name.

In deference to their rank, the crowd had made way for the chiefs in whose company he was. At a sign from Sitting Bull, it now gave way further, and Vipan was able to approach within easy speaking-distance of the prisoners.

"Oh, for God's sake, Mr Vipan, save me from torture! Kill me—put me out of my misery at once!"

Vipan stared at the utterer of this agonised prayer. In the distorted features, cut and bruised out of all knowledge, and livid with the dews of bodily and mental anguish, in the strained eyeballs staring from their sockets in deadly fear, he could hardly recognise the unfortunate Geoffry Vallance.

A curious change passed over the adventurer's face, so curious that even many of the Indians standing around noticed it and wondered.

"I am the last person in this world, of whom *you* ought to ask a benefit," he said curtly.

Had there been time for reflection, poor Geoffry might well have been amazed. Now, half-frenzied with terror, he only moaned:

"Save me from the torture! Kill me, that is all I ask you!"

"I cannot if I would," was the answer, in a more relenting tone. "How did you manage to let them capture you?"

"It was the day the camp was taken," gasped the wretched prisoner. "I was lingering behind and got lost, and then my horse ran away when I was dismounted. I don't know how it was, but I looked up and found myself in the middle of the Indians."

"Well, I can do nothing for you. Mind me, though. I knew a chap in your position once. He managed to roll his tongue back into his throat and choke himself. He escaped the fire that way. Try it. It's your only chance."

The despairing moan with which this gloomy alternative was received was drowned by a loud cry from the other white man.

"Colonel Vipan. Git us out of this fix, for the Lord's sake! I kin put you on to a good thing, I kin!"

The adventurer turned in amazement. He saw what was a villainous countenance at the best of times, and now with the shaggy beard matted with saliva and gouts of blood, it was hideous and horrible in the extreme. He recognised the man he had felled in the liquor saloon at Henniker City — Bitter Rube.

"How in thunder did you get into this hobble?" he said.

"It's this way, Colonel. The red devils jumped us at our *placer*. They scalped the other three."

"Burntwood Creek?"

"That's it, Colonel. You get me out of this, and I'll make you a rich man for life. There's gold there worth millions and millions."

"Glad to hear it, Bitter Rube," was the unconcerned reply. "I know the place all right; going to work it by and by. It's where your mate jumped me and got laid out for his pains. Remember your scheme to lynch me, eh, Bitter Rube?"

"Oh, Lord, Colonel. It was the other chaps. See here now—"

"Well, I can't even repay the little service you were going to render me—a short shrift and a long rope," interrupted Vipan, the scowling glances and increasing murmurs of the throng convincing him of the peril he himself was incurring. A frantic yell burst from the prisoner.

"You snake-spawned white Injun! Here's a white man being cut into chunks before your eyes. I'll haunt yer! I'll ghost yer! I'll make life a hell to yer!"

The miserable wretch went on to bellow the most frantic blasphemies. One of the young Indians, stepping up behind him, thrust a red-hot faggot into his open mouth. This was greeted as an excellent joke by the onlookers, who shouted and screamed with laughter. Then one of them applied a light to the victim's unkempt and shaggy beard. It frizzled and flared up, burning the wretched man frightfully about the face and head. The mirth of the spectators became well-nigh uncontrollable.

"How! white brudder," said a burly buck, grinning hideously into Geoffry's face, and patting him fraternally on the shoulder. "Injun brudder hab heap fun. Injun brudder not hurt you first. Other man hurt first—you see him—you hab heap good fun. You hurt first, you no laugh—other hurt first, you plenty laugh—Injun brudder plenty laugh. How—how!"

Then the wretched Geoffry understood that with a diabolical refinement of cruelty the savages intended that he should witness the torture and death of his companion in adversity before his own turn came. He could only raise his eyes stupidly to the grinning countenance of his addresser.

Two squaws now stepped forward—hideous hags whose long flattened breasts fell in disgusting flaps below their waists. They were nearly naked, and each held in her hand a sharp knife. Advancing to the sufferer they made an incision down each of his sides, and proceeded to skin him alive as coolly as a butcher would flay a dead sheep.

The anguished shrieks of the victim were terrible to hear; but no spark of pity did they stir in the hearts of the ruthless fiends who crowded around, gloating over this diabolical performance. They danced and laughed, leaping high in the air, hurling taunting epithets at the miserable victim, and exhorting the other prisoner to observe what was in store for him. And in their hellish glee the women, if anything, surpassed the younger and more ferocious of the warriors.

For nearly an hour the scene went on—varied at intervals by the passing of a lighted torch along those portions of the victim's body already laid bare. The piercing shrieks of the tortured wretch sunk into laboured and hollow groans—then ceased altogether. He had fainted.

A glance having sufficed to show them that he was not dead, the performers stood back, contemplating their handiwork with a grin of ferocious satisfaction. And so deftly had they done it, that from chin to feet, the front and sides of the sufferer's body was entirely denuded of skin, which hung from his shoulders in a bleeding and ghastly mantle. Yet this was only the first stage of his torture.

Vipan, who had perforce witnessed this hideous spectacle, felt seized with a violent and well-nigh uncontrollable nausea, and would have turned away. But as the exhibition of the slightest repulsion or feeling would have been not merely inexpedient, but highly dangerous, he was constrained to master himself. Besides, a sort of horrible fascination rooted him to the spot—an overmastering and morbid curiosity to see how the other prisoner would fare.

Sitting Bull, who with a few other chiefs had been witnessing the hellish performance with grave impassiveness, must have read his thoughts.

"They are not King George men," he remarked laconically. "They are not your countrymen, Golden Face."

Vipan made no reply. The remark suggested an idea. He might be able to save Geoffry by claiming him as a fellow-countryman. A strange struggle took place within him. Why should he? If he attempted to do so it would be at deadly risk to himself, and even then would he meet with success? And apart from these considerations, as he himself had told the unfortunate one, he was the last man from whom the latter should claim any assistance.

Then the bloodthirsty rage of the barbarous horde took a fresh turn. Their one victim was for the time being insensible to pain, but there was another. Him they had been reserving with this end in view. Shouts were raised that it was time to begin upon him.

With a wild-beast laugh, the two fiend-like hags approached the new victim, their reeking knives in hand, the yells and roars of the crowd urging them on. The miserable Geoffry, bound immovably to the stake, watched their approach. His eyes protruded from their sockets, a cold sweat rained down his distorted countenance, and there was a strange hoarse rattle in his throat. It was a sight to haunt the spectator for a lifetime. Then his head fell heavily forward on his chest.

Seizing him by the hair, one of the female fiends forced it back. It was as lead in her grasp. Then the truth became apparent. The miserable captive was stone-dead. He had died of sheer horror and fright.

A moment of silence, then with a wild yell of disappointed fury the ferocious crowd flung itself upon the corpse and hacked and mutilated it into a shapeless and gory mass. Then the blind madness of their bloodthirsty rage fairly let loose, they turned once more to the first victim. The scalp was torn from his head; knives and burning splinters were stuck into his flesh;

and the yet warm and palpitating heart was plucked out and reared aloft on the point of a lance. Then bundles of dry brushwood were piled around both of the mangled corpses, and set alight, and soon the red tongues of flame—whose roaring and crackling was drowned by the frenzied yells of the savages as they danced and leaped around like devils let loose from the nethermost hell—shot upward, licking around the cruel stakes of torture, and a horrible and sickening odour of burning flesh hung upon the air. A great volume of smoke mounted to the heavens, and, after watching it for a while, the whole fiend-like crowd surged back to the village, there to hold a gigantic scalp-dance—bearing the reeking trophies aloft on lance-points.

All that remained of the border ruffian and the unfortunate Geoffry Vallance were two little heaps of calcined bones.

Chapter Thirty Five
The Sun Queen

A month had gone by. The mountain air had become thin and steely, and the gorgeous glories of the golden-hued woods were falling fast. Winter was in the atmosphere.

In the villages of the hostiles time was of no account. Dancing and warlike exercises, gossip, story-telling and gambling, and hunting in the adjacent mountains, thus this great gathering of savages on a war-footing solaced their leisure hours—which were many. Bands of warriors, under some favourite chief or partisan, would strike the war-post, and sally forth on some more or less desperate foray, returning in due time with scalps or plunder, or both. Once they brought with them a wretched prisoner, who was promptly done to death under the usual circumstances of revolting barbarity.

Now, of this life Vipan had become heartily sick. Accustomed as he was to come and go at will among the camps and villages of the Sioux, the restraint of knowing himself a prisoner galled him. For although allowed a certain amount of liberty, and rather ostentatiously treated as a guest, he was carefully watched. But it is doubtful whether another cause had not more to do with his weariness and disgust. That was no mere passing passion whose expression had so nearly escaped him when standing in the dug-out with Yseulte Santorex. By an inexplicable rebound from his wild and reckless life, this man's mature mind and strong nature had sprung to the other extreme. Well he knew—none better—his position, or, rather, the utter lack of it, did he return to civilisation, and there were times when he felt tempted to throw himself in heart and soul with his Indian friends, to lead them on the war-path, and in ferocity and daring excelling even the savages themselves, to devote the remainder of his life to acts of vengeance upon that civilisation whose laws had placed it in the power of a specious hypocrite to drive him forth from its midst a pauper and an outcast—acts of barbarous and bloody vengeance that should render his name a terror to the whole of the Western frontier. What had he to do with softness—with love—at his time of life? Yseulte Santorex would be safe in her English home by this time, probably recalling—when she did recall it—their acquaintanceship only as a passing romance embedded among her other adventurous experiences. With such reflections would he lash and torture himself.

More than once when accompanying some of their hunting parties into the mountains he had been seized by a wild impulse to make a dash for liberty. But the cat-like watchfulness of the Indians never flagged, and upon such occasions a glance was enough to show the impracticability of any such scheme. The first step would be the signal for a volley of bullets through his body—moreover, he was never allowed the use of anything but an inferior steed.

And now, day by day, his situation became more precarious. Sitting Bull, Crazy Horse, and the other chiefs had somehow waxed more than doubtful of late as to whether his services in regard to a possible British intervention would be of any use at all—and this idea was insidiously fostered by his enemies, who were many and powerful—Mountain Cat, the Ogallalla war-chief, and Crow-Scalper, who hated all whites, and the band of young desperadoes who had attached themselves to the fortunes of War Wolf. The latter brave's bumptiousness had become simply overwhelming. Full of the recently-acquired importance conferred upon him by his captivity among the whites and subsequent escape, he would strut and swagger around, bedecked in all his war-paint and finery— passing Vipan with a contemptuous laugh or a remark of covert insolence. The only consideration that restrained the latter from inflicting summary chastisement was the certainty that the hour he did so would be his last. And his friend and protector, Mahto-sapa, was frequently absent on warlike or diplomatic expeditions. The sullen and hostile feeling growing around him was written on every grim and scowling face. He felt as helpless as a fly in a spider's web.

Pondering over these things, he was seated one day alone in the lodge of his host—the latter being away upon one of those absences which constituted such a peril to himself—when a shadow darkened the entry and a feminine voice inquired in English:

"May I come in?"

He started, as well he might. The accent was pure and refined, the tone firm and pleasing. For answer he rose and bowed, and the speaker entered.

Strange as it may seem, during all this while Vipan had seen his host's white wife by no more than a few stray passing glimpses, and then at a distance. It had always struck him that she avoided him with design, and he had respected her motives. She dwelt in two *teepes*, which she occupied all to herself—an unwonted luxury—and was attended on by a Shoshone slave girl of unrivalled hideosity, captured on one of the chief's forays into the country of the Snakes.

He saw before him a tall, fine-looking woman who might or might not have been under forty. She was habited in the tasteful Indian dress, and the tunic and leggings of soft doeskin, beautifully embroidered, brought out every line and curve of a splendidly-moulded figure. Her face, browned and hardened by exposure to the sun, and a life not altogether free from privation, was lighted up by a pair of clear blue eyes, and must formerly have been one of striking beauty. But the chief attraction was her hair. This was not arranged in two long plaits after the Sioux fashion, but rippled over her shoulders in a heavy redundant mass, forming a very mantle of sheeny, ruddy gold, explaining to the astonished spectator the name she bore among her adopted compatriots, The Sun Queen. But—Heavens—what an apparition to meet with in the camp of the hostile Sioux!

"Thanks," she said, simply, seating herself upon the pile of robes which Vipan had dragged forward for that purpose. Then pausing a moment to see if he would break the silence, she went on: "You do not seem to remember me."

"Pardon me. I am not likely to have forgotten you," was the quiet reply, with an undercurrent of cutting satire. "Who that had seen her could ever forget the beautiful Miss D'Arcy—the Belle of the Island?" She broke into a bitter laugh. "Is that what they used to call me? I had forgotten—it seems such a long, long time ago. Could it have been myself? I, Isabel D'Arcy, who held the whole island in thrall; Government House, the garrison—all—all my humble devoted slaves, now the wife of a painted savage! In a word, an Indian squaw!"

"And because I declined to make one of the crowd of your humble devoted slaves you ruined my life. You blighted my whole career as a sacrifice to your ruffled vanity. One word from you would have exonerated me—yet you did not speak it."

"Why did you not defend yourself? Why did you not explain the matter fully?"

"I was a fool not to, perhaps. In fact, I am sure I was. Well, you see—it was no part of my creed to give away a friend, nor yet a woman—for it was in a secondary degree on your account that I kept silence and set up no defence."

"On my account?" she echoed.

"Yes. Your only chance of getting clear out of the business was to deny the whole thing and stick to it. If I had cut in with the story of the other man borrowing my charger for the occasion, especially as owing to our striking resemblance we were often taken for each other—why the whole murder would have been out. No, there was nothing for it but the denial."

"And—and have you never explained a word of it since?"

"Never. What was the use? I was already condemned. Your uncle, Sir George, had more than enough influence for that, and I was practically cashiered. I must, however, give him credit for the astute way in which the business was hushed up. Barentyne, I suppose, couldn't clear me for fear of giving *you* away."

"And what became of Major Barentyne?" she asked eagerly.

"He left the service soon afterwards. He's a governor-general now, a sort of viceroy, and all sorts of things; while I'm—well, a fair specimen of a Western border ruffian. Thus, in this world, is the saddle clapped upon the wrong horse, and the scapegoat is jerked forth into the wilderness—and it doesn't much matter."

There was no heat, no upbraiding in his tone. After the first touch of satire underlying his recognition of her he spoke in an even, almost monotonous voice, puffing slowly at his long Indian pipe with the impassiveness of the red men themselves. Then a silence fell between them. The meeting, the conversation, seemed to have bridged over the weary, hopeless years of captivity of the one, the aimless and chequered wanderings of the other. By magic the Indian *teepe*, with its confusion of *parflèches* and robes and cooking-pots and wicker-beds, seemed to have disappeared, and once more their minds were back among the Government House state and the garrison festivities of the island colony, and many a familiar, but long-forgotten, face and memory of other days. And now the once beautiful girl who had queened it there, the descendant of a good old line, was the weary, middle-aged wife of a Sioux chief, doomed to live and die among the red barbarians. Truly the whirligig of Fortune was executing a strange freak when it brought these two face to face thus.

"I have, indeed, injured you," she said at length. "But I can yet make some amends?"

He shook his head.

"Listen," she went on. "I can do this. I can give you in writing a full and true statement of the whole affair. Then you can return home and clear yourself."

"And to what end?" he answered. "Nothing on earth is to be gained by raking up old troubles already forgotten. Besides, you are forgetting; I am a prisoner here, and, candidly, have very small hope of ever knowing liberty again. My time is about run out. Do you know that from hour to hour I live in unceasing apprehension of treachery? Any moment may be my last. See, I have an old pistol here—only one shot. I am keeping it for myself, if necessary, for I will never figure at their hellish stake."

She shuddered.

"But," she urged, lowering her voice, and speaking quickly, "but what if I can help you to escape?"

He looked up, a flash of hope in his eyes. Then he shook his head.

"I'm afraid it can't be done. They would be certain to detect your agency in the matter, and then what would be *your* fate?"

"What, you can still make that a consideration!" she exclaimed in amazement. Then, suddenly she burst into a flood of tears.

"Forgive me," she said, quickly recovering herself. "I am very foolish. But you are the first of my race I have conversed with for eight long years. The only white faces I have seen during that time have been those of wretched prisoners brought in for torture and outrage, or of horse thieves and border ruffians, more repulsive and villainous than those of the savages themselves."

"I had no idea of your identity," he said, "until you came in here just now. Then I recognised you, for I never forget a face. I am not easily astonished, but I was then. If the subject is not painful I should be glad to know the circumstances of your being here at all."

She laughed drearily.

"Oh, no! Feeling is pretty well dead by now, and happily so. The story is that of many another, only I suppose I ought to reckon myself fortunate when I think of what I have seen others go through. In an evil moment I arranged to come home from the Islands with some friends, who were anxious to do the trip overland. We landed at San Francisco, and all went well until we reached this side of the mountains. We were a small party, so small that the people at Fort Laramie tried all they could to dissuade us from going on, as most of the tribes were on the war-path. We were attacked on the banks of the North Platte, about two days out from Laramie. It was early in the morning, and we had just hitched up for a start. The spring waggon containing ourselves was a little behind the rest. Suddenly a band of warriors, hundreds of them it seemed, charged in upon us yelling like fiends. The teamsters were shot dead in a moment. Mr Elsdale, under whose protection I was travelling, was run through with a lance almost before he had time to fire a shot, and his wife and I were at the mercy of the savages. Even now I would rather not think of what she had to go through."

"And yourself?"

"I fainted, mercifully. I must have remained unconscious for hours, for when I came to I found myself tightly held by a powerful Indian in front of his saddle. The party was travelling at a considerable pace, and some of them carried freshly-taken scalps, those of our unfortunate outfit. My captor smiled good-humouredly as I opened my eyes, and, with signs and a word or two of English, told me not to be afraid, they were not going to kill me. Even then it struck me that he had a fine face. There was an expression of humanity and kindness in it totally absent from the hideous and painted visages of the rest. That man was Mahto-sapa."

She paused, and seemed to make an effort to proceed. Her listener, keenly interested, still smoked gravely without speaking.

"That night, when we halted, there was a frightful scene. Mrs Elsdale was a prisoner too, but I had not seen her until then. Well, you know Indians and their ways. She was dead before morning. That I escaped the same brutal treatment was due to the chief. It appears that he had captured me with his own hand, and he claimed me as his exclusive property. There was nearly a fight over me, and I have since learned that it was little short of a miracle that he carried his point. Well, I was taken to their head village unmolested, for the chief protected me unswervingly the whole way, and then he took me as his wife. What could I do, at the mercy of a band of ruthless savages? Some women might have killed themselves, but I was a full-blooded creature and clung to life; besides I always had a strong dash of the Bohemian in me."

Vipan remembered how that very thing used to be said of her among the envious gossips of the island colony, who had predicted all sorts of queer futures for Isabel D'Arcy. Surely, however, that which had befallen her was many degrees queerer than even they had ever designed for her.

"The chief was a splendid-looking man," she continued, "and I felt genuinely grateful to him when I thought what he had saved me from. So

I made a virtue of necessity, and resolved to make the best of the situation; and that I succeeded in obtaining a certain amount of ascendancy over him you may judge from the style in which I am allowed to live. He has always treated me well, and I have never been molested in the smallest degree from the time it was an understood thing that I was his property. I have more than once been the means of saving a wretched prisoner, not from death—that would be beyond even my power—but from the frightful ordeal of the stake. The reason why those two unhappy wretches were done to death outside the village the last time instead of here, in its midst, was on my account. The horrible sights I have witnessed here would make even you turn sick. Well, I laid myself out to acquire influence among the Indians, doctoring them in a small way and teaching them various little things; and once my position assured I took no small pains to keep up its dignity. They soon named me The Sun Queen."

"And do you never contemplate a return to civilisation—to your friends?" said her listener as she paused in her narrative.

"Never. Friends! Why, I never had a real one; and as for relations, they would spurn me from their door. No, I am accustomed to this life now, and I shall live and die among the Sioux, the squaw of a savage. Rather a contemptible object, am I not?" she ended, with a harsh and bitter laugh.

"No, I should not say that," said Vipan, slowly, puffing out a great cloud of smoke.

"What!" eagerly. "You do not despise me in your heart?"

"Certainly not. Look here. Let us put the case fairly and without prejudice. Supposing you had lived the ordinary society life. You might, as hundreds have done before you, have married some vulgar *parvenu*—we'll say from force of circumstances—or a fellow who got drunk on the quiet and threw empty bottles at you, or some execrable gutterling who happened to be rolling in money. Civilised men and Christians, mind. I am brutally frank, you see. Or again, more than one Englishwoman of birth and breeding has been known to espouse some slant-eyed, sallow-skinned Oriental for the sake of his rank and jewels, sometimes not even that. Well, you have allowed that Mahto-sapa, as a man, is not contemptible either in aspect or qualities. Now I call him a king in comparison with such as I have just mentioned. Of those who would define him as a heathen and a savage, not one in a hundred could boast half his good points. My opinion is that you have shown sound judgment in making the best of the situation."

"Do you know, you have taken a weight off my mind. I had often thought of what you now say, but required someone else's opinion. No, I shall live and die among these people. But you? I will think out and form some plan for you to escape, but I do not disguise from you that it will be difficult and risky. And should you find yourself threatened with immediate danger, do not delay, take refuge at once in my lodge. I believe they would hesitate to pursue you there."

She rose from her seat with a lithe, rapid movement, grasped his hand, and glided from the lodge.

Chapter Thirty Six
A Tardy Reparation

Vipan, left alone, felt drowsy, and kicking up the lodge fire into a blaze, rolled himself in a blanket and lay down in the long wicker basket which did duty as his bed. But sleep refused to come. This strange meeting had something weird about it. That this woman, whose selfish reticence had ruined his life, to screen whom he had sacrificed his prospects up to blighting point, as to whose whereabouts he had long ceased to speculate, should appear before him alone in the camp of the hostile Sioux—living there as one of themselves—struck him as little short of miraculous, and a superstitious feeling seemed to warn him, eagerly as he strove to dismiss it, that an occurrence so startling, so entirely out of all reckoning, portended some grave crisis to himself. Was her appearance after all these years destined to herald some other turning-point in his life? Thus musing, sleep at length overcame him, and still his dreams were haunted by the sad face of the ex-society belle, doomed to spend her life among savages, even resigned to that deplorable destiny.

A stealthy form wormed itself quickly through the opening of the *teepe*. Vipan, who slept with one eye open, never moved, but his hand tightened on the stock of the pistol in his breast. Only for a moment, though; for he recognised the hideous lineaments and beady eyes of the Shoshone slave girl.

"Rise quickly, Golden Face," whispered the latter. "The Sun Queen sends for you. Come at once."

Prepared for any emergency, he obeyed without a word. It was already dusk, and at the other end of the village were signs of a gathering of some sort which was about to take place. Unobserved, he entered Isabel D'Arcy's tent.

Enjoining caution by a sign, she beckoned him to a seat. The firelight glinted on her shining hair, and he noticed that her still handsome face was clouded with anxiety. The *teepe* was furnished in quasi-civilised style. There was a camp bedstead instead of the Indian wicker basket, a table, two trunks, and even a few books.

"I have just learned something," she began, "that renders it necessary for you to make the attempt at once. Listen. Time is short, and we must lose none of it. There is to be a big scalp-dance to-night in the Ogallalla camp. Hark! They are beginning now. Afterwards you are to be seized and put to the torture. I know the plot—never mind how. Nothing can save you. The Ogallallas have fourteen hundred warriors in the village, and are all-powerful. The whole of our band, except about fifty, are away with Mahto-sapa, and even he could hardly protect you if he were here. Mountain Cat, War Wolf, Long Bull, and a dozen others are all in the plot. Now, quick—quick, I say!" stamping her foot. "Obey me or you are lost. Take as much as you can carry of this," handing him a *parflèche* half full of dried meat. "And this is the only weapon I can find."

With a thrill of satisfaction he found himself in possession of a large navy revolver, loaded in every chamber.

"But," he objected, "if I get clear will they not visit it upon you?"

"No. They dare not. Quick. You have only an hour's start, with the best of luck. You may not have ten minutes. Roll your blanket round your chin, so as to hide your beard, and put on this."

She handed him an Indian head-dress of beadwork and cloth, from whose summit rose a tall eagle-feather. Fixing it on, he stood there transformed into a stalwart savage.

"Now, my plan is simple—in fact, ridiculous. You must personate an Indian larking with my slave girl here. She will pretend to run away, and you must pursue her. She will lead you to the nearest herd of ponies; you must catch one and trust to luck. Now, good-bye. God speed you!"

He thought he detected a quaver in her voice as she grasped his hands, and would have lingered. She stamped her foot angrily.

"Go, go! You are endangering both of us, and the plan will fall through." And she almost pushed him from the lodge.

A mischievous cackle, and the dark form of the Shoshone girl glided round the outside of the *teepe*. Vipan, entering thoroughly into his *rôle*, started boldly in pursuit. So well did he act up to it that a group of squaws whom he passed within ten yards screamed with laughter at the sight of a stalwart buck larking after the Sun Queen's hideous slave, no less than at the broad jests which he was gruffly hurling after her as she ran.

The dark figure still glided on between the *teepes*, hardly visible in the falling gloom. To those who did see it the sight was an everyday one, so that beyond a shout of mirth and a boisterous wish for his success, no notice was taken of it.

The last line of *teepes* was passed. In front lay the timber belt, then a subdued "crunch, crunch," betokened the proximity of a group of ponies. The dark figure of the Shoshone girl had disappeared. "The nearest," his deliverer had said. His lariat rope was ready. Gently, soothingly, he approached the one he reckoned the best. Up went the perverse brute's head with a resentful snort, as it sidled and backed away. He tried another, with the same result. His heart was in his mouth. The ponies had stopped feeding, and were gazing at him in alarm. The least thing might stampede the herd and arouse the attention of its owners. There was no time to lose. Whirling the noose around his head he let fly. The coils tautened out. The affrighted animal thus noosed, plunged, and fell heavily. He was upon it like lightning. Avoiding the kicking hoofs, he wrenched a bight of the rope into its mouth, jerked the trembling and terrified steed to its feet, and was on its back like a circus-rider. The rest of the herd trotted away, snorting and throwing up their heels.

Suddenly a wild, shrill whoop went up from the village. Ah! now for the race for life; but what were the odds in his favour? They had discovered his flight.

On, through the darkness, the fugitive urged his unwilling steed, whose bucking and plunging would have unseated any less skilful horseman. And as he fled, carefully picking his ground with the instinct of a consummate plainsman, he strained his ears through the darkness to catch the first sounds of pursuers behind, of a possible manoeuvre to outflank and head him in front. But the discovery had not, in fact, been made. The wild shouts were the yells of the scalp-dance just beginning. Fainter and fainter behind him sounded the savage chorus, then died away, and amid the solitude of the grim mountain waste only the soft hoof-beats of his steed, and the occasional scream of a panther among the craggy heights, broke upon the dead and ghostly silence of the night.

Chapter Thirty Seven
Between the Living and the Dead

With the first lightening of dawn, the fugitive realised that it behoved him to exercise tenfold wariness. Save one brief halt to rest his steed, he had ridden the night through, and now he intended to lie hidden in some snug retreat until darkness again should cover his flight beneath its friendly folds. A shallow stream flowed close at hand, now losing itself in the timber, now gurgling along a grassy bottom, to emerge a few hundred yards further down. Into the water Vipan now guided his steed, and riding down stream, emerged a mile or so further on. This manoeuvre, executed with the object of hiding his trail, he had performed already twice that night.

The morning dawned but slowly; dark and cold, for a thick mist had settled down on the land. And now it seemed to Vipan that the ground was becoming less precipitous. Could he be getting clear of the mountains already? Suddenly the murmur of guttural voices struck upon his ear, and strangely enough they sounded ahead of him.

Softly he checked his horse. Then to his unbounded amazement the subdued murmur arose again. This time *it was behind him.*

A puff of air drove a space through the mist, and now Vipan's heart stood still. On either side of him, all around, gigantic in the filmy wrack which swept over them in thickening or decreasing folds, loomed shadowy horsemen. Their deep-toned conversation, their plumed heads and painted faces, were only too familiar to this man who was flying there for his life. *He was riding in the very midst of a war-party.*

Their strength he could not estimate. Ghostly forms appearing and disappearing as the mist thickened or partially dispersed, no clue could he obtain as to their numbers. One even called out to him a remark. He answered with a laconic grunt, and in his heart fervently blessed the foresight of his deliverer which had invested him with the eagle-crested head-dress. The savages evidently took him for one of their party. Fervently, too, did he bless the welcome fog and its kindly aid, for the fraud could not have lived a moment in broad daylight.

Gradually, imperceptibly, he checked his steed. Any moment the fog might lift. He must back out of this perilous escort as imperceptibly as he had entered it. But, just as he reckoned himself clear, a fresh group of figures would start up on his rear, and canter forward in the wake of those who had gone before. These ceased, and by the time the fog began fairly to roll back beneath the dispelling power of the rising sun, Vipan, to his inexpressible relief, found himself alone. Then spying a confused heap of rocks and bushes high up on the slope of a hill he made for it. As a hiding-place it was perfect. Entering its welcome shelter, he secured his tired steed in such wise that the animal could crop the green herbage growing in the cool shadow of the rocks. Then he lay down and fell fast asleep.

When at length he awoke it was with a shiver of cold. The sun was not an hour from the western horizon. He had slept the whole day.

Cautiously he peered forth. His hiding-place, being at a considerable elevation, afforded a wide view of the surrounding country. The blue line of the Black Hills cleft the sky to the south-eastward, and he could make out the granite cone of the towering Inyan Kara. His course had so far been an accurate one.

Suddenly a moving object caught his eye. Was the land absolutely bristling with enemies? Advancing along his trail far down in the bottom came a file of mounted figures. Though nearly three miles off, there was no mistaking them or their object. Then he chuckled sardonically. The trail of the war-party, under whose escort he had so unwillingly travelled for ever so brief a space, would obliterate his own a hundred times over.

Nearer and nearer they drew, riding at an easy canter. He made out forty-one Indians in war-costume. He watched them with a sneer and a chuckle.

Suddenly, when nearly abreast of his position, the leader halted, gazing intently at the ground. The band clustered round him, then scattered, as if searching for more trail. Then a smothered curse escaped the lips of the watcher. In obedience to a rapid signal, the whole band had diverged from the trail of the war-party, and was heading straight for his place of concealment. It was all up with him. They had lighted upon his trail. It was time to give them the slip.

He sent one more glance at the party. Strung out in single file, the warriors were riding along his trail, like a pack of hounds with their noses to the ground. In their leader he recognised his implacable and untiring foe, War Wolf.

"All right," he muttered between his teeth, as he twisted the lariat rope into the horse's mouth. "All right, my friend. You're bound for the Happy Hunting-Grounds this time. We'll get there together."

His horse, fresh and rested, bore him bravely as he dashed forth, leaving the hill and the covert between himself and his pursuers. Well he knew what would happen. The Indians would not ride straight up to the bushes. They would halt and cast round the hill to see if his trail led away again. This would give him a start.

The face of the country on this side was a series of rolling slopes freely dotted with clumps of straggling timber. Some distance ahead he noted a long dark line of forest. Night was at hand; could he reach this in time he might yet hope to escape.

Then a long, pealing whoop went up. The Sioux had discovered him, and with exultant shouts each warrior lashed his pony into the utmost speed.

For half an hour the furious chase continued. Vipan, glancing over his shoulder, became aware that his pursuers were slowly gaining on him. On—on. The forest belt would soon be reached, and meanwhile the dusking shadows were lengthening around.

He gained the first straggling patch of scrub. A few hundred yards and he would be within the welcome refuge, when his horse put a foot on the crusted surface of a mud-hole, turned a somersault, and his rider came whizzing to the earth.

Vipan arose. Throughout the horror of the shock his self-possession did not desert him, for he retained firm hold of the lariat rope. He was on his feet again, active as a cat, though stiff and bruised, but his steed stood shaking with alarm, using its right foreleg limpingly.

A yell of exultation went up from the pursuers. Half-a-dozen warriors, better mounted than the rest, were some distance ahead. So easy a capture would be that of the unarmed fugitive that they had not troubled to hold a weapon in readiness. Now they began to whirl their lassos ready for a throw.

Vipan, perfectly cool, crouched behind a bush, his revolver pointed. On they came, War Wolf leading, a grin of triumph wreathing his fierce features. A hundred yards—then fifty. A ringing report—a jet of flame in the glooming twilight. War Wolf threw up his arms and lurched heavily forward upon his horse's neck. The terrified animal, snorting and rearing, dashed away at a tangent, dragging his rider, who had somehow become entangled in the caparisonings.

And what a howl of rage and consternation rent the air! They had not bargained for this, for they believed the fugitive to be unarmed. Panic-stricken for the moment, they halted, then some of them dashed off to the succour of their leader. But they need not have done so. The bullet had sped true. The young partisan had shouted his last war-whoop.

Profiting by this temporary check, the hunted man had again sprung on the back of his horse. Lame or not, the animal must carry him further yet. On—on. The forest belt was gained. He plunged beneath its shadows, only to find it was mere straggling timber—not thick enough for hiding purposes. The frosty air cut his face and the leaves crackled crisply under his horse's hoofs. He drew his knife and pricked the poor brute furiously in the hinder quarters. The fierce yells of the savages drawing nearer and nearer told only too plainly that they had no intention of relinquishing the pursuit, and the horse was beginning to go dead lame.

"Cau—aak!"

He glanced involuntarily upward. A huge raven disturbed on its roost flapped away in alarm. But another sight met his eye. Extending horizontally from two sturdy limbs of a Cottonwood tree, cleaving the wintry sky, was a long dark object. Vipan recognised one of those platforms on which the Indians deposit their dead—like Mohammed's coffin, midway between earth and heaven.

His mind was made up in a flash. Checking his horse he dismounted, and tearing a bunch of thorns from a bush, proceeded deliberately to insert them beneath the poor animal's tail. Then, as the horse galloped off in a perfect frenzy of pain and terror, he slipped up the tree and gained the burial platform, literally flattening himself against its ghastly burden. It was a hideous alternative.

Scarcely had he gained this gruesome refuge than the pursuers passed beneath. They were barely fifteen feet below him as he lay flattened there, not even daring to breathe as the savages swept by, guided by the frenzied gallop which, seeming to have gained redoubled speed, they could hear still ahead of them. It was a desperate expedient, but it had answered so far.

"Cau—aak! Cau—aak!"

Like an evil spirit let loose beneath the frosty heavens came the black swoop of the raven he had disturbed, and the hunted man saw it with a cold shiver. He dared not even turn his head. The warriors might return at any moment from their fool's errand, and then even a breath might seal his fate. A strong shudder of disgust ran through his frame. The hideous croak of the ill-omened bird brought back vividly that other scene—the two grinning blood-stained skulls lying there in the dark forest by Burntwood Creek, and the startling challenge of their would-be avenger. Involuntarily he turned his head, and a revulsion of horror caused him to shrink back in spite of himself, and nearly to fall from his precarious resting-place. For within six inches of his face his glance lighted upon a fearful sight. A human countenance scowled upon him—but such a face. From the blackened and mummified skin drawn tightly over the protruding bones, the glazed eyes seemed to glare anew with menace and hate towards the violator of their resting-place. Shadowy yet distinct in the light of the new moon this horrible countenance, peering as it were from the fantastic cerements of barbarous sepulture, was enough to unhinge the stoutest nerves. A grisly skeleton-claw raised in mid-air, as though about to grapple with the impious intruder, completed the horror, while overhead, like the fierce spirit of the departed warrior yet hovering around its decaying tenement, the grim raven flapped in circles, emitting its gruesome croak.

"Pooh!" said the fugitive to himself, making a strong effort to overcome his not unnatural horror. "Pooh! While the country's swarming with live redskins hunting for my scalp, am I going to be scared by one dead one? Not much—not much!"

An hour wore on—then two. Wolves howled dismally over the midnight waste, and still that grisly countenance glared menacingly in the moonlight—and still they lay side by side, the dust of the half-forgotten dead, and the living, breathing, vigorous frame—welded together in that weird partnership—its object the saving of a life.

Thus they lay, side by side—the dead warrior preserving the life of the hereditary enemy of his race.

Chapter Thirty Eight
Another Bomb for the Rev. Dudley

Once more we must peep into the library at Lant Hall.

Mr Vallance sat in his accustomed chair, thinking. His gaze would wander from the window to the blazing fire and back again, and the frown of anxiety deepened on his features. Without, the wind howled shrilly through the bare boughs, and a few scattered flakes of snow whirled in the air.

"Why did we ever let him go?" he exclaimed aloud. "Why did we ever let him go?"

Even as when last we saw him, Mr Vallance was terribly anxious on behalf of his son. His former misgivings had been allayed by the subsequent receipt of a letter from Geoffry; which missive, however, had given him to understand that it was the last the writer would have an opportunity of sending for some time—in fact, until he should be on his way home again. Characteristically, too, this letter contained only vague and general information that the writer had fallen in with and joined Winthrop's outfit; and of his meeting with Yseulte Santorex, not a word. It was of no use worrying about the matter, decided the Rev. Dudley. Any post might now bring intelligence that the boy was on his way home. It was poor comfort, and again he found himself repeating:

"Why did we ever allow him to go?"

Of the other affair which had so sorely troubled him—his cousin's unexpected and preposterous claim—he had heard no more. His apprehensions first were lulled, then subsided altogether. The whole business was palpably a "try on."

A sound of subdued voices outside, then a knock.

"A gentleman wishes to see you, sir."

In his then frame of mind, Mr Vallance could not but feel startled by the interruption.

"Who is he, James?" he asked, quickly.

"He wouldn't give his name, sir. He said as how you'd be sure to see him, sir."

"Quite right, quite right," said a deep voice, whose owner entered behind the astonished flunkey. "Er—How do, Dudley!"

If Mr Vallance had been startled before, the expression of his features now betokened a state of mind little short of scare. His face had turned as white as a sheet, and his jaw fell as he stood helplessly staring at his visitor.

"Why—bless my soul—Ralph," he stammered. Then advancing with outstretched hand, "Why—Ralph—I'm—I'm glad to see you. I hope you have come to stay with us for a time."

The visitor's reception of this friendly—this hospitable overture, was singular. Standing bolt upright, he deliberately put his hand behind his back.

"Glad to see me!" he echoed, with a sneer. "No, you are not. Why tell a—tarra-diddle. Such a tarra-diddle, too—and you a preacher—er—I beg your pardon—a *priest*, it used to be, if I remember right. You would sooner see the devil himself at this moment than me."

Under the sting of this reply, the parson recovered a certain amount of dignity.

"Really," he said, stiffly, "your behaviour is strange, to put it mildly. May I ask, then, the object of your intru— your visit."

"Certainly, if it affords you any satisfaction." Then glancing around the room, and finishing up with a look out of the window, he went on. "Say, cousin Dudley, this is a pretty shebang enough. The object of my visit is this: You've bossed up this show about long enough. Suppose you abdicate now and let me have a turn?"

"Have you taken leave of your senses?"

"Not much. Have you?"

There was a sternness about the speaker's laconic reply which caused Mr Vallance to quail involuntarily. He made a step towards the bell-pull. The other laughed.

"No, no. Don't exert yourself. I'm not going yet—and if you bring in all the pap-fed flunkeys and swipe-guzzling stable-hands on your establishment, the poor devils'll only get badly hurt without furthering your object. I mean what I say—you've got to quit sooner or later. If you're wise it'll be sooner."

"Indeed! And why?" was the answer, given with cutting politeness.

"Well, it's this way. If you agree to clear at once, I'll give you five hundred a year—no, I'll make it six—out of the property for your life. That and the parsonic pickings will keep you in clover. If you mean fighting, I'm your man. But I warn you I'm prepared to plank down ever so many thousands of pounds to get you out—and when I've got you out I'll come down on you for every shilling of arrears, by George, I will!"

"Oh, you will?"

"You may bet your life on it."

For some moments the two men looked full in each other's faces without speaking. The sneer of conscious power on that of the one was matched by the expression of defiance, hatred, mingled with fear, on that of the other.

"Well, well," said Mr Vallance at length. "Take your own course. Only, let me remind you that you are in England now, and that in this country we don't settle important matters in any such rough and ready fashion."

"Oh don't make any mistake; I'm not going to *hurt* you, if that's what you're thinking about. You see, I've been knocking around a goodish few years, and now I've a fancy for settling down—settling down *in my own place*, you understand."

There was a smug smile of triumph on the parson's face now. His cousin was merely "bouncing" to extort terms. It would come to that in a few minutes. But the look aroused a very demon in the other. His eyes burned like live coals, though when he spoke his voice was under perfect control.

"Again, I say, you needn't be afraid," he said. "Everything shall be done in due course of law."

"But—but, my good fellow, surely you are aware you haven't a leg to stand on?"

"I reckon I'm the best judge of that. See here, most reverend Dudley. Do you remember our last interview, here, in this very room? Safe in the triumph of your successful fraud—fraud, I say, if you prefer it, forgery—you jeered at me, jeered at the man you had robbed. Remember?"

"'Fraud!' 'Robbed!'" sputtered the parson, trying to lash himself into anger to drown the sinking sense that had come over him. "Do you know, sir, that you are using actionable words?"

"Ah, ah! History repeats itself. That is precisely as you spoke on the former occasion, friend Dudley. I will say it again, call in witnesses if you like. Having defrauded and robbed me of my patrimony by lies and intriguing, *and* worse—you, a preacher of the Gospel, a teacher of Christian morality—you threatened me with the law. You made your lawyers write to threaten me with an action for libel if I dared so much as venture an opinion on your behaviour. Do you remember my words to you as I left this room?"

Well, indeed, did he remember. And now at the sight of the deadly wrath on this man's features, all the more terrible because so completely held in hand—of the towering form with its back just half a yard from the door, precluding alike entrance or exit—again Mr Vallance could not restrain a shiver of physical fear.

"I told you my time would surely come, didn't I? How many years ago was it? Nearer twenty than ten—yes. You slandered my name and stole my possessions—you, a sacred dispenser of sacraments—and I went forth a beggar, followed by your jeers of triumph. If you go where I have been during those years, and take the trouble to enquire, you will learn that few persons have played me a scrofulous trick without bitterly rueing it. You have played me the most scrofulous trick of all, and you are going to rue it."

"Well, I must trouble you to let me pass, please. I shall ask you to excuse me wasting my time any longer," said Mr Vallance, making a move as if to leave the room. But the other only smiled.

"Not yet. Not quite yet," he said. "By the way, Dudley. Heard anything of Geoffry lately?"

The tone was easy—smiling—but it struck a chill to the parson's heart. He glanced up quickly at his interlocutor's face, his own white with deadly fear. His lips parted, but he was powerless to articulate. The other stood immovable—smilingly enjoying his apprehension, but the smile was that of a fiend.

"Not heard anything of him?" he said, slowly, while like the hellish hiss of red-hot irons in quivering flesh there passed through his mind the recollection of his cousin's defiant sneers over the successful intrigue that had robbed him of his patrimony, there in that same room, whose very walls seemed to echo their refrain even now. "Not heard anything of him? Well I'm not surprised, for—he's dead."

"Dead?" echoed Mr Vallance blankly, as though in a dream.

"As the proverbial door-nail."

"Murderer!" gasped the wretched man, spasmodically clutching the air with his fingers, and gazing at his tormentor as through a far-off mist.

"Oh, no. You are under a delusion," was the cool reply. "It's odd that it should devolve on me—on me above all people—to give you the latest news of him. He died at an Indian stake."

Even the pitiless, revengeful heart of the man who stood there smilingly unfolding his horrible news was hardly prepared for the awful metamorphosis that came over the smug, smooth-tongued, purring parson at those words. With a scream that rang through the house from top to bottom, and froze the blood of all who heard it, the miserable man leaped at his tormentor's throat like a wild cat at bay. But he might as well have leaped at a rock. The powerful arm was raised, and the mere shock of the recoil sent the poor wretch sprawling. He lay—his livid features working in mania—the foam flying from his lips in flakes.

The other glanced at him a moment, then opened the door.

"You, James?" he said, coolly, to the trembling flunkey, who had not been many yards from the door during the interview. "You, James? Your boss is taken bad, I guess. Better see after him. Tell him, when he comes round, I'll call again by-and-bye, and give him further particulars."

With the same easy smile upon his lips he passed through the crowd of frightened women-folk who met him on the stairs, and who shrunk back before his glittering eyes and towering form, and gained the front door. Then he smiled in fearful glee.

"The last time I passed out this way," he said to himself, half-aloud. "The last time I passed out this way, I was saying my time would surely come—and it has. Aha! my exemplary and most reverend cousin I think I'm nearly even with you now—very nearly!"

Chapter Thirty Nine
In the Twilight Oakwood

Yseulte Santorex was slowly wending her way homeward through the now leafless oak woods which overhung Elmcote.

The lonely ride looked ghostly and drear in the early dusk of the November afternoon. A chill and biting wind moaned through the covert, and now and again a pheasant or rabbit scuttling among the undergrowth, raised a stealthy rustling sound that would have been somewhat startling to any other of her sex who should find herself belated in that lonely place. But in this solitary pedestrian it inspired no fear, only a sweet, sad recollection — albeit reminding her of the most perilous moment in her whole life. For it brought back vividly, by an association of sound and surroundings, the shadowy timber belt, and the stealthy tread of the grim painted savages advancing to seize her on the lonely river-bank in the far Wild West.

But what a change had befallen her! The happy, even-tempered girl who had so gleefully left her home in keen anticipation of a period of adventurous travel amid new and stirring scenes had disappeared, and this pale, wistful-eyed woman walking here seemed but the mere ghost of the Yseulte Santorex of yore.

Often in her dreams she again goes through those terrible experiences — the perilous flight with the scout across the rugged ranges, momentarily expecting the volley of the lurking Sioux ambushed in the dense timber. Often in her dreams she is once more fleeing for dear life across those wild plains, the war-whoops of the painted fiends ringing in her ears, the thunder of their pursuing steeds shaking the ground. Often in her dreams she is again entering the frowning portals of that dread Thermopylae, where one man had unhesitatingly laid down his life in order that she might reach a place of safety. Often, too, she is once more amid her genial, kindly, travelling companions, only to wake up with a start and a shiver to the remembrance of their horrible fate.

But never as long as she lives will she forget the moment when her brother, finding her out at Fort Vigilance, brought the news which had confirmed her fears to the uttermost. He who had offered his life for her was dead—dead amid the horrid torments of the Indian stake, as the savages themselves affirmed—and to her, thenceforward, life seemed a grey and valueless thing. There was nothing further to be gained by opposing her brother's wish that she should at once accompany him home to Lant-Hanger. Travelling through the British possessions safe beyond the reach of the hostile Sioux, who still carried terror and pillage over the plains of Dakota and Wyoming, they had set forth on their journey and had reached home in due course.

Shocked out of even his philosophy by the change, nothing could exceed the affectionate consideration her father had show for her since her return. Even her mother forgot to grumble and scold in her relief at having the girl back again safe and sound, for George had judiciously put them up to the real state of affairs. It was not in the nature of things that her parents should be well pleased that she had buried her heart in the grave of an unknown adventurer, who had, moreover, met with a horrible death, but time, they hoped, would work a gradual cure, and she was young yet. Then, too, apart from this unfortunate affair, her experiences had been terrible for a refined and luxuriously-nurtured English girl. So no care or trouble was spared to induce her to forget them.

But Yseulte herself was the last to second these well-meant efforts. She would brace herself up to appear cheerful and at ease, but seemed never so happy as when alone, rambling for hours through the fields and woods, to her parents' concern and alarm. But any expression of the latter would be met by a wan smile and a remark that one who had heard the war-whoop and shots fired in grim earnest, and had twice been chased by red Indians on the war-path, felt pretty secure among the peaceful lanes and meadows of tame Old England. And one other thing noteworthy was that she avoided Lant Hall and its denizens with a horror and a persistency that was little short of feverish. She had never divulged poor Geoffry's presence with the waggon train, and shrank morbidly from doing so now. He might have escaped, but that he had fallen in the general massacre which overtook the unfortunate emigrants she could hardly doubt.

This evening she was returning from a long walk, having gone out to join at luncheon her father and brother, who were shooting some distant coverts, and who would drive home by the road. She, preferring her solitary ramble through the fields and plantations, had left them early in the afternoon.

The sharp air had brought a tinge of colour to her pale cheeks, as, defying its rigours in her warm winter dress and toque, she stepped along the woodland ride with the easy grace of a perfect physical organisation. An owl dropped softly from overhead, hooting as it glided along on noiseless pinions, the bark of a fox echoed from the depths of the brake; but these weird sounds amid the gathering mists of night caused her no uneasiness, let alone fear. She even stopped to listen to them with a wistful yearning, for in the cry of the wild creatures of the woods, and the swirl of the wind through the denuded branches, she seemed to feel once more borne back to those nights of peril and of fear—but oh! how sweet the recollection—in the wild and blood-stained West, to walk alone in the spirit presence of him whom her mortal eyes should never more behold.

"Would to God we had died together!" she exclaimed aloud, her eyes dimmed with a rush of blinding tears. "Ah, why did I not die with him when it was still in my power to do so? Ah, why?"

And the owl flitting ghostly through the brake, answered:

"Tu-whoo—whoo-whoo!"

A sound smote upon her ear as she turned the bend of the path—a sound as of the footfall and snort of a horse. She looked up, and the sight that met her eyes rooted her to the ground, while the blood at her very heart stood still. But not with fear. Yet—what was that but a phantom—a phantom horseman—advancing towards her at scarce thirty paces? For the noble proportions of the coal-black steed there was no mistaking—and his rider—ah!—through many a night of horror and anguish she had seen in her dreams that towering frame, mangled and mutilated by the barbarous vengeance of the red demons, that splendid face, drawn and livid in the throes of an agonising death. Rider and steed had been parted in life—here in the lonely woods, in the glooming twilight, they were together again.

Her eyes met those of the phantom. An ecstasy shook her frame, and she was powerless to articulate. A sweet smile played on her lips; her gaze was strained upon the apparition, as though in the very strength of her yearning she could constrain it to remain with her, could retard its return to the shadowy unknown.

"Yseulte—love—I am no spectre," said the voice she knew so well. "I have come straight to you as soon as I learned where to find you. Come to me, darling!"

He had sprung to the ground, and stood awaiting her. The spell was broken. A loud cry rang through the wood, and then she was in his arms—laughing, weeping, sobbing, then laughing again. Words were out of the question.

The wintry night fell black upon the glooming oakwoods, weirdly musical with the mournful hooting of the owls. But there was no gloom in the hearts of these two who now stepped from those thickening shades.

A crunch of wheels on the gravel, a flash of lamps, and the dog-cart deposited the two shooters at the front door.

"Hallo, Chickie! What's in the wind, now?" exclaimed Mr Santorex, staring in amazement, as his daughter, hardly giving him time to alight, had flown at him and flung her arms around his neck, her face all aglow with more than the happiness of former days.

"Father! *He's* in there. Go in and see him!"

"*He?* What the deuce! In where? Give a fellow a chance! Who's *he?*"

"Mr Vipan."

"Oh, ah—I remember. The champion scalp-hunter. Come to life again, has he? Let's have a look at him."

As the door opened a tall figure rose from a chair, advancing with outstretched hand.

"How do, Santorex?"

He thus unceremoniously addressed stared, as well he might. This was Western brusquerie with a vengeance, he thought.

"Confound it! am I altered so dead out of all recognition?" said the other with a careless laugh, standing full in the light.

"Why, no—that is, yes. We none of us grow younger in twenty years. Well, well, Ralph. I'm heartily glad to see you, heartily glad." And the two men grasped hands in thorough ratification of the sentiment.

"No, by George! I should never have known you," went on Mr Santorex. "And Chickie, here, called you something else just now—what the deuce was it?"

"Vipan? Yes, it was an old name in the family at one time. I've revived it lately for my own convenience. That's how I was known out West."

"Think you'd have known the child here?" went on "the child's" father, turning to Yseulte, who had followed him into the room, and was now staring in amazement at this new revelation.

"Well, I've had rather the advantage of her; a mean advantage she'll say."

"She" was incapable of saying anything just then. That photograph of the disinherited Ralph Vallance, which, since her return home, she had managed to conjure out of her father's boxes of old correspondence, and had treasured because it bore some slight resemblance to her dead lover, now turned out to be nothing less than his actual portrait. Yet during all their daily intercourse, so well had he guarded his secret, that not a shadow of a passing instinct had ever warned her of his identity. It was astounding.

"Been to call on Dudley yet, Ralph?" said Mr Santorex, with a twinkle in his eye.

"Oh, yes. We had a talk over old times. By the way, that's another misnomer. My real name's Rupert. They used to call me the other for short. Heaven knows why, but they did, and I dropped it when I went West. Shan't revive it."

If ever there was a snug family party gathered together, it was that at the Elmcote dinner-table that night, when Rupert Vallance, as we must now call him, yielding to general request, but especially to an appealing glance from Yseulte's blue eyes, narrated his experiences from the time of his capture to his escape from the camp of the hostiles, only generalising however as to the agency of this latter event, and omitting for the present all mention of poor Geoffry's horrible death. But when it came to the narrator literally tucking himself in with the grisly denizen of the Indian grave, in the ghostly silence of the darkling forest, Mrs Santorex shivered and announced her intention of fainting; however, this effect was soon dispelled by the more pleasing *dénouement* of the stirring tale, how just in the nick of time, when alone, dismounted, barely half armed, and the savages still in search of him, he had been found by Smokestack Bill, who all this while, in hourly peril himself, had unweariedly watched his chances of coming to the aid of his friend. Smokestack Bill, too, with no less a companion than old Satanta, who had been wandering the country ever since his escape from the Ogallalla war-party, defying white or red to capture him, until, seeming to recognise his master's friend, he ran whinnying to the latter of his own accord.

"He's a grand fellow, that scout," said Mr Santorex. "Why didn't you bring him over with you, Rupert?"

"Wouldn't come. He's going as chief scout to an expedition just about to be sent against the hostiles. I made him promise, though, to come over directly after the war."

But the acme of this marvellous and stirring life's romance was reached when later—after the ladies had retired to bed—Rupert Vallance recounted, in strict confidence, the circumstances of his meeting in the Sioux camp, the unfortunate woman who had ruined his career hitherto by allowing him to suffer for another's intrigue.

"By Jove!" said George Santorex, junior. "I've heard of that party. Always supposed, though, she was a common sort of woman. A lady! and prefers to live among a lot of dirty redskins! Why, the tallest yarn of old Mayne Reid's is skim-milk to this. But I guess she pretty well wiped out old scores by chousing the reds out of your scalp in that clever way, eh, Rupert!"

He nodded. "That's so."

Just then there was an interruption. A messenger had arrived from Lant Hall. The Rev. Dudley was not expected to live through the night, and particularly wished to see Mr Santorex.

"Phew-w!" whistled the latter. "I suppose I must go. What on earth can he want to talk to me about? Perhaps it's about you, Rupert."

"Maybe it is," replied the latter, puffing out a cloud of smoke with as complete nonchalance as though they were discussing the weather. And George Santorex, junior, furtively watching the unconcerned, relentless face, thought he could well understand the reputation which this man had set up in those Western wilds which had been for so many years their common home.

Chapter Forty
Conclusion

Summer has come round once more, and again, amid all the glories of a cloudless evening, we stand beside the banks of the rippling Lant—howbeit not without misgiving, for are we not about to enact the part of eavesdroppers towards those two strolling languidly, contentedly, there by the shining water?

"It strikes me, child, you seem inclined to find life rather a happy thing," a voice well-known to us is saying. "And you've no business to."

A loving pressure of the strong arm on which she is leaning is the only answer Yseulte deigns at first to make. Then:

"Why not?"

"Because you've done a very wrong thing. If the late lamented Dudley were alive, he would tell you that a man may not marry his grandmother, and by parity of reasoning a woman may not marry her grandfather. Now this is just what you have done, and it's very wrong of you."

She gave his arm a pinch.

"I never liked—boys!" she replied with a sunny smile. And then she sighed. For it was on this very spot, beneath this same spreading oak here on the river-bank, that poor Geoffry had made his passionate and despairing declaration barely a year ago. And now at the thought of the poor fellow and his miserable end far away in that savage land, she could not repress a sigh.

"By Jove!" cried Rupert Vallance, flinging a stone into the river. "Something here seems to remind me of that evening when I came upon you staving in the red brother's grinders with the butt end of a fishing-rod. I wonder, by the way, what became of that same weapon? I expect Mountain Cat's band still keep it as a big medicine-stick. Deuced bad medicine it was for the buck you were laying it into. Ho, ho!"

"Don't remind me of that horrible moment," she said, coming closer to him with a slight shiver. "Let us go home, it's getting cold."

The Rev. Dudley Vallance was dead. The shock of learning his son's horrible end had brought on a stroke, and the following day he had breathed his last—not, however, before he had made what reparation he could for the wrong he had done his cousin, who, by the way, had so far relented as to satisfy him that he had borne no hand in poor Geoffry's death, and, in fact was powerless to prevent it; added to which he had himself rescued him from the same fate on a previous occasion. So on his death-bed he had signed a hastily drawn-up will, bequeathing the Lant property to Rupert Vallance absolutely, save and except a yearly charge on the estate for the support of his widow and daughters. To this Rupert had added with ample liberality. Once "the old man had climbed down," as he euphemistically put it, he himself was willing to let bygones be bygones, and had endowed the widow accordingly; needless to say, without earning the slightest degree of gratitude from the latter.

They strolled homeward across the meadows in the falling eve, and, lo, as they entered the gate of the home paddock there arose a whinny and a stamp of hoofs.

"Dear old Satanta!" said Yseulte, stroking the velvety black nose which the noble animal thrust lovingly against her hand. "You have well earned your ease for life, at any rate."

"I should rather think he had. No more arrows flying in his wake. No more brack water or willow-bark provender. All oats and fun for life. We shall have to give the war-whoop occasionally, just to remind him of old times."

"Please, sir," said a man-servant, meeting them in the hall. "Postman says was he right in leaving this, sir?"

His master took the letter, glanced at the address, and exploded in a roar of laughter. It bore the United States stamp, and was directed—

> "Judge Rupert Vipan, Lant Hall,
> Brackenshire County,
> Great Britain."

"Nat Hardroper's fist! Come along, Yseulte, and let's see what that 'cute citizen's got to say. 'Judge!' Great Scott! With infinite trouble I got him out of calling me Colonel, and now he's elevated me to the judicial bench! 'Vipan,' too! The old name seems to stick, anyway."

He broke open the letter and began to read—

Henniker City, Dakota, 14th July, 1876.

Dear Rupe,—Seems to me you're fixed up pretty tight and snug, after "baching" around all these years. My respects to Madam.

May be you'll not be sorry to hear I've sold your interest in the Burntwood Creek Mine to a New York Syndicate for two hundred and fifty thousand dollars, and five hundred fully paid-up shares in the new Co. If you weren't so keen on settling down in Great Britain again I reckon this find would make you more than a millionaire. However, I've banked the specie here, where it'll be safe enough till you undertake to ship it to Great Britain—safe enough, that is, while I'm Sheriff of Henniker City—though they did "hold up" the bank in Jabez Humbold's time.

The pesky Sioux are still on the war-path, as I judge you'll have learned even in Great Britain, but they're in a fair way of being soundly whipped. And now I've got to tell you what you'll be dead sorry to hear.

Yseulte, watching her husband's face, marked the change that came into it, as he turned the sheet and glanced hurriedly down it. A terrible frown—a frown similar to that which she had seen there when, dismounted and alone, he had turned to face the savage pursuers at the entrance of the cañon that never-to-be-forgotten evening of her escape. Mastering himself, he continued to read:

Your old pard, Smokestack Bill, is rubbed out. He fell at the Little Bighorn with Custer and his command, and I reckon the red devils have had many a dance round his hair by this time. Poor Bill! I allow it's kinder rough when men have been pardners all the years you and he have; but he fell in fair fight, and that's better, as he himself would allow, than dying of a slow sickness, or being knifed in the back by some slinking wall-eyed rowdy in a saloon. Well, well! There wasn't a straighter, stauncher, all-round man, nor a better scout on this continent than Smokestack Bill, and if so be as any man says there was, why he'll be ill-advised to make the remark anywhere around this section. I judge that's about all the news you'll care for just now, and with my respects to Madam, now as ever, old hoss, your sincere:

Nathaniel J. Hardroper, Sheriff of Henniker City.

For some time Rupert Vallance stared vacantly at the hateful paper in dead silence. All the stirring experiences they had gone through together crowded upon his mind, and the fate of his friend, staunch, unswerving, true as steel, moved him more than he cared to show, even to his wife.

"Ah, well!" he said at last, laying down the letter with a sigh. "It's bitterly rough on a fellow. For upwards of a dozen years we've chummed together like twin brothers, in tight fixes and out of them, and now the poor chap's wiped out. Yes, it's rough!" An arm stole round his neck. "Darling, can I forget that the noble, unselfish fellow saved your life and brought you back to me! And don't think me unfeeling, but if I had never gone out there you might be lying there too, at this moment, having shared the poor fellow's terrible fate."

"That's so," he assented. "I hadn't thought of it in that light."